Curiosities of the Mind

By Keith A. Wollen

© August 8, 2022

FOREWORD

Keith has led a life of rich experience, from notable achievements to tragedy, and everything in between. Having worked with Keith on this project for nearly a year, it has been a joy to see this anthology of short stories come into a single volume. As a fellow writer, I have become an admirer not only of his prodigious story-telling, but also of his character—his humility, his willingness to share his life, his gentle character, his humorous wit, and his sharp perception of the human soul. I've said it many times over the past several months—there's something in this volume for every reader, no matter the age or background. Enjoy!

Gerrit Hansen, June 2022

PREFACE

The workings of the mind have always fascinated me. After retiring from a professorship in the psychology department of Washington State University, I became interested in writing short stories about emotions and curiosities of the mind. Since my first works were met with enthusiasm from friends and colleagues, I decided to write more and assemble them into this book. I've endeavored to write interesting and informative tales. I hope you enjoy reading them as much as I enjoyed writing them.

Keith Wollen, June 2022

DEDICATION

To my family, sons Craig and Bruce, and my late wife, Fran, and son, Doug.

TABLE OF CONTENTS

- 15 The Grumpy Neighbor
- 20 The Maiden and the Mask
- 25 The Woman in a Red Coat
- 31 Two Diaries
- 36 Stranded
- 44 Footsteps in the Attic
- 49 Clyde
- 52 Invasion of the Ants
- 57 Ransom
- 63 The People Next Door
- 71 Thief
- 75 Unicorn Peak
- 83 Conner's Adventure
- 88 Dark Mountains
- 97 Survival
- 101 The Maid
- 105 The Gathering
- 107 Nostalgia
- 111 The Letter
- 113 It
- 115 Reunion
- 118 Waiting
- 121 My Journey with Alzheimer's
- 125 Voices
- 133 Desdemona
- 137 My Son Pete
- 143 Encounters in the Fog
- 148 The Chamber
- 152 Peril on the Farm
- 157 The Gift
- 162 The Visitor

173 Never is a Long Time
181 Confession
185 Threats
190 Death's Legacy
195 Obsession
198 A Fortunate Accident
202 Ryan's Secret
206 Missing
210 Nothing Left
214 The Magic Box
218 The Riddle Murder
223 The Contribution Machine
227 The Hand
231 The Mysterious Trunks
234 The Pinochle Game
237 Acknowledgments

The Grumpy Neighbor

Moving from the city to a small town meant adjustments for the Williams, but the opportunity to leave dead-end jobs to run a thriving restaurant was too good to pass up. Moreover, it was a better environment to raise a child, away from gangs and big city temptations.

On moving day, their son, Kyle, a streetwise and unusually self-confident six-year-old, was eager to see his new home. As soon as his stepfather parked in front of the apartment house, Kyle bounded up the stairs. Rounding a corner, he slammed into Runar, an 81-year-old who lived down the hall.

"Watch where you're going, kid," Runar huffed.

"Okay, *Gramps*."

"What? Don't your folks teach you manners?"

"Do you live here?" Kyle asked, ignoring the question.

"No, I just like to walk in this hall for fun," he replied sarcastically.

"Are we going to be neighbors?"

"I hope not"

"Why are you so grumpy?" Kyle asked.

"Why do you ask so many questions?" the man snapped, continuing down the hall to his apartment.

Not one to be easily cowered, Kyle continued cheerfully greeting Runar, but the old man's responses were always acerbic. When Kyle told his mother about their grouchy neighbor, she suggested he take a plate of cookies to him. Runar opened his door with a scowl.

"You again?" he growled. "What do you want?"

"My Mom baked these cookies for you."

"Well, thank your *mother*," he grumbled, snatching the plate and slamming the door.

Smiling, Kyle returned to his apartment, convinced his neighbor's bark was worse than his bite.

The following week, his mom awoke one morning with a high fever, belly pain, and vomiting. Alex, Kyle's stepfather, had to take her to the hospital but realized it wouldn't work to take Kyle since he had no idea how long he would be away. But who could he leave him with? In a panic, he realized the only person he knew was Runar. Apprehensive, he took Kyle to their neighbor's apartment and knocked loudly.

Runar, aroused from a nap, mumbled as he went to the door. He startled upon seeing Kyle and his father, Alex.

"I have an emergency and need to take my wife to the hospital. She's very sick. Would you mind looking after Kyle?" He didn't wait for an answer.

"Uh, I ..." Runar stammered.

"Thanks so much," Alex shouted over his shoulder, running to get his wife.

"Well, don't just stand there—come in," Runar muttered with a sigh.

"This is great," Kyle chirped, bounding into the living room. "What'll we do?"

"We? I'm going to read the paper. I don't know what you'll do."

"Do you have any games?"

"Games? What would I do with games?" Runar groused.

"Play with me."

"I have better things to do than play games."

"Then, I say we play twenty questions."

"Oh, all right, if you'll stop pestering me."

"I'm thinking of something old."

After asking twenty questions but failing to guess the correct answer, Runar gave up.

"Okay, you got me. What is it?"

"You," Kyle answered.

Despite himself, Runar laughed, the first time Kyle had seen a dent in his gruff demeanor. However, he quickly reverted back to his usual frown.

Later, Alex called to say he would be gone longer than he thought. With a life-threatening ruptured appendix, his wife required immediate surgery. He wanted to stay with her and asked Runar if he could keep Alex for a few days and see that he got fed. Runar reluctantly agreed.

"Why do you look so unhappy?" Kyle asked when Runar ended the call.

"Because I have to take you to dinner," he snarled.

"Oh goody! Can we have pizza?"

"I guess, if you promise not to bombard me with your relentless questions."

Looking over the menu at Paccelli's Pizza Parlor, Kyle asked if they could order pepperoni with extra cheese. Unfamiliar with pizza of any kind, Runar acquiesced. He found it surprisingly delicious, so much so, his frown faded with each piece he gobbled down.

"That was great," exclaimed Kyle. "Did you like it?"

"Yeah, it was okay," Runar answered, unwilling to let his guard down.

Back at the apartment, Runar got some bedding for the couch, Kyle's bed for the night.

"Do I have to sleep in this lumpy thing?" Kyle asked. "Why can't I sleep in your bed? It's king sized with plenty of room for both of us."

"Listen, Kid. You're either sleeping on the couch or the floor. Your choice."

Alex stayed at the hospital for three days. Kyle loved his time with Runar, but Runar was at his rope's end.

At breakfast, Runar placed a box of corn flakes in front of Kyle.

"I don't like corn flakes. What else do you have?

"Eat this or go hungry," Runar insisted.

At lunch, he made sandwiches using wheat bread.

"Do you have any white bread?" Kyle asked.

Runar threw up his hands.

"Look, kid, since you're in my apartment, you'll just have to eat what I have. Quit being so picky."

As days passed, Runar remained grouchy but had to admit it was nice having company, even if it was exasperating. After Kyle's parents returned from the hospital, Runar missed the excitement of having a youngster around. For his part, Kyle missed goading Runar into doing things he didn't want to do and went to visit him a couple of times.

One sunny day, Runar agreed to take Kyle for an ice cream cone while his mother napped. They had just started down the street when Kyle realized he had forgotten his cap. His mother insisted he wear it for sun protection. As he hurried back to Runar, he tripped, fell down the apartment stairs, and broke his arm. Wondering what was taking him so long, Runar went to investigate and found him lying at the bottom of the stairs holding his left arm.

"Oh my God, are you okay?" he asked.

"My arm hurts bad," Kyle whimpered.

"Looks broken." Runar grabbed his phone to call Kyle's dad.

"Alex, Kyle had an accident."

"What happened, Runar? Is he okay?"

"He's fine, but I think he has a broken arm. I can take him to the emergency room and meet you there. He'll get to a doctor faster that way."

When Alex arrived at the hospital, Runar explained what had happened. Fidgeting, they sat in the waiting room until the doctor came to tell them the arm was set and should heal fine.

With his arm in a splint for six weeks and not knowing others his age because of his recent move, Kyle spent time with Runar, who now was much more receptive to him. Kyle took his board games to Runar's apartment where they played for hours on end. No longer wearing a scowl, Runar took his young friend on trips to the zoo and the ice cream store.

After his mother recovered, Alex's folks invited Runar to a festive dinner. During the meal, it came up that Kyle's birthfather was a man named Dankworth who had died in an automobile accident four years earlier.

"Dankworth? What was his first name?" Runar asked.

"Hugo."

"My God, you were married to my son?" Runar struggled to catch his breath. "I lost track of him years ago. We never got along, especially after he became an alcoholic."

Kyle's mother jumped up from her chair.

"What? You're my father-in-law? Kyle, do you know what this means? Runar is your grandpa."

Since our initial impressions of people are often wrong, it is best to withhold judgment until we get to know them. As pointed out in this story, the world is sometimes smaller than we realize.

The Maiden and the Mask

"Mom, have you seen my blue rain jacket?" Cara asked. Packing for a one-month vacation at Lonely Pines Resort was taking a toll. She stormed around the room gathering clothes and throwing them into a suitcase. Frustrated, she sat on the edge of her bed with her head in her hands.

Why did I promise to do this? I don't want to go.

A 26-year-old barista at Starbucks, Cara relished time away from work, but she did not like the idea of going to a resort where she would be around a lot of people she didn't know. Not one to relate easily with others, she much preferred to stay home and read a book. She shunned parties and had few friends. Part of the reason may have been her looks. She was on the heavy side with a big nose and an overbite.

Precisely for these reasons, her folks had given her the trip as a birthday present thinking it would encourage her to be more outgoing. Advertisements for the resort stressed the many opportunities for meeting others.

Driving to the vacation spot, her mother spoke continuously about the great time Cara would have, but she remained silent.

As advertised, the camp provided many activities. On the first day, a sing-along took place in the living room. Not interested in singing, Cara went to her room. Since her roommate had the TV on, she left to go on a walk where she could be by herself.

Choosing one of many paths, she walked by the resort's workshop where she saw the back of a young man in overalls. When he turned around, she was shocked to see he wore a mask. Startled, she turned away.

"Hi, I'm Brennan, the handyman for the resort," he said. "I'm sorry if I frightened you."

"I'm Cara. Why are you wearing a mask?" she asked.

"My face is scarred from an accident. Please join me for a cup of coffee. I don't get many visitors."

Feeling unsure but not wanting to offend, she entered. He placed cups on a small table with an oilcloth covering. The delicious smell of coffee permeated the air. Opening a tiny refrigerator, he removed a carton of cream and added it to the sugar already on the table.

He motioned to a chair.

Looking closer, Cara saw that under the coveralls, he had a muscular build. Brown hair flowed down to his shoulders. Calloused hands were a testament to his work.

As they drank coffee, he through a straw, he told stories of how the resort started, his voice warm and calming. Cara, torn between staying and leaving, enjoyed the conversation but felt she should not be visiting with a strange man wearing a mask. Before long, she excused herself and left.

"You're welcome back any time—the coffee is always on," he said, waving to her.

Back in her room, Cara asked others about the masked handyman. Several people who had seen him felt he was creepy and urged her to avoid him.

The following day, none of the activities interested her, so she retreated to her room to read. Unable to concentrate, she decided to walk on a different path. It was a beautiful day, with sunlight filtering through tree branches and birds singing. The ubiquitous sound of croaking frogs added to the ambience. Before long, she came upon a pond, with an arched wooden bridge from which koi could be seen swimming among waterlilies. After walking for nearly an hour, she saw the handyman's workshop ahead and realized she had gone in a circle. She forged ahead, hoping to avoid Brennan. She had passed the building when she heard his voice behind her.

"Cara, won't you join me for coffee?"

Should I? I would love to know what his mask is hiding. Perhaps he'll remove it.

"Okay," she said, turning and walking back to the shop.

As before, he was charming. They had talked for 25 minutes when Cara excused herself and left.

For two days, she stayed in her room, reading a book and leaving only for meals. As time wore on, she became increasingly uneasy, putting the book down and pacing the floor. She even tried joining a treasure hunt put on by the resort. However, that soon wore thin, and she returned to her room. At night, she lay in bed, staring at the ceiling, finding sleep difficult. Finally, she decided to visit Brennan again.

The following morning, she took the path to the workshop. She knocked on the door but got no answer. As she turned to leave, Brennan came down the path pushing a wheelbarrow filled with mulch.

"Hi Cara, I haven't seen you for a while. Won't you come in for a bit?"

Confused by her feelings toward the masked man, she tripped on the doorsill and fell. Grabbing under her arms. Brennan easily lifted her up, holding onto her longer than necessary and looking into her eyes.

He seems so...nice. And why do I feel...this way?

Unhurt except for embarrassment, she joined him in conversation for nearly an hour. For the first time in her life, she found visiting with someone easy and enjoyable.

When she returned to her room, she pondered the encounter for hours, still wishing he'd take off his mask. She did not understand the feeling in her stomach. Sleep became difficult and reading impossible.

Eager to see him again, she went back to the shop on Sunday but could find no sign of him. Deciding to wait, she sat for an hour on a bench beside the door. He never appeared. Dejected, she returned to her room and flopped into her bed. Three days passed with no Brennan. Beside herself, Cara realized she was falling in love with a man she hardly knew, a man whose face she'd never seen. Why did he insist on wearing the mask? She stopped by often, hoping to see him, but he was gone.

Finally, he returned to the resort, explaining he had gone to the city to help his parents move. Glad for the simple explanation, she talked with him all afternoon until he indicated he had work to do. He grabbed her hand to help her up from the chair, then continued to hold it between his.

Oh my god, could he have feelings for me too?

Cara returned to the resort's dining room, dazed and upset. How could she fall for a masked handyman? It didn't make sense.

During the second week of her vacation, Cara and Brennan spent as much time together as they could. It became clear both were in love. Yet, despite repeated requests, he still would not remove his mask.

One evening, they walked to a nearby lake where they sat on a rock gazing at the stars. He seemed more distant than usual.

"Cara, I can't help it. I'm deeply in love with you, but I don't see how it can work out."

"Why not? We get along so well together," she protested, tearing up.

They discussed their relationship for a while before heading back to the resort. At the evening's end, Cara felt encouraged that he would change his mind.

The following day, Cara went to the shed as usual, but things were anything but usual.

"Cara, I've given this a lot of thought. I love you deeply, but this just isn't going to work."

"Why?" she protested, tears forming. She reached for his hand, but he pulled away.

"Have I done something?"

"No. It's me. My face. It just wouldn't work."

"Brennan, please take off your mask."

"I can't. Please leave now."

"The mask, Brennan. Take it off."

"For God's sake, Cara. It's over. Leave."

"I will when you remove your mask."

"Damn it, Cara, here," he said, ripping the mask from his face. "Satisfied? Now get out of here!"

She stood looking at him as her eyes moistened. Then, she slowly approached him, her gaze steady. Standing directly in front of him, she reached up only to have him pull away. Again, she reached up and gently ran her fingers over the scars on his face.

"I love you," she whispered in his ear. Then, for the first time, she kissed him, a long tender kiss.

Weeping with his head on her shoulder, he hugged her so hard she had trouble breathing.

"You are the loveliest person I have ever met," she said, crying. "But please get rid of that mask."

* * *

Three months later, a special event took place in the resort's famed Flower Garden. An azalea-lined path led to an open space encompassed by flowering shrubs. The gurgling of a forty-inch waterfall created a relaxing atmosphere for the 35 guests sitting in folding chairs on the lawn. Voices hushed as the last guests arrived.

"Is that Brennan?" a waiter at the resort's restaurant whispered.

"Yes," replied a manager. "He hasn't been around because we started a go-fund-me campaign so he could get plastic surgery."

"I've never seen him without a mask. He looks great."

The crowd quieted as the ceremony unfolded.

"I now pronounce you man and wife. You may kiss the bride."

Applause rang out as Brennan and Cara embraced.

"You once told me your parents insisted you come here," Brennan whispered.

"Best present ever," she cried, hugging him with every ounce of affection and gratitude she possessed.

How often have we felt discomfort around people with unpleasant features or been attracted to those with good looks? All too often, I suspect. By concentrating on the inner person rather than on external appearances, we may find real beauty and happiness.

The Woman in a Red Coat

Heading to work, David boarded the 7:22 train to Portland. An attractive woman in a red designer coat sat down nearby. He opened his book but couldn't keep his eyes off of her.

A 45-year-old bachelor, David had never married, not that he wouldn't have liked to. But he lacked self-confidence around women. It all began in childhood. Other kids made fun of his cleft lip and didn't include him in their activities. Things didn't improve as an adult, largely because of shyness and appearance. His receding hair line, paunch, limp from an old football injury, and lip, obvious despite his mustache, all contributed to his low self-esteem.

Quit dreaming. She would never be interested in me. She's probably married, anyway.

He tried to concentrate on his book, but to no avail.

As days went on, he kept seeing her, always in the same red coat, always with a book.

Why can't I stop thinking about her?

One day, the train was particularly crowded except for an open seat beside the woman.

Oh my god, I can't sit there.

He stood for a while, shifting about trying to reduce the pain in his knee. Giving up, he finally took the seat.

I hope she doesn't think me forward.

While taking off his coat, he accidently brushed against her leg.

Did she notice? Should I apologize?

His shyness prevailed and he said nothing. Ill at ease, he attempted to read, but all he could think about was the woman sitting beside him.

After fifteen minutes, she put the book in her lap and looked at him.

"I noticed you're reading a John Steinbeck novel. My book is also by him."

Nodding, he said nothing.

"My name is Amanda." She extended her hand.

"Ray," he replied, trembling.

Her hand feels so soft—I could hold it forever.

"Have you read other books by Steinbeck, Ray?"

"Yes, he's my favorite author."

*She is so beautiful. Why is she talking with **me**?*

"Mine too. His stories are so moving," she nodded. The conversation continued until they both got off at the same station. Ray warmed up during the conversation but hurried off to escape his lifelong discomfort.

The following day, he took his seat and had just started reading when Amanda entered and sat beside him, although other seats were available.

Why would she want to sit by me?

Settling in her seat, she brushed against his arm.

Was that intentional?

Heart racing, his face turned red. Amanda kept the conversation going despite Ray's reluctance.

"I take it you live in Hillsboro?" she asked.

"Yes."

"Did you grow up there?"

"No. Until college, I lived in Redding, California," he replied looking down.

"I spent my younger days near Bend," she offered. "My adoptive parents owned a large ranch. I miss the open spaces and the opportunity to go horseback riding. That's where I learned to fly my dad's Cessna. He even let me pilot it to Seattle for our monthly symphony concerts."

The conversation was interrupted by the train arriving at their station.

"See you around," Amanda said cheerily.

God, I hope so.

Over the following weeks, the two continued sitting together and conversing. Ray grew more comfortable talking with her, but still couldn't bring himself to ask her for a date. Then, the unthinkable happened. He didn't see her on the train for two weeks. Crestfallen, he fell behind at work and tossed and turned at night. Realizing she could not possibly be interested in him, he tried unsuccessfully to put her out of his mind.

Near the end of the month, he boarded the train and noticed the red coat a few rows ahead of him.

Should I sit beside her? Perhaps she's trying to avoid me.

Shaking and with butterflies in his stomach, he decided to at least say hello and see where that led.

"Good mor-morning." He barely got it out.

"Oh David, I'm so glad to see you. Do sit down. My dad died unexpectedly, and I had to go to Bend for the funeral and to be there for my mom. I didn't have any way of contacting you to let you know what happened."

She held his hand in both of hers.

Does she actually have feelings for me?

He turned his head a bit to hide his tears, then lost it and broke down.

"Why David, what on earth is wrong?"

"I'm...fond...of you...but didn't think...you could possibly...like me. When you didn't...show up on the train...I thought...I thought...maybe...you were trying to avoid me." He had a difficult time talking.

"Dear David, nothing could be further from the truth."

"Would you go out with me?" he blurted.

"I'd love to."

They had their first date at a pizza parlor in Hillsboro. After driving her home, they stayed in his VW talking for hours. Trembling as he walked her to the door, he wondered if he should kiss her. Because of his cleft lip, he had never dared to kiss a woman. Suddenly, she solved the situation by grabbing his shoulders and planting a long, heart-felt kiss.

He walked back to his car in a daze. Never before had he experienced such feelings.

After the pizza date, they had many more. On one, David brought up an issue bothering him.

"Amanda, I love you dearly, but I don't see how this can work. You come from an affluent background, used to fancy clothes, airplanes, and nights at the symphony. I can't provide such things."

"You silly thing. I don't care about any of that. I care for you. I can't hug a plane or kiss a symphony."

Those words removed the last of his qualms.

"Will you marry me?" he stammered.

"You know I will," she answered, flinging her arms around him and smothering him in kisses.

The wedding was a simple affair, with her folks and a few friends in attendance. They bought a house in Hillsboro and continued working in Portland. Immensely happy, they talked about starting a family, but put it off since they both worked long hours.

One day a letter arrived in the mail. David's mother wanted to come for a visit.

How on earth did she find out where I live?

He had no desire to see her since she abandoned him for drugs. Amanda, however, urged him to go through with the visit, saying his mother had probably changed and regretted losing him. After much cajoling, he relented and arranged a meeting.

Arriving in an old Chevy, his mother sat in her car, her brow furled and fingers drumming on the steering wheel. Eventually, she walked to the door and rang the bell. David answered, his stomach jittery.

"Huh…hello," he stammered.

She reached out to embrace him, but he pulled away. They stood, looking at each other.

"Is it okay if I come in?"

"Oh…yes." He stepped aside and showed her to the living room.

"Ha…have a seat."

"Thank you for seeing me."

An awkward silence prevailed until his mother broke the silence.

"I'm so sorry I abandoned you. At the time, I was strung out, not caring about anything but my next fix. But ten years later, I went into rehab and realized what a mistake I had made by leaving you and your sister." Her eyes moistened with tears.

Sister?

"I didn't know I had a sister."

At that moment, Amanda entered the room.

"This is my wife," he announced proudly.

"Hello, I'm Amanda," she said, extending her hand.

"David's sister was also named Amanda," his mother pointed out.

David fidgeted while Amanda engaged his mother in uneasy conversation. After a few minutes, the woman from his distant past departed, leaving her phone number and address.

Upset, David took his wife by the hand.

"She said her daughter was named Amanda. You don't suppose…?"

"Don't jump to conclusions, David."

"But I can't help wondering."

Amanda spent the next two months trying to find information about her birth mother, but without success. The authorities refused to reveal anything other than her birth date and adoption details. Hoping to settle the issue, she contacted David's mother and arranged to go to her home. They conversed more easily with him absent and soon established that Amanda's birth date agreed with the one mentioned by his mother.

"Amanda, do you…do you have a penny-sized birthmark on your left thigh?"

"Oh my God," she said, rushing to give her mother a hug. Then the initial euphoria gave way to the realization she had married her brother. Back home, she hugged her husband while confirming his suspicions.

"What should we do?" he asked in a halting voice.

"Absolutely nothing, except love each other and refrain from having kids," she replied."

"What will people think?"

"Who cares? Besides, no one needs to know we're siblings."

With misty eyes, he embraced his wife.

Trains have been the source of many mystery stories, but seldom other genres. I wanted to write a story about a romance that begins on a train.

Two Diaries

Ben—January 15, 2021: Today, I moved into The Pines, a retirement community. Since my wife died, I wanted a living arrangement free of the responsibilities of a large house and yard. The complex is huge, about 100 apartments. Meals are offered, so I don't have to cook. Unfortunately, my move comes in the midst of a pandemic, so I'm quarantined for two weeks. Boxes everywhere. After much trial and error, I have the main furniture arranged. It seems like a nice place to live, at least once the pandemic subsides.

Angela—February 22, 2021: I moved into an apartment in The Pines independent living facility. My living room is attractive, with enough room for my couch, love seat, rocking chair, and TV. My kitchen is convenient, although I don't plan to cook—one of the virtues of living here. Hated to give up my house, but it was just too much to keep up. People seem friendly.

Ben—March 11: At dinner, I sat with Angela, who lives down the hall from me. We had a pleasant conversation. We both go to eat at the same time each night. I may try to sit with her again.

Angela—April 22: I am finally settled in and enjoying my new life. I had a good conversation with Ben, a gentleman I met at dinner. It's nice being able to make new acquaintances.

Ben—May 7: At dinner, I was seated with Angela again. She's an attractive woman. I like visiting with her.

Angela—June 22: At dinner, I was seated with Ben. I mentioned that my daughter, Claire, had been a javelin thrower at the university. Ben asked what years she was there and indicated that his son, Tyler was a discus thrower at the same time. They surely would have known each other. Small world.

Ben—June 22: Seated with Angela, I was surprised to learn that her daughter threw the javelin at the University. She was there at the same time as Tyler and they would have known each other. I also learned that Angela and I both grew up on a farm. I'd like to get to know her better.

Ben—June 28: Angela showed me photos of her daughter. Like Tyler, Claire earned All American honors at the U. Both died young, Claire at 53 and Tyler at 51. The similarities are uncanny.

Angela—June 28: After dinner, I showed Ben pictures of Claire and the Rose parade honoring her and others for being organ donors. We talked for a while about our kids. He seemed genuinely interested in learning about Claire.

Ben—July 18: Because of covid, we are now restricted to having only one person at a table. Since the tables are far apart, visiting is impossible. I hate eating alone.

Ben—July 21: Learned that two people can sit together. Although the chairs are eight feet apart, conversation is possible. Since Angela and I go to dinner at the same time, I asked if she'd like to sit together to avoid the isolation. She agreed—much nicer than sitting completely alone.

Angela—July 21: Started sitting with Ben. We had an interesting conversation about our farming backgrounds. At my age, I feel rather strange being with a single male, although he seems pleasant.

Ben—Aug. 15: It was announced that we can resume sitting four to a table, making my excuse for sitting with Angela no longer apt. Not wanting to give up being with her, I asked if she'd still want to dine together. She said that was up to me. Pleased, I indicated that would be my choice.

Angela—Aug. 15: Now that we can resume sitting with others at a table, Ben asked if I'd like to continue sitting with him. I wonder just how interested he is in me.

Ben—September 1: Helped Angela with a TV problem. It took several hours since we had to get a new cable box and install it. I relished the opportunity to spend so much time with her.

Angela—September 1: My TV quit working. Ben spent hours fixing it. I appreciated his help since I would have been without TV for several days if he hadn't solved the problem.

Ben—September 17: The food choices didn't look good tonight, so I asked Angela if she'd like to eat takeout. We had delicious Mexican food in my apartment.

Angela—September 29: Our living facility puts on entertainment on the weekends. This week it was songs of the fifties. I took a seat near the back and Ben arrived later and sat next to me. Because our apartments are close, we walked back together, conversing along the way. I still feel uncomfortable being around a single man. Could this develop into something?

Ben—August 12: I saw Angela walking and asked if I could join her. We had a pleasant conversation—no awkward pauses.

Ben—September 3: Angela and I have been doing things together. Today we went to our facility's happy hour. As usual, the conversation was good. I wish I knew whether Angela had the feelings for me that I have for her.

Angela—September 14: We walked on the waterfront today. Then we sat on a bench to enjoy the sunshine and watch people. Ben sat down first and I sat close to him. He put his arm on the back of the bench and around me. I think he's interested in me. Should I be encouraging him? Does it make sense for people our age to be involved with one another? I'm satisfied with my women friends and daily routine.

Ben—September 14: After walking, we sat on a park bench watching people and visiting. Angela sat close to me. Does that mean anything? I don't want her to think I'm presumptuous, especially since she has indicated that she is learning how to be around single men. She hasn't even ridden in a car with a single man. I really like her. What should I do?

Ben—October 1: We've gone on a couple walks together. I'd love to hold her hand, but I don't know if she'd like that. I'd hate to turn her off because I was too forward.

Ben—October 7: We went on a short walk today. For the first time, I actually held her hand. Oh joy! I think it was okay with her since she gripped mine.

Angela—October 7: Ben asked me to go on a walk and held my hand for the first time. I'm becoming more comfortable with him.

Angela—October 23: Ben routinely holds my hand when we walk. I wonder if we'll eventually kiss. I'm willing, but I'm not sure he is.

Ben—November 12: I took Angela to a history museum. We had fun looking at the exhibits. Afterward, we had a drink at a café. I enjoyed holding her hand when we walked. She's enchanting.

Ben—November 25: I asked Angela over for dessert. We had a wonderful visit for over an hour. We seem to have so much in common. When she left, I asked her if she'd mind if I hugged her and she agreed. I don't know what I'd have done if she had turned me down.

Angela—November 25: Went to Tyler's apartment for pie and a great visit. Afterward, he asked for a hug, which was nice. I'm feeling more comfortable with him and enjoy his company. It's fun getting out and doing things, especially since I have no car.

Ben—November 30: I'd love to kiss Angela but I'm worried that she'd think I was too brash. I don't want to do anything that would jeopardize our relationship. I now feel comfortable holding her hand.

Angela—December 3: Ben invited me to his apartment after dinner. He expressed his feelings for me. I could tell he was reluctant to take the next step, so when I stood to leave, I brought my face toward his and we kissed. I had wondered when that would happen. Even in death, our children brought us together. If it hadn't been for them, we might never have become close.

Ben—December 3: We kissed for the first time! Finally, I feel completely comfortable and relaxed with her. I expressed my feelings for her in the following poem:

> I thrill to the touch of her hand as she grips mine,
> To the warmth of her body, the caress of her lips,
> Her smile drives away darkness, lighting up my day,
> And my heart sings with the exhilarating music of love.

Seniors, especially those living in retirement homes, often feel alone. Many have lost a spouse after many years of marriage. Plagued with fears about intimate interaction with the opposite sex, they can appear bumbling to young people. However, love at any age is beautiful.

Stranded

"Dad, Ben and I have been thinking about taking a trip to Wallowa Lake," Jason started. "Would it be okay to take the Miss Behave?"

"How long do you plan to be away?"

"Three days."

"Well, I trust you to be safe, as long as you promise to wear life vests."

"Thanks, Dad," Jason beamed, an unmistakable bounce to his gait as he rushed to phone his friend with the news.

Since Jason was generally responsible, his father had few reservations about granting permission. Jason had taken the boat out before and had always been careful.

The two boys, both high-school seniors, had a three-day weekend because their school was closed on a September Friday for plumbing repairs. A quiet teen, Jason excelled in school. On the other hand, Ben was an average student, popular with his peers, but had a rebellious streak. Companions since third grade, they planned to camp two nights, explore the lake, and water ski. The Miss Behave, a bowrider motorboat, was perfect for such activities.

On a sunny Friday in September, they threw their gear into Jason's pickup and headed out from Lewiston, Idaho. On the way, Ben brought up the possibility of going to the Snake River instead of Wallowa Lake.

"But I told my dad we were going to the lake," Jason protested.

"We've been *there* several times, but never to the Snake," Ben pointed out. "It would be fun to do something different." The discussion went on for several minutes.

"My dad will kill me if we change our plans."

"He doesn't need to know," Ben grinned, his voice silky and his tone persuasive. Little by little, Jason's opposition wilted, and he admitted he'd like to see the canyon. So, it was settled.

Arriving at the put-in site, they launched the boat.

"Put on your life vest, Ben," Jason insisted as he donned his.

"I'm not going to wear one. I hate those things."

"Ben, I told my dad we'd wear vests. Put it on!"

"Oh, okay, but I don't see why we need them."

Starting out, the going was smooth. They had a good time, expecting to find a camping spot upstream. After an hour, they encountered some Class I rapids. The boys whooped and hollered as the boat bounced on the waves. Later, they came upon some Class II rapids, providing more thrills, though Jason, uneasy, frowned as he steered the boat. Stopping at a sandbar, they enjoyed a lunch of ham sandwiches and canned pop. Afterward, they lay on the beach, enjoying the sunny day.

"Keep a lookout for a place to camp," Jason said as they resumed their trip.

"What's that noise?" Jason asked as they progressed. Rounding a bend, they shouted warnings to each other. "Oh my god, we can't navigate that," Jason screamed above the thunderous roar. "Class IV rapids!"

"Keep to the right of that big rock," Ben yelled back. "We'll be okay."

Jason hesitated, then decided it'd be better to turn around. But it was too late. The waves flipped the boat, tossing the boys into the icy water and washing them downstream. The life vest raised Jason to the surface first.

"Ben, Ben…Ben?" No answer. Frantically looking around, he spotted his friend floating but unresponsive. Jason splashed toward the unconscious boy and grabbed his vest. Struggling as wave after wave plunged them under, he eventually got him to quieter water just as Ben regained consciousness, coughing and spitting.

As they floated downstream and the rapids gave way to calmer waters, Jason pulled Ben to the side, but the bank was too steep for them to climb. Eventually, they came to a sand bar and wearily threw themselves ashore, panting hard and coughing. Since the sun was hidden by clouds and they were soaking wet, they started shaking, partly from fright, partly from cold.

Ben felt a lump on his head and winced in pain. Blood trickled onto his cheek. Jason held his left arm which had an ugly twelve-inch gash. Both were covered with scrapes and bruises.

"The boat's gone," Jason wailed, lying on his back with his hands over his eyes. "Why…why did I let you talk me into this? What'll I tell my dad?"

"Right now, we need to get out of these wet clothes," Ben answered. "I'm freezing." They put their clothes to dry on rocks still hot from the sun. Stomping their feet to get warm, they cursed as dark clouds rolled in. After 45 minutes, they put their clothes back on, still damp but tolerable.

"What'll we do now?" Ben said in a barely audible voice. "We can't stay here."

"Let's get to higher ground. Perhaps we can spot a house or a road."

The uphill climb was tough, their shoes squishing with every step. The wind whipped at their shirts and the sagebrush swiped their legs.

"I need to rest," Ben complained, heading toward a large boulder.

"Stop!" Jason yelled, yanking him backward.

"What's the matter?"

"A rattler, sunning itself on the rock you were about to sit on."

The menacing rattling sound filled the air as they backed carefully away.

"Oh my god," Ben rasped. "That was close!"

Jason put his hand up to shield his eyes from the sun as he peered up the canyon.

"Do you see a road or trail?"

"Nothing but sagebrush and dried out shrubs. Let's go higher. Perhaps we'll see something from there." He pointed to a ridge above them.

After gaining more elevation, they still could see no sign of civilization.

"Wait a minute. What's that?" Jason pointed southwest. "It almost looks like the roof of a house. Let's check it out."

As they got closer, they could tell it was, indeed, a building of some sort. After another 700 feet of elevation gain, they arrived at an old miner's cabin situated on a slight incline. Hanging by one rusty hinge, the door nearly fell off when Jason opened it. Inside, a shelf held several rusty cans, their labels gone. A crude handmade table and a bunk with the remains of a rat-infested, straw mattress rounded out the contents. Slivers of sunlight filtered through the roof.

Ben stepped on a loose board on the floor. Curious, he picked it up to discover a spring flowing under the floor.

"Well, I'll be damned. A cabin with running water. That'll come in handy," he exclaimed. There was one window with most of the glass missing. "Must have been vacant for years," he added, looking around at the empty shack covered in cobwebs and dust.

They removed some of their clothes and spread them out to dry. While Ben cupped his hands to drink from the spring, Jason sat on a box with his head in his hands.

"What's the matter, Jason?"

"What's the matter?" he snapped. "My dad's boat is gone, and we're stranded here on the side of a canyon. No one will come looking for us for three more days since we aren't expected back until Sunday night. When they do look, it'll be at Wallowa Lake, not the Snake River. Even if rescuers search the Snake Canyon, they won't expect us way up here. Finally, we're beat up and have no food. Other than that, nothing is wrong, Ben, nothing at all!" Jason sniffed and wiped his nose on the back of his hand. "I should never have let you talk me into changing our destination." His icy glare could have frozen hell itself.

Ben turned away, hanging his head but saying nothing. What could he say? Jason was right. They sat silently for an hour. Almost in a whisper, Ben broke the silence.

"I'm really sorry, Jason, but we couldn't have stayed near the river without shelter."

"Probably not," Jason conceded, putting his hand on Ben's shoulder. "And I'm sorry I exploded."

"I wonder what's in those rusty cans?" Ben commented minutes later. "Let's open one."

Without tools, Jason took a can outside to look for a sharp rock. Finding one, he struck the can. Beans spilled out, some on the ground. He tasted one. It seemed okay, so the boys ate hungrily. Jason insisted on saving the rest for later.

"We need to decide what to do about sleeping," he pointed out. "Throw out that old mattress. I'll gather some shrubs and grass to pad the boards. The bunk is narrow, but I think we can both squeeze in." After collecting and arranging the cushioning, he tested the bed. "It's not the most comfortable, but it'll have to do."

The sun had already disappeared behind the canyon wall. They had no way of making a fire since all their equipment was lost when the boat capsized. As darkness descended, they crawled into the bunk, shivering from the cold. All they had for warmth was each other and the clothes on their backs. Eventually, they fell into a fitful sleep.

Saturday morning, they awoke, barely able to move from the beating they had taken. Their miserable bed had added to their stiffness. Jason nearly collapsed as he rose. Ben fingered the enormous lump on his head. Wincing, Jason examined the wound on his arm. After they loosened up, they shared another can of beans.

"What'll we do now?" Ben asked, continuing to finger his head. "Should we try to hike out?"

"We can barely walk, and there are cliffs we couldn't pass," Jason replied. "Besides, when lost, one should stay put. Let's make an SOS. A plane flying overhead might see it."

They set about clearing a large area of brush and gathering rocks for the sign. It wasn't as visible as they would have liked since they could only use rocks small enough to carry, but they agreed it was the best they could do. Before long, they were complaining about their hands blistering from all the shrubs they had pulled out and the heavy rocks they had carried.

"Let's see if there is a road or trail higher up," Jason suggested when finished. Their injuries made walking torturous. After climbing three hours, black clouds had rolled in, hiding the sun. Rain started—light at first. Visibility was still good, but they could see no road or trail. They started back down to the cabin. Before long, the rain became a torrent, with blinding flashes of lightning and earsplitting thunder. They slipped and slid their way back to the cabin and arrived soaking wet, exhausted, and discouraged. Jason opened two cans, one of which was peaches and the other beans. They ate in silence.

After eating, Jason noticed his buddy scratching his legs.

"Ben, pull up your pantlegs." A red rash with ugly welts oozing liquid covered both legs. "Dude, that's bad news."

"What is it?"

"Poison ivy. Don't scratch it."

"I can't help it. It itches like crazy."

"I know, Ben, but scratching spreads it, making the itching worse. Wash it as well as you can in the spring." In the night, Jason heard him whimpering quietly.

Sunday morning, Jason saw that Ben was in bad shape. Unable to sleep, he continually complained about the itching and the impossibility of being rescued. Jason opened the next to last can of food, but his companion refused to eat. To top it off, it started to rain again. Water poured in through cracks in the roof. Jason did his best to plug them with pieces of the empty tin cans and boards lying around in the cabin. They huddled in the lone corner that remained relatively dry.

An hour later, Ben started retching. Jason joined him shortly thereafter.

Food poisoning. Damn!

Jason did his best to clean up the mess using water from the spring.

The rain fell in sheets and continued long into the evening. The cabin was almost as wet inside as out. Making matters worse, Ben couldn't resist scratching, which only increased his misery. They spent another restless night.

On Monday morning, the boys passed most of the day lying about. The only diversion was the sound of an occasional passenger jet far above. From time to time, Jason scanned the river for any sign of life, but he hadn't seen a boat since they arrived.

* * *

The search for the missing teens began in earnest on Monday. Search and Rescue boats ran the length of Wallowa Lake, hoping to see some sign of the boys—a campfire, debris, anything. Nothing. They scanned the lake with sonar. Nothing. As darkness approached, the rescue parties agreed to meet at sunup on Tuesday.

Early Tuesday morning, a fisherman launched his boat in the Snake River and proceeded to his favorite spot. There, he saw a box floating in the water. Curious, he pulled up alongside and lifted it into his boat. Opening it, he found camping gear. As he scanned an eddy nearby, he saw Ziplocs containing sandwiches. Alarmed, he tried to phone authorities. No service. He then motored downstream until he had a signal and called 911.

Since it was well known that two boys were missing from a boating vacation, Search and Rescue diverted their attention to the Snake River Canyon. A jet boat and a helicopter were dispatched.

An hour later, Jason heard a new sound. As he got up, the sound grew louder. He ran outdoors, scanning the sky. The familiar whomp, whomp, whomp of a chopper gave him hope as it moved upriver. He waved his arms, jumped up and down, and hollered, despite knowing there was no way his voice could possibly be heard. However, the helicopter continued upstream. Dejected, he considered making his way down to the river so the rescuers could see him on their way back. But knowing that would take hours, he realized the chopper would return long before he could reach the water's edge.

Why didn't we make an arrow pointing uphill? Or an SOS near the river?

He went back into the cabin to tell Ben what had happened, but a faint whirring returned. Running back outside, he saw the chopper heading his way. He jumped up and down, waving his arms. It kept coming—straight toward him. Once it landed, Jason ran toward it and hugged the first person he saw, tears flowing.

"Thank you," he managed to blurt before choking up.

Have you had a teenager who got in trouble doing something foolish? Most people have, including me, which provided the motivation for this story. The setting is based on my experience going on a jet boat up the Snake River to Hells Canyon and on a backpacking trip in the Wallowa Mountains. During the latter, I happened upon a cabin similar to the one in the story, including the spring flowing under it.

Footsteps in the Attic

"What a neat house! Can we get it?" Darlina pleaded as she marveled at the old Victorian mansion. "It would be like living in a castle,"

"We'll see," her father answered. "It's been empty for years and would need a lot of work."

From the outside, they saw the two-story mansion had an attic. On the left was a round tower with a conical roof. An enormous chimney reached to the sky. On the right, a large porch led to the front door. In the back, a storage shed for yard tools adjoined the building. Not far away was a greenhouse with missing glass panes. Rotten windowsills, a moss-covered roof, loose siding, and other problems meant lots of renovation work.

Inside, what had once been an ornate grand staircase ascended to a landing where it branched left and right to the second floor. A huge, tarnished chandelier and a marble fireplace graced the living room.

Darlina, a sparkling five-year-old, with freckles and pigtails tied with red ribbons, was in constant motion, running from room to room. After exploring the winding stairs in the tower, she sprinted up the main staircase to explore the second floor. She immediately fell in love with one of the bedrooms on the east side. It had French doors that opened onto a balcony from where she saw ducks swimming in a small lake. Despite filthy, floral wallpaper hanging in strips, torn carpet hiding the original oak floor, many cobwebs, and a closet missing a door, the room showed promise of elegance.

"Can I have this room?" she asked.

"Slow down, we haven't decided to buy the place yet," her father laughed, as he surveyed the room.

After much debate, her parents decided to make a low offer on the house. To their surprise, it was accepted.

They spent a year renovating and installing appliances to make it sufficiently livable. They knew it would likely take two more years to have it in the condition they wanted.

Darlina picked out wallpaper for her room. The refinished oak floors and new French doors opening onto the balcony made stunning additions.

On moving day, Darlina skipped around and waved her arms excitedly. She knew exactly where she wanted her furniture and ensured the movers got it right.

The first night, she refused to turn off the light, wanting to relish the looks of her room. She got out of bed repeatedly to move her dresser slightly or adjust a picture on the wall. Finally, her energy spent, she settled down into restful sleep.

On the second night, she heard footsteps in the attic and called out for her parents. They came running.

"What's wrong, Darlina? "

"The footsteps are keeping me awake."

"What footsteps?"

"In the attic," she answered.

"Honey, no one is in the attic. This house has been vacant for years," her father assured.

"Maybe it's a ghost," Darlina argued.

"But sweetheart, ghosts float. You can't hear their footsteps," her mother interjected. "Perhaps the shutters blew in the wind. Now try to get some sleep. She pulled the blankets to her daughter's chin and kissed her forehead.

Over the course of several days, Darlina insisted she heard footsteps, whereas her folks tried to convince her she was imagining things. Becoming concerned at her insistence, they took her to see a psychologist. After several sessions, the therapist concluded she was a perfectly normal girl with perfectly normal imaginations.

One night, Darlina was startled by a shadow moving in her room. A man, standing at a distance with his hands raised in surrender, wore a warm smile.

"Don't be scared. My name is Treyvon. I'm not going to hurt you. I cud tell you was upset, hearing my footsteps n all, so I came down to talk with you—explain what's going on. Since I'm homeless, da previous owners of this house let me live in da attic. Don't worry about my footsteps. I ain't mean it if I scared you. What's your name?"

"Darlina."

"That's uh pretty one."

"You talk funny," Darlina said, laughing.

"Different folks talk different, but we all say da same. This is da way I wuz brought up."

The man was so gentle and nice that she quickly felt at ease. Treyvon explained that a wall in the tool shed was actually a door that opened up to a ladder going to the attic, enabling him to come and go without bothering the owners. Having nowhere else to live, he stayed after the house was put up for sale. He explained the home had been a safehouse for slaves escaping to the north—a cog in the underground railroad. He also told her about the well-disguised door in the hall ceiling with a drop-down ladder.

Enthralled with the man's stories, Darlina talked with him for over an hour until Treyvon said he should leave and let her get some sleep.

Treyvon came each evening and regaled her with tales. He told stories about the underground railroad, the role her parents' house played in it, and exploits from his own life.

After several visits with Treyvon, Darlina dared to tell her parents about him.

"I have a new friend. His name is Treyvon."

"Oh, really? Is this someone you met at school?"

"No, he comes to my bedroom. I talk with him every night. He's really nice."

Her parents, concerned that she was slipping into an imaginary world, talked again with the psychologist, who again reassured them that young children often had vivid imaginations and that it was nothing to worry about.

As the renovation projects continued, the house gradually regained its former glory. Restoration was nearly complete on the outside and first floor inside. They were about to begin work upstairs when an electrical short started a fire in the pantry below.

Flames soon spread to the kitchen and living room, including the stairs. Smoke alarms screeched, awakening Darlina's parents, who left their bedroom coughing from the smoke.

"I'll get Darlina!" her mother shouted as she started up the flaming stairs. Her father ran after her and pulled her to a stop.

"The fire is too intense, we can't go that way," he shouted over the roaring flames.

"We can't just leave her," she sobbed between fits of coughing.

"I'll get a ladder and see if I can get...." The burning timber drowned out his words. A neighbor came to fight the fire with a garden hose, but it couldn't quench the blaze. He soon gave up in defeat. Neighbors gathered in the street, shielding their faces from the heat, watching in horror. The shrill siren of a fire truck grew louder as it neared.

Running to the west side of the house near the origin of the fire, her father found a wood ladder, but it was burning. Grabbing an aluminum ladder, he cursed and dropped it, his hand blistered from the hot metal.

Dashing to Darlina's balcony on the east side of the house, burning debris from the collapsing porch fell from above, nearly hitting him.

Meanwhile, Treyvon, raced to Darlina's room.

"Don' worry honey, ah'll git choo out," he said in a calm voice.

He picked her up and headed for the stairs but met a wall of flames. As the ceiling collapsed, he raced to the attic stairs and to the secret ladder.

"Okay, darling, there ain't room for both of us, so I'll go first. That way I can catch you if you start to fall. Think you can go down this ladder?"

"I think so," she cried.

Once they made it down, Treyvon picked her up and carried her to her parents who were standing below her balcony shouting her name.

"Here...she is...she's fine," Treyvon said, gasping for breath.

Darlina clung to her mother, crying.

"Watch out," her father exclaimed when the balcony crashed to the ground with a thunderous roar. They fled to the street just as a fire engine arrived. After catching their breaths, they turned their attention to Treyvon.

"Who are you?"

"I'm Treyvon."

"What are you doing here, and how did you get Darlina?" he shouted above all the commotion.

"Well, sir, I've been living in da attic for years. I went to her room n carried her up into da attic n down uh secret latter to da tool shed n here we are." He went on to explain that, years earlier, the house had been used in the underground railroad to hide slaves escaping to the north. Since he was homeless, the owner let him stay in the attic.

"I knew I shouldda moved out when you bought da house, but I had nah place to go. I'm sorry. I'll go now."

Darlina, leaving her mother's embrace, ran to Treyvon and wrapped her arms around his legs.

"He's my friend. Can he live with us?"

"Well, Treyvon, we owe you a huge debt of gratitude. I don't know where we'll live now, but I hope you stick around and we'll see how things work out. In the meantime, you can stay at the Hillside Motel on us."

Who hasn't been intrigued by tales of old mansions with hidden passageways and creepy sounds? I thought it would be fun to write such a story. Rather than base it on supernatural events, I wanted it to have a rational explanation. Everything about the tale is fiction.

Clyde

He stood out from the crowd, did Clyde. With a protruding forehead, widely-spaced eyes, thick lips, a pug nose, and above all, intellectually disabled, he attracted unending ridicule from his peers. In stature, Clyde was short and stocky with the most distinguishing feature being an unusually large butt. Since he lived in Lone Pine, a town of only 2,012, everyone knew him. Although generally ignored by adults, younger kids teased him unmercifully, especially the Three Amigos—Joe and his buddies, Bill and Dexter. Known as the town's bullies, they enjoyed asking Clyde to do outlandish things.

As Clyde and his eleven-year-old brother, Lester, walked on Main Street to the dime store, they chanced upon the Three Amigos.

"Hey, dog face, we need someone to direct traffic," Joe said, looking around to insure no adult would hear him. Pulling a toy badge from his pocket, he gave it to Clyde and told him he was now a police officer and to go into the street to direct traffic. With his ubiquitous smile, Clyde entered the main intersection and proceeded to wave his arms directing traffic. Since the drivers were local people who knew him, they were careful to avoid an accident. After a bit, Joe called Clyde to return to the sidewalk.

"Way to go, dog face. You're a great policeman. See that person who just walked into the dime store? He's wanted for murder. This is your chance to be a hero. Arrest him."

Clyde went up to the man, showed his star, and said he was arresting him for murder.

"Alright, Clyde, but first let me get some candy for my daughter," the man said, realizing someone had put him up to the stunt.

"Okay, I'll arrest you tomorrow," Clyde answered, agreeable as always.

Alarmingly, Lester never objected to his brother being treated in such fashion; in fact, he often joined in.

On another occasion, Joe and his cohorts in crime encountered Lester and Clyde in the town's park.

"Hey Big Butt, pretend you are a dog and go fetch this stick in your mouth." Joe threw the stick about fifty feet and Clyde ran to get it, put it in his mouth, and returned it to Joe several times.

"Okay, Dog Face, now bark like a dog." Clyde barked and Joe petted him on the head.

"Now wag your tail."

"Don't have a tail," Clyde replied, looking behind himself.

Such shenanigans occurred every few days. But one day, they came to an end. On the edge of town, the bridge crossing the Inesh River attracted daredevils who liked to exhibit their bravery by crossing the bridge on its six-inch railing. One day, as Joe attempted the dare, he saw Lester and Clyde approaching.

"Hey Big Butt, come walk the railing with me." Though Lester usually didn't object to people ridiculing Clyde, this time he insisted his brother stay on the sidewalk.

"Come on Big Butt," Joe persisted, you can fly, so there's nothing to be afraid of."

His attention on Clyde, Joe put his foot down on the edge of the railing, lost his balance, and plunged 35 feet into the river below.

"Oh my god, Dexter, save him," Bill exclaimed, "I can't swim."

"I ain't committin' suicide by jumping into that river," Dexter retorted.

Clyde jumped up on the rail and dove headfirst into the water. He swam like a fish.

People ran to the scene, reacting to the yelling and waving of arms at passing cars. Then the boys raced across the bridge and down to the river's edge. Clyde was struggling to hold onto Joe while fighting the current. When he reached the bank, two adults grabbed Joe, unconscious, and laid him on the ground. They were about to begin CPR when he came to, confused about what had happened. Bill explained that he had fallen into the river and Clyde had dived into the river to save him.

"He dove from the bridge?" Joe asked incredulously. "Big Bu..., er Clyde...." At that point, he reached for Clyde and hugged him, thanking him over and over. Patting Clyde on his back, the adults praised his bravery. For his part, Clyde, smiling as usual, wondered what all the fuss was about.

As school got out the next day, some kids saw Clyde and started teasing him.

"Knock it off or I'll make ya wish ya hadn't gotten up this morning." Joe, standing nearby, sent them scattering with a menacing glare.

Though fictionalized, I knew a person like Clyde when I was young. Many, but not all, of the episodes described herein actually happened. Writing the story gave me the opportunity to show the cruelty of bullying and teasing. Everyone has redeeming qualities. All place names are fictitious.

Invasion of the Ants

Spreading photographs of rentals on the counter, the agent ended his sales pitch.

"You can't go astray with a Honeymoon Chalet."

Despite wincing at the cheesy motto, David and Elena decided on one especially picturesque unit.

"Excellent choice," the representative said. "It's our nicest cabin—a bit more expensive, but hey, you only get married once. You can reserve it with a fifty-percent deposit. The rest will be due at the end of your stay."

Showered with rice as they left the wedding, the newlyweds left their cellphones behind and joyfully made their way to their honeymoon site in the Cascade mountains. Turning off I-90, they continued on forest-service roads for several miles until arriving at their destination just before sunset.

"Just look at that, David. What a lovely setting."

The luxurious cottage had a large deck looking out onto a flock of Canadian geese swimming in a gorgeous lake. A great blue heron perched on a rock near the water and snowcapped peaks loomed in the distance.

"Wow," David exulted. "The photos didn't do it justice."

After unloading the car, they embraced passionately, finding the king-sized bed suitable for their amorous activities. Thirsty, Elena went to the kitchen to get a drink. A look of surprise crossed her face as she peered intently out the window.

"Strange, the backyard is full of big lumps."

"Who cares?" David replied. "As long as the bed isn't lumpy, I'm happy. I think we can occupy ourselves inside." Nevertheless, he ambled over to see what she was talking about. His brow wrinkled as he took in the sight.

"That's bizarre. The front yard wasn't that way," he agreed.

"David, do you know if the cabin is equipped with ant bait?"

"Why? You anticipating problems?"

"No, I just saw one in the kitchen."

"Just kill it, Elena."

"I did."

David prepared dinner in the well-stocked kitchen, stopping frequently to look out the window, puzzling over the mounds.

After a candlelit meal, he stomped his foot.

"I just killed another—perhaps a friend of the one you did in," he joked.

As the sun set, Elena went to the kitchen to get a glass of water. Something caught her eye.

"David, look."

"Look? Where?"

"The floor, there." She pointed.

He saw several ants milling around. Irritated, he swatted them with his shoe.

"You'd think a honeymoon cabin wouldn't be infested with ants," he grumbled.

"David, do you hear that?"

"What?"

"That chirping sound," she exclaimed, grabbing him.

"Yeah, what is it?"

"I don't know, but it's getting louder." She held him tighter.

David got up to look for the source of the noise. Peering out the window, he saw movement in the faint light but couldn't tell what it was.

"Honey, would you bring me the flashlight from the bed stand?"

Shining the light out the window, he saw thousands of ants emerging from the lumps in the yard.

"My god," he exclaimed, "those mounds are ant hills. Solid lines of the things are streaming toward the house. That racket is coming from them." As he looked around, he saw ants pouring in under the door.

"Elena, we have to stop these damned ants. Shut all the windows and block any cracks you see."

He shoved a throw rug against the bottom of the front door, but it didn't stop them. The eerie sound kept getting louder.

"See if there's tape of any kind that we could use."

Yanking open several drawers, Elena found only a small roll of adhesive tape.

"Ouch," Elena yelled, frantically pulling up her robe. "They're biting my legs!"

"Me, too," he cursed, slapping at the nasty pests.

"Maybe they're after food. Let's toss it into the yard," he cried, dancing up and down to avoid getting bitten further.

They opened cabinet doors, grabbing all the edibles and piling them on the counter.

"When I open the window, we need to fling everything out as quickly as possible and squash any ants that get in. Ready? Here goes." More insects streamed in.

"They're biting my arms," Elena screamed.

"Mine too," he said, brushing them from his arms. Turning on the kitchen faucet, he grabbed the sprayer and washed them off Elena and then turned the spray on himself. Their arms and legs were covered in red, painful welts.

Loud banging on the front door startled them.

"What's that?" David yelled.

Elena shined the flashlight through the glass in the door.

"My god, it's a man!" she exclaimed, reaching for the lock.

"No, Elena! For god's sake, don't open the door. You'll let in more of them."

"But...he'll die."

David grabbed the light and shined it on the stranger. The creatures were crawling in his mouth, nose, ears—even his eyes. The man convulsed and collapsed on the porch. He moved no more.

"He's gone," David said firmly.

"They're coming in under the baseboard," Elena screamed. "Quick, tape it."

"We're out. Stuff rags in it instead."

Finding nothing but their clothes, she tried to force them into the cracks.

"It's not working. The crevices are too tight."

In a frenzy, they swatted the creatures for hours until the floor was black with their dead bodies. The smelly sight nearly made them retch.

"We can't keep up with them. Let's go into the loft. Maybe they haven't gotten up there yet," David bellowed. He scrambled up the ladder and reached down to help Elena. She whimpered and David cursed as they examined the bloody welts on their arms and legs.

Directing the light beam on the ladder, David panicked. The critters were halfway up the ladder. He tried to kick it free but couldn't.

Elena wept and they held each other waiting for the inevitable.

"Do you think we'll make it, David? I keep thinking of that poor man."

"I don't know. If they get up here…."

The first sunlight peeked over the foothills and through their lakeside windows. As if flipping a switch, the ants stopped their advance, lingered, and then started to retreat.

"They're leaving!" Elena shouted. "They're leaving!"

"Nocturnal ants?" David mused, hugging his wife and rejoicing at the unexpected turn of events.

Once the creatures left the cabin, David and Elena grabbed their clothes and rushed to their car. After killing more of the insects that had made their way inside, they sped away.

"I feel sick and my tongue is swollen," Elena sobbed, her pent-up emotions finally finding release.

"Me too. I think we're reacting to the bites. I'm heading to the emergency room."

Hustling them into the ER, medics administered epinephrine to stop their allergic reactions. Cold compresses helped reduce the swelling on their arms and legs. Hydrocortisone cream and antihistamines reduced the itching. After two nights in the hospital, they were discharged.

As they limped into their apartment, the telephone rang and David answered.

"Hello."

"Is this David?"

"Yes."

"This is Jeff Whittingham from Honeymoon Chalets. I've been trying to reach you for two days. You haven't paid the second...."

Cursing, David slammed down the receiver.

Having experienced the vicious stings of ants and seen Hitchcock's movie, "The Birds," I thought it would be fun to write a story about an army of the insects attacking humans. What could be more poignant than to have the onslaught take place during one of life's most thrilling events—a honeymoon?

Ransom

Steering her Lexus around curve after curve on US 101, Mary Pickering thought about her next con job. She had to come up with a bigger payday than her last trick, a measly ten grand. That didn't go far these days.

At 42, Mary was meticulous about her façade of respectability—designer clothes, a shapely figure to match, a studded wedding band—despite not being married. Her partner in crime, Jill Hancock, had blond hair cascading down her back, a mini skirt, and a blouse with a plunging neckline, helpful in certain swindles. She looked ten years younger than her actual age of 38. For nine years they had worked together, getting by, but unable to live the lifestyles they wanted.

As they rounded yet another curve, the car ahead of them hydroplaned and careened down a bank, rolling as it plunged. Always on the alert for possible capers, they stopped to investigate. Slipping and sliding down the steep bank, they arrived at the upside-down car, its wheels still spinning.

In the front seats, Mary found two men, both bloody, both presumed dead. Then she checked the man in the back.

"Oh my god, this is Frank McPherson!"

"You know the guy?" Jill asked.

"I saw his picture in *Fortune*. He is the CEO of Infodyne, the IT company. He's worth billions!"

"Is he alive?"

"I think so…he has a pulse and I don't see any blood. Do you realize what this means?"

"No, what?" Jill answered.

For a con artist, she's not the brightest bulb in the building!

"Lady luck is with us." Mary smacked her lips.

"What are you talking about?"

"Ransom, Jill. Anyone worth billions is worth a big payday."

Excited chatter followed until they settled on a plan. First, they had to get the unconscious man up the steep bank and into their car. Fortunately, passing cars couldn't see them or the wreck from the highway.

Each woman grabbed an arm and together they dragged him up the bank. Their feet slipped on the muddy slope and soon they were gasping for air from the exertion. Keeping him out of view of the highway, they waited for a lull in traffic before pushing him into the back seat of their car. Exhausted, they leaned against the car, their heads hanging low. Next, they tied his arms and legs and blindfolded him. The plan was to keep him in Mary's cabin deep in the mountains, about a two-hour drive from San Francisco.

Arriving at the cabin, they pulled McPherson from the car, carried him inside, and tied him to a bed. Before removing his blindfold, they donned Halloween masks to hide their faces.

"My head!" McPherson moaned, coming to.

"You hit your head and were unconscious for over an hour," Mary answered.

Jill added, "I have some nurse training. We'll take good care of you."

"What happened? Why am I tied up? Who are you anyway?" he asked, pulling at his bonds.

"We are holding you for ransom," Mary answered. "You don't need to know our names. Just do as we say and you'll be fine—at least if the ransom is paid."

"Where are we?"

"No more questions," Mary snapped.

Jill put an ice pack on his head to relieve the swelling. Mary offered him Tylenol and a glass of water. They had to ensure he stayed healthy; no one paid ransom for a dead person.

The two women went outside to discuss their next steps.

"How much should we ask?" Jill questioned. "One million?"

"One million?" Mary snorted. "Remember, he's worth billions!"

"Well, what do you suggest?"

"I think more like one billion," Mary replied.

They continued to discuss the amount until deciding on 100 million, enough to last them nicely for the rest of their lives without raising too much resistance from his benefactors. All seemed possible until Mary realized they had no idea whom to contact for the ransom.

Looking in his wallet for information, she discovered his address, several credit cards, a photo of his wife, and $650, but no phone number. She tried looking online to no avail, but then thought of looking up Infodyne's address and sending the ransom note there.

To compose the note, they cut letters from a *Time* magazine. Careful to remove all fingerprints, they drove 300 miles to Redding to mail the letter, which read:

We have Frank McPherson. He is in good health. If you expect to see him alive, deposit 100 million dollars in bitcoin to wallet address Qi35&32uvTlZ!@479fe56 by 5:00 p.m. on 9/18/2021. Once we verify the deposit, we'll tell you where to pick him up.

They included a photo of McPherson eating an elaborate meal.

The CFO and other officers at Infodyne discussed what to do about the note. Since it did not indicate McPherson's location or how to contact his captors, negotiation was impossible. They contacted the police who advised against paying the ransom because doing so would not guarantee his safe return and could lead to more ransom requests. After hours of discussion, they decided not to pay the ransom.

Two Infodyne officers went to McPherson's home at 3:30 p.m. to inform his wife about the ransom request and their decision.

"Oh my god, how long have you known about this? Is he okay?" she asked.

"We received the ransom note at 11:30 a.m. and immediately notified the police. The ransom note indicated he is fine, which seems accurate given this photo accompanying the note. The police advised against paying the ransom and we agree. However, you are free to do whatever you want."

Without hesitation, she said she would pay and phoned her accountant to make the deposit.

After verifying the deposit, Mary and Jill celebrated by downing a bottle of champagne. One key step remained—where to leave McPherson. After much discussion, they chose an abandoned warehouse on the outskirts of Redding. Since the ransom note came from Redding, they knew police would focus their attention there, far away from their planned escape to Mexico.

They opted to transport him at night, thinking it would be less likely anyone would see them and become suspicious. After tying his arms and blindfolding him, they took him to their car. Fearing their intentions, McPherson flailed his arms and legs, cutting his hand on a broken taillight lens. Cursing, Mary went into the cabin to get a bandage so he wouldn't get incriminating blood on the car. Eventually, she convinced him the ransom had been paid and they were taking him to the transfer location. Once in the car, the rest of the trip was uneventful.

Arriving at the warehouse, they made sure no one was around before taking McPherson, still blindfolded, into an office. Tying him to a chair, they added a gag. Just as they were leaving, they heard a noise coming from an adjoining room.

"Damn, sounds like we have company!" Mary whispered. They tiptoed to the door and peeked in, careful to remain unseen. A disheveled man sat on the floor drinking from a bottle of rot-gut wine and singing off key.

"What'll we do, kill him?" Jill asked.

"No need, he's so drunk he won't even remember being here," Mary replied. "But we'd better tie him up. We don't want him to see or hear us. Hand me that board."

Quietly, Mary crept up behind him and smacked him on the head, knocking him out. After tying and gagging him, they jumped in their car and headed for Mexico, an eleven-hour drive.

Ecstatic, they sang along to the radio, boasting about their perfect crime. Bitcoin could not be traced, and McPherson had not seen their faces. In a few hours, they would be in Mexico. Only one thing remained, to tell his wife where to find her husband.

A few miles before the border, they drove into a rest stop. Mary noticed a pay phone and made a call to Infodyne revealing McPherson's location and instructing the company to inform his wife. Then she drove to the border check.

Upon receiving the call about her husband's location, Mrs. McPherson phoned the Redding police who reached the warehouse within minutes.

"Can you identify your kidnappers?" an officer asked while releasing McPherson from his bonds.

"Not visually. They either blindfolded me or wore masks, but I know they were women. One of them said she had nurse training."

"How many were there?"

"Two that I know about."

"What happened to your hand?"

"I cut it on the lens of their taillight."

"Do you know which side?"

"They put me in the rear seat on the right side, so it had to be the right."

The officer called for an APB for two women, possibly others, driving a car with a broken right rear taillight lens. Since a large ransom was involved, he suggested informing Canadian and Mexican border security in case a car with that description attempted to escape the country.

Mary, getting antsy, hadn't anticipated the long wait at the border. When she finally reached the checkpoint, a border patrol agent noticed the damaged light and directed them to another lane. Police surrounded the car and took them into a building for questioning.

"Why did you stop us?" Mary asked. "We weren't doing anything."

"We're looking for two women in a car with a broken right taillight," the detective answered. "There's been a kidnapping."

"A broken taillight?" Jill exclaimed, her eyebrows raised in disbelief. "That's how you found us?"

"A 100-million-dollar taillight," Mary grumbled.

Driving on highway 101, I was struck by how curvy it was and how easy it would be to have an accident. I took this idea and wove it into a story.

The People Next Door

"Look at this, Jane." Pulling back the curtain, Brian Smith peered out the window at the small moving van parked next door. "It looks like we have new neighbors."

Joining her husband, Jane watched the unloading of boxes and unusual furniture.

"The legs on that table couldn't be more than eighteen inches long," she commented. "Of what use would that be?"

"I have no idea," he replied. "Did you see chairs or anything to sit on?"

"Now that you mention it, no. I didn't see a bed either—just a mattress. Maybe some things will come in another vehicle."

"I doubt it," he said. "That's a small truck. I don't think they'd use two—they'd just use one larger one." A couple wearing capes with red and blue stripes walked toward the house. "Oh, they must be the ones moving in. What on earth are they wearing—blankets?"

The following day, Brian saw the man get in a car with vinyl peeling off the roof, one bumper missing, several dents, and a cracked windshield. Black smoke billowed out the tailpipe as he drove off.

"What? I've seen better cars in a junk yard," he exclaimed.

A week later, the Smiths couldn't contain their curiosity about the individuals next door. Armed with a plate of cookies, they rang the doorbell. A smiling man wearing a cloak decorated with brightly colored birds answered. Brian stepped back but quickly recovered and shoved the plate of cookies into the newcomer's hands.

The man stepped back, too, eyes wide with alarm.

"Me Judvk Mytabe," he stuttered awkwardly. "Please, coming in." His accent was heavy.

The Smiths entered the living room where a teenage girl was reading a book in the corner, never showing her face. A woman sat on a cushion on the floor, sewing. The room was otherwise devoid of furniture.

"Please, sitting. Wife Radyv."

Looking around, Brian couldn't see anything to sit on other than the pads. He struggled to get down and had to put his hands behind himself to prevent falling backward. Jane remained standing.

"What country are you from, Judvk?" Brian asked.

"Adzerbe."

Brian struggled to converse with him, finally giving up and leaving. As near as he could tell, the Mytabes had fled Adzerbe when a coup established a ruthless dictator as president. A refugee program was providing funds for rental of the house until they could get on their feet.

"Just our luck to have foreigners next door," Brian remarked to Jane once they returned home. "I don't trust 'em. They can't even speak English. They're not like us at all."

"Dad, you are so prejudiced!" his nineteen-year-old daughter grumbled, her bruised jaw clenched.

"Shut up, or I'll give you another whupping," Brian snarled.

* * *

Weeks later, Judvk awoke early. Peering out the window, he saw six men with extensive tattoos streaming into his neighbor's house.

What's going on—drugs? Suspicious.

Concerned, Judvk watched the Smiths' home every morning for three weeks. Early each Monday, individuals sporting tattoos visited, leaving an hour later. They wore tattered clothes and jackets with a strange symbol on the back. One even had a gun conspicuously displayed on his belt.

"Did we escape drug cartels in Adzerbe only to end up next door to a drug den in America?" Judvk complained in his native tongue, throwing up his hands in exasperation.

"I think we should report them, but how?" Radyv responded.

While shopping at a neighborhood grocery the following day, Judvk struggled to explain his concerns to its friendly proprietor. The man gave Judvk the number for the police and suggested he call them. After much hand wringing, he did so.

"Third precinct, Sergeant Peters."

"I Judvk Matabe. Suspect drugs."

"What do you mean? Speak English. The sergeant's voice was harsh.

"House by me maybe drugs."

After several attempts at understanding the caller, the exasperated sergeant said he'd send someone to interview him and slammed the receiver.

A burly policeman, arms covered in tattoos, arrived later that day to try to make sense of Judvk's complaint. After forty minutes, he finally realized that Judvk suspected his neighbor of selling drugs. When Judvk indicated he hadn't actually seen transactions of illegal substances, the officer left, shaking his head.

After reading the report of the interview, the chief decided further inquiry was warranted and sent a detective to interview the Smiths. Brian said he held religious services once a week, emphasizing they used no drugs of any kind. Rolling his eyes, the detective asked a few more questions before departing.

When Judvk learned that the Smiths were having devotional services, he was relieved but somewhat dubious, his doubts fueled by the appearance of Brian's yard. Why would someone who held spiritual sessions not be conscientious enough to keep it up? Now more than twelve inches high, it hadn't been mowed for weeks. He resolved to keep an eye out for suspicious activity.

A month later, Judvk arose early to go for a walk. Looking out the window at the neighbor's dimly lit driveway, he saw Brian struggling to put something rolled up in an old blanket into the trunk of his car. After tossing in a shovel and closing the lid, he looked around, finally staring intently at Judvk's window. Furrowing his brow, Judvk quickly ducked behind the curtain.

Did he see me? What could be in that bundle?

That evening, as he peered through the Smith's kitchen window, he saw Jane sobbing uncontrollably. Suddenly, it all made sense.

I bet his wife is crying because Brian murdered their daughter, wrapped her in a blanket, and buried her.

Remembering his experience with the cops when he reported suspected drug dealing, he kept silent. But he did keep a lookout for the daughter. Days went by with no sign of her. Finally, his conscience got the better of him and he contacted the police.

"Me Judvk Matabe. Think neighbor…murder daughter."

"Who's your neighbor?" the gravelly voice on the phone asked.

"Brian Smith."

"What makes you think he murdered his daughter?"

"Put…heavy thing…in car, cover…blanket. Wife sad. No more…daughter." He struggled to find the words.

"When did you observe this?"

"June 15, 4:30 am."

"Today is June 20. Why'd you wait so long to report it?"

"Possible wrong," Judvk said, fidgeting and biting his lip. "Maybe daughter…come back."

"Name and address."

"Brian Smith…," Judvk replied.

"No!" the officer interrupted, banging his fist on the table. "*Your* name,"

"Judvk Matabe, 1024 Elm Street."

"We'll send someone out," he said, sighing.

A detective arrived later that afternoon just as rain clouds darkened the sky on an already humid day. Rivulets of sweat ran down Judvk's furrowed brow as he showed the officer into the living room.

"Please, have sit," Judvk said, biting his lip.

"Sit? Where? I don't see any chairs," the detective questioned.

"My country, sit pad," Judvk answered, motioning. Frowning, the detective started to get down but then changed his mind, saying he preferred to stand.

As Judvk explained what he had seen, the detective scribbled notes in a dogeared notebook before going next door to question Brian.

* * *

"Judvk Matabe claims he saw you put something wrapped in a blanket into your trunk and drive off. Is that correct?"

"Yes," Brian replied as he played with his hair.

"What was in the blanket?"

"Chip."

"Chip?" the detective answered, jerking to attention.

"Our pet dog," he nodded mournfully.

"Dog? Why'd you wrap your dog in a blanket and put it in the trunk of your car?"

"He died. I wanted to bury him in the woods where we used to walk."

The detective's steely eyes glared at Brian for a minute before he continued the interrogation.

"Do you have a daughter, Brian?"

"Yes."

"Where is she?"

"She took a job as a live-in maid in Steubinville."

"How can she be reached?"

He wrote down the information, and after several more questions, the detective left.

* * *

Back at headquarters, he dialed the phone number to check Judvk's story about his daughter.

"Hello," a voice answered.

"I'm Detective Marlow from the Manville Police Department. I'd like to ask you a few questions, if that's okay."

"Sure."

"Does a woman by the name of Matabe work for you?"
"Yes."
"May I speak with her?" the detective asked.
"She isn't here right now. She took the week off to go to the beach with her boyfriend."

After hanging up, the detective called Judvk to inform him that Brian's story checked out.

Flushing, Judvk apologized for taking up the detective's time.

* * *

After a restless night, Judvk paced the floor, frowning. Upset at having been found wrong twice, he still had a nagging feeling about the Smiths.

The following night, he tossed and turned, eventually arising to get a glass of milk. Taking care not to be seen, he peered through the kitchen window into Brian's back yard. There, his neighbor was shoveling dirt into a large hole. When finished, he planted two dozen pansies in the loose dirt. Then, looking around, he retreated to his house.

Judvk's lips grew thin and firm, and the ache in his belly told him something was grievously wrong.

That looks like a grave. What should I do?

Finally, he couldn't stand it any longer and phoned the detective—again.

"Judvk, stop calling me with your conspiracy theories," he bellowed. "I've had it with you."

"But...but...grave?"

"Grave? What grave?" he demanded, leaning forward.

Judvk described what he had seen and pleaded with the detective to check it out.

"Oh, all right, we'll investigate. But I'm warning you, if you're wrong, I'm going to charge you for making frivolous claims that interfere with police work." Frowning and his palms clammy, Judvk hoped he'd done the right thing.

* * *

After knocking at Brian's door, the detective looked at his watch repeatedly while waiting for Brian to answer.

"Brian, I have a few more questions. May I come in?"

"Sure," he replied.

The detective asked several trivial questions. Then, looking out the window at his back yard, he broached the reason for his visit.

"You have a big back yard. Would you mind showing it to me?" he asked, noting Brian's darting eyes. Once outside, the detective commented about several features before settling on the flowerbed with freshly tilled soil.

"The pansies are pretty," he observed, looking around at the rest of the overgrown yard. "Well, I'd better get back to the office." He didn't want to reveal his suspicions until he had a search warrant. With it in hand, he and another policeman returned to dig up the site.

"Sir, there's something that looks like hair," the junior officer said.

"Careful not to destroy evidence—dig around it," the detective replied.

"Well, I'll be damned—it's a dog!" the other exclaimed.

"Is this the dog you said you buried in the forest?" The detective's icy stare and tight lips didn't faze Brian.

"I had two dogs," Brian replied, looking down. "That's Duke. He was sick and in pain, so I put him out of his misery."

Stroking his beard and frowning, the detective pondered Brian's explanation. Things did not make sense. Why would Brian go to elaborate lengths to bury one dog in the forest but lay the other one to rest in his back yard? Could his daughter somehow hold the answer? He called her employer to inquire about her again.

"I called you before about the Smith's daughter and you indicated she'd gone to the beach. Has she returned?" he asked, drumming his fingers on the table.

"No. She said she'd be gone seven days, but it's been weeks and she hasn't returned. I'm worried. It doesn't seem like her."

The real breakthrough in the case came when a hunter saw a button near freshly-dug dirt in the forest outside of town. Investigation of the site revealed the body of Brian's daughter buried in a shallow grave.

* * *

The excited murmuring in the courtroom silenced at the booming voice of the bailiff.

"All rise. The U.S. Court for the district of Manville is now in session, the Honorable Judge Miller presiding." The judge entered and sat down.

"Be seated," he said. "The prosecution will present its opening statement."

"Ladies and gentlemen of the jury, the prosecution will show that Brian Smith willfully, and in cold blood, shot his daughter and buried her in the Chahana National Forest. On July 12, 2021, she went home to get her swimsuit, hoping to have fun on the beach. Alas, that was not to be. Instead, her father, Brian Smith, shot her. Why would he do such a thing? Because she threatened to expose the fact that he had repeatedly raped her from the time she was twelve. He then wrapped her body in a blanket, put her in the trunk of his car, and buried her deep in the forest. Suspecting that he had been seen putting the body in his trunk, he shot his dog and buried it in his back yard, hoping he could convince us that the body he had placed in his car was his dog, not his daughter. We are confident you *will* find the defendant guilty of murder in the first degree."

> *Prejudice, sexual abuse, and murder are major problems in our country and the world. They're often compounded by baseless suspicions of people that look different from us.*

Thief

"Act normal or I'll shoot. I have a gun in my pocket, and I won't hesitate to use it." A single 35-year-old male with a landscaping business, Justin was insistent.

"Wh...What do you want?"

"Shut up. Get in your car and drive home. I'll follow in mine. I know where you live and how to get there, so no funny stuff. When you arrive, pull into your driveway. I'll park behind you. One more thing—give me your phone."

Michael Grayson did as instructed. An eccentric millionaire, he had earned a reputation for swindling people out of their homes and not trusting banks. After arriving at Michael's home, Justin kept his hand in the pocket of his jacket, firmly poking Michael's back as they walked to the entrance.

They were met at the door by Julie Grayson.

"Step back, ma'am. Everything will be fine."

"Please don't shoot. If you want money, I have some in my safe," Michael pleaded, his voice quavering.

"Take me there. You have to come along, too, ma'am."

Michael's hand shook as he turned the safe's dial.

"Here's $200,000. That's all I keep here."

"I want $162,000."

"Not all of it?"

"Are you hard of hearing? $162,000."

Michael counted the money and shoved it at Justin.

"Now, go to the living room and sit down—both of you." Once there, Justin pulled a roll of Gorilla Tape from his pocket and tied Michael's arms behind his back. He also bound his legs. "I'm sorry, ma'am, I'll have to tape you also." Strangely, he took special care to ensure she was comfortable.

"Please don't worry about how you'll get free. A couple of hours after I leave, I'll use your phone to call someone to release you. Understood?"

They nodded.

Opening the door to leave, Justin became alarmed. Dozens of cars parked everywhere, including in the driveway, blocked his exit. Rock music blasting from next door suggested a party. He shut the door and leaned against it, heart racing. This was one contingency he hadn't considered. He went back into the living room.

"It looks like you'll be tied up a little longer." Justin removed his jacket, exposing a *Justin's Landscaping* logo on his shirt and revealing his identity. Recognizing his mistake, he blanched.

Damn! First, I can't get away and now they know who I am.

"I have a headache," Julie said. "Could you get me some ibuprofen and water?"

"You're always bitching about headaches," Michael snapped.

"Don't worry ma'am. I'll get the pills for you. Where are they?"

"In the bathroom cabinet."

"I hope this helps your head," Justin said, returning with the medicine.

"Her head needs help, alright," Michael spat, "but not that kind."

Walking to the window, Justin saw that his car was still blocked.

"Why are you always so mean, Michael?" Julie asked.

"Because you are so bird brained and lazy," he responded. "I wouldn't be surprised if you knew this thief and suggested he rob us."

Justin rolled his eyes.

"You're always tearing me down," Julie whimpered. "You're no angel, cheating people out of their homes. And I'm tired of making up stories to explain these bruises," she said, pulling up her sleeves to reveal yellow and purple splotches.

"Simmer down, you two. And you," Justin pointed at Michael, "shouldn't talk that way to your wife."

"So, a common thief is telling me what to say to my wife? I suppose you always talk nicely to your spouse?"

"I'm not married," Justin replied, glaring at Michael. Their caustic exchange continued for more than an hour.

"People like you should get a job," Michael continued, "Instead, you rob those of us who've found success."

"I'd hardly call cheating people 'success.' You think you're so high and mighty just because you have money, but you treat your wife like scum."

"Look who's talking—an armed robber. I'll bet...."

"I'm not armed," Justin smirked, "unless you think a finger in my coat pocket is a weapon. And I've never stolen a thing...until now, that is. It gives me great pleasure to relieve you of some of your ill-gotten money."

"You're expect me to believe that I'm the first person you've robbed?"

"That's right."

"Why me?"

"You got your millions by swindling people who didn't have the money to fight back."

"Everything I did was legal."

"Legal, perhaps, but extremely immoral."

"And robbing me is moral?"

"No, but I had to do it."

"*Had* to do it? How can you talk about morality and maintain a straight face?"

Justin walked over to the window and looked out.

Damn. Still blocked. When will that party end?

Michael continued his tirade.

"One thing I don't get. Why only $162,000?"

"That's all I need."

"Need? For what?"

"For my mother's operation."

"What operation? A face lift?"

"A heart bypass. She'll die soon if she doesn't get the procedure. She's only 52. She has no insurance and doesn't make enough cleaning houses to pay for it. My landscaping business doesn't provide enough for me to afford it either."

Julie choked up.

Looking out the window at 3:00 a.m., Justin noticed that the car blocking his exit had left.

"You won't get away with it, you know," Michael warned. "After I report it to the police. you'll be in jail by sunrise."

"He won't be jailed," Julie exclaimed firmly.

"And why is that?" Michael snarled.

"Because he isn't going to steal the money—I'm going to give it to him, all $200,000."

Agape, Justin stared at Julie.

"But I only need $162,000,"

"Give the extra to your mother. She can use it to pay for help while she recovers." Julie's tone was adamant. "And I'm leaving you, Michael. I realize now that men can be decent and caring."

"You not only steal my money, you steal my wife?" Michael sputtered.

"Who said anything about going with this man? I'm leaving *you*, something I've thought about for some time. Hand me that tape, Justin." After slapping it on Michael's mouth, Julie said triumphally. That'll stop you from badmouthing me."

Robin Hood stories have always held a certain appeal to me. Combining that with abused women I've known provides the basis for this story.

Unicorn Peak

Dreaming about falling off a cliff, Ken bolted awake, feeling every one of his 73 years. Outside, the warm glow of the sun peeked over the horizon—a perfect day for a hike in the Olympic Mountains. However, he worried his shrinking muscles and arthritic knees might not be up to the task. Sighing, he crawled out of bed.

Despite his doubt, the Olympics beckoned to him, especially Unicorn Peak. Glancing at the dresser, his eyes misted at the photo of him and his wife taken on their fiftieth anniversary, two years before she had died of Alzheimer's. Caring for his ailing spouse had kept him from returning to the area for ten long years.

After dressing, he downed three eggs and a stack of pancakes before packing a lunch of three bagels, trail mix, two hard boiled eggs, a chunk of Swiss cheese, a chocolate bar, and an apple. He put his daypack, boots, and trekking poles in his Jeep and drove to the trailhead, troubled. Was it because of his bad dream?

Putting on his boots and daypack, he started up the paved trail, enjoying spectacular views of the Bailey Range along the way to Hurricane Hill. From there on, he went cross country. The route dropped 1200 feet over uneven terrain. Halfway down, he caught his foot on brush and fell. He thought about turning back, but decided to go on, his knees protesting all the way. His ankles burned from continually being bent sideways, and his lungs ached from inhaling ash from a forest fire two years earlier. Wiping sweat from his eyes, he climbed over one downed tree after another.

Stopping at the base of Griff Peak, he removed his sweaty shirt, making him prime mosquito bait. Several bites later, he put it back on.

Next, he started up Griff Peak, fighting dense undergrowth as he climbed 600 feet to the summit. He experienced a wave of sadness as he realized the hike would be too difficult for him in the future.

After a short rest, he followed the ridge west until it descended 100 feet to the base of Unicorn's summit block. After gaining 160 feet of elevation, he noticed a man sitting dangerously close to a sheer drop over a rocky basin several hundred feet below. The disheveled man had an unkempt beard, long hair, and a tattered jacket with a shoulder patch showing a cue stick and an eight ball. Ken approached cautiously, not wanting to startle him.

"Hi there. Great view," he said, instantly regretting his comment since the man seemed upset. "Are you okay?"

"Don't bother me," the man grumbled.

"Alright, are you okay?"

The man didn't answer.

"Do you mind if I sit down?" Ken asked. "My legs need a rest."

The man turned toward him, wide eyed and trembling, but relaxed after Ken sat. Since he looked to be at least 85, Ken marveled that he had made such a difficult hike. He sat quietly trying to decide what to do or say.

"I've come here several times. I love the Unicorn summits and the view. I live in Port Angeles. Where are you from?"

Getting no answer, Ken decided to be more direct.

"My name is Ken, what's yours?" Silence followed, so he kept talking.

"Have you been here before?" Ken didn't wait for an answer, assuming he wouldn't get one. "The hike in was easier before the burn. So many blowdowns."

"Look, please leave me alone!"

Encouraged he at least got a response, Ken continued.

"I don't mean to be nosey, but we are both hikers, and hikers assist one another. It seems something is wrong, and I'd like to help if possible."

"No one can help me."

"Why not? What's wrong?"

"She's gone," he replied, hanging his head and weeping.

"Who's gone?"

"Silvia."

"Was she your wife?" Ken asked.

"She died two months ago," the man added.

"I'm sorry," Ken replied, fumbling for the right words but finding none. "Please give me your name so I know what to call you."

"Bob. Now leave me alone."

"I can't very well do that, Bob. Here we are on a mountain in the middle of a wilderness with nobody for miles around. You've got me curious…you look like you might be in your eighties…this isn't an easy hike. What brings you here of all places?"

Getting no answer, Ken offered to hike back to the trailhead with Bob, but the man indicated he had no intention of leaving. Ken asked if he planned to stay overnight but got no answer.

Moving a bit closer to make it easier to talk, he sat down. He learned Bob had been married 63 years to a woman he described as gentle, kind, intelligent, and beautiful. They had met in a college literature class where she had asked him for a date. After two years of dating, Bob was drafted into the army and sent to France. A few months later, Silvia flew to Europe where they were married. Bob indicated they had Army leave to travel all over the continent. After his service, he returned to the States and taught psychology at a small college. Ken confided he, too, was a college professor.

"Is that your wife?" Ken asked, seeing Bob clutching a photo.

Saying nothing, Bob held it up. Ken moved beside him to see their wedding photo.

"She was indeed beautiful. What a handsome couple!"

"I'll never see Silvia again!" Tears again crept into Bob's eyes.

"I understand the grief you feel," Ken said softly.

"You can't possibly understand what I'm feeling!" Bob replied, shaking his head.

"I think I can, Bob, I lost my wife to Alzheimer's three years ago and my son eight years ago." He paused, "What caused Silvia's death?"

"Cancer. They had to remove ten inches of her colon. She was unconscious in intensive care for 5½ months with multiple organ failure and sepsis. Eventually, I had to pull the plug. I didn't even get to say goodbye." His weeping resumed.

Ken waited in silence until Bob calmed down.

"That's hard. But I'm concerned about you right now. What's your plan?"

"Wait for the sun to set."

"And then?"

"Jump."

"Why after sunset?"

"I think it will be easier in the dark."

Ken pointed out that someone would have to make a difficult trip to deal with his body if he went through with his plan—a horrible thing to inflict on anyone. Bob said nothing, and Ken refrained from saying more to let his message sink in.

Finally, Bob broke the silence by asking Ken about his wife's Alzheimer's.

"At first, she had nothing more than mild memory problems. As time went on, she had to stop driving, had difficulty walking, became incontinent, and had to be fed. Then, worst of all, she no longer knew me."

"Did she die of Alzheimer's?"

"Indirectly. Food got into her lungs causing pneumonia." Ken paused. "She died two days later" he added, his voice shaking.

"What do you think Silvia would want you to do?" No answer.

"Do you have children?"

"Yes."

"If you jumped, don't you think they'd miss you? It isn't easy for kids to part with their father, especially this way. They might be consumed with guilt the rest of their lives, thinking they should have done something."

Bob didn't reply. Both sat silently for a while until Bob again asked to be left alone. Ken explained he wouldn't have time to make it out before dark, and he definitely wouldn't leave without him. The man merely stared at him.

Ken knew he had to get Bob to a safer place. Then he could worry about making the best of a night in the open without sufficient food or water.

"Bob, how about getting off this rock?"

"I can't live without Silvia."

"I felt the same way when my wife died. I think about her every day and miss her terribly, but gradually, I found new interests, and once again, life seemed worthwhile. You'll always miss Silvia, but the pain subsides over time."

Ken sensed Bob's resolve weakening.

"I'd love to do things with you. We're both retired and have time on our hands. We could play pool, go on hikes together, eat out. I'd appreciate the company. What do you say?"

Bob turned toward Ken and then looked away, saying nothing.

"We're both cold. Let's at least get to a more comfortable place while awaiting sundown," Ken implored.

Bob stood, looked around, and stepped away from the precipice. Although Ken was concerned about slipping, they both made it off the rocky pinnacle. Ken found a sheltered spot behind a boulder near some trees. They sat on a log, not talking for a while.

"Why are you doing this?" Bob asked as Ken looked for some fir boughs to provide insulation from the ground.

"Doing what?"

"Spending time with me and saying you would do things with me?"

"Because we have so much in common—college teachers, hikers, pool players. More importantly, we both lost our wives and are lonely. I think we'd get along well." Hesitating, he added, "I've never told anyone about this, but I have mild cognitive impairment which means I'll eventually end up with dementia. In the meantime, I'd love to have a friend with whom I could do things."

Bob turned toward Ken and looked at him intently. Divulging his destiny seemed to make an impact on Bob.

"How long have you known this?"

"Eleven months, as far as I know," Ken replied, staring at the ground.

"My mother had dementia. I'm sorry you have to go through that," Bob offered.

Abandoning his moment of gloom, Ken rose, encouraged that Bob was no longer thinking about Silvia or suicide. He started making a lean-to using their trekking poles, branches, and brush. He took inventory of his remaining food and shared a bagel and some of the trail mix with Bob, keeping the rest for the hike out. Bob had no water, but Ken had filled his bottle at a spring about a quarter of a mile from the base of Unicorn. He shared half, saving the rest for morning.

They talked into the evening, with Ken doing most of it. Bob seemed to have given up on his suicide plan. Eventually, they lay down on their bed of boughs and covered themselves with Ken's space blanket. It didn't provide much insulation, but the foil reflected back some of their body heat.

After a cold, uncomfortable night, they ate half of the remaining food, leaving the rest to eat along the way. Ken ate less because he knew Bob needed it more. After tearing down their lean-to, they went to the spring to drink and fill their water bottles.

By the time they got to the base of Griff, Bob was hurting, yet the worst stretch lay ahead of them. They rested for ten minutes, finished the trail mix, and started uphill through the burn and downed trees. After an hour on the side hill, they stopped to eat the remaining food. Ken hated to think about what would happen if Bob gave out. He knew they'd be home free if they made it make it to the top of Hurricane Hill.

Bob dragged his feet, stirring up the ash and making breathing painfully difficult. Tripping while trying to step over a small deadfall, he cut his hand on a sharp-edged rock. Ken carefully bandaged the gushing wound.

Though his knees burned with pain, Ken hid it as best he could since Bob was in worse condition.

Arriving at the top of Hurricane, Bob collapsed, totally exhausted. After a twenty-minute rest, Ken pulled Bob to his feet and started downhill, trying his best to prevent him from collapsing. A teenager, seeing their struggles, offered to help. With Ken on one side of the exhausted man and the teenager on the other, they managed to get him down successfully.

After reaching the trailhead, Ken put Bob in his Jeep and headed back to Port Angeles. Once there, he put him in his guest bedroom, not bothering to remove his clothes. He knew food would have to wait because Bob, nearly unconscious from fatigue, fell asleep instantly.

Ken scarfed down some leftovers, took a shower, and collapsed in bed. After sleeping ten hours, he awoke stiff and sore but dressed and limped to the kitchen to prepare a breakfast of eggs, pancakes, and sausage. He went into the guest bedroom to awaken Bob.

"Wha...Where am I?" Bob mumbled.

"You're in my house in Port Angeles. How do you feel?"

"Awful! I hurt all over. Why am I here?"

"You were too exhausted to drive home, so I brought you to my place. I have some breakfast ready. Are you hungry?"

"I feel sick."

"No wonder, but some food ought to help. We didn't have much to eat yesterday."

"I don't want to be a burden—I'd better leave."

"Nonsense. I've already fixed breakfast. After we eat, I'll take you home so you can shower before we get your car."

* * *

Ken saw Bob daily for a period of months, during which time Bob's depression slowly diminished. They played pool often, with Bob, the better player, giving Ken pointers. They hiked frequently, but never to Unicorn Peak or Hurricane Hill, and they never talked about their first meeting.

Ken gradually slipped into dementia and moved into a facility for memory care. Although frail, Bob visited him daily.

Nine years after their first meeting, Bob made his way to the facility. He opened the door to Ken's room to be greeted by a vacant stare, as had been happening for months.

"Hi Ken. It's Bob."

Ken said nothing but looked at Bob and smiled weakly.

"I brought a book I think you'd enjoy. Let's sit over here on the couch." Ken opened the book and started reading.

"This one is by Dr. Seuss:

The sun did not shine,
It was too wet to play,
So, we sat in the house,
All that cold, cold, wet day...."

When done with the book, Bob slowly closed the cover, wiping tears from his eyes.

"Time for dinner, Ken," a caretaker announced as he entered the room.

"See you tomorrow, Ken," Bob said, his voice trembling. Just want you to know that I love you. You are like a brother to me,"

Although not the highest mountain in the Washington State Olympics, Unicorn Peak has a spectacular summit block that rises steeply 650 feet above the surrounding terrain. One side has a sheer drop. Since access is mostly cross country, it is seldom visited. Unicorn Horn is a mere quarter mile away. I went to Unicorn Peak three times, twice on day hikes and once backpacking. It seemed a good background for a story. I incorporated elements of my wife's Alzheimer's, her colon surgery, and my son's death into the tale.

Conner's Adventure

"How many pairs of socks should I take?" Conner shook his hands, unable to contain himself. At nine years of age, he couldn't wait to go on his first backpacking trip. His father, Nick, expected Conner to carry his own clothing and sleeping gear while he had all of the common equipment they'd need. Conner's pack weighed in at sixteen pounds, a reasonable weight for a young boy on his first trip.

Packs loaded in their Jeep, they headed west from Port Angeles, turning south at the Elwha River and going toward Observation Point west of Lake Mills. Arriving at the trailhead, they shouldered their packs and began the gentle climb to *Olympic Hot Springs*, a two-mile hike. Conner stopped frequently to examine flowers, rocks, trees—so many exciting things. Nick, delighting in his son's enthusiasm, made no attempt to hurry.

Despite Conner's delays, they soon reached *Olympic Hot Springs*, a chain of natural, hot-water pools with steam rising from each. Conner wanted to soak in them, but since they had over three miles to go to reach their camp at Boulder Lake, his father said they'd better keep going.

"Perhaps we can enjoy the springs on our way out," Nick offered. Not too disappointed, Conner continued on, looking forward to the fascinating things along the way.

They arrived at Boulder Lake by 4:00 p.m. and pitched their tent at a site near the lake. After filtering water, gathering wood for a bonfire, and getting things ready for night, they lit the stove to boil water for Camper's Stew and cocoa.

"The cocoa tasted great," Conner exclaimed, "but the stew? Ugh! Dad, can we go up Boulder Mountain tomorrow?"

"Well, there's no trail, but I think we could go cross country okay."

"Fantastic. I bet there's a great view from the summit."

They roasted marshmallows and talked until 9:00 p.m. when they crawled into their sleeping bags.

They rose the following morning at 7:00. The day was still somewhat dark, for the mountains blocked the sun. Nick prepared a breakfast of pancakes and freeze-dried eggs.

"Dad, the pancakes are great, but the eggs are yukky."

Laughing, his father told him to eat them anyway because he'd need the energy to climb Boulder Mountain. Little did he know how apt his advice would be.

After breakfast, they picked their way up a ridge to the south. From there, it was above tree line and relatively easy going to the summit, about 1,000 feet above their camp.

"Wow, you can see forever from here," Conner remarked.

"Well, not quite forever," his father replied. "Lizard Head Peak is to the north, and that way," he pointed south, "is Mt. Appleton, the highest mountain we can see. Mt. Olympus is higher, but it is beyond Appleton so we can't see it."

They sat on a rock eating lunch while Conner kept peppering his dad with questions. A magpie swooped down and grabbed a bite of the bagel Conner was eating, delighting him.

"You really have to watch your lunch closely or the magpies will steal it. That's why they're called camp robbers." Once again, his father took much joy in seeing his son so happy.

They returned to camp by a different route, going north along a ridge and then dropping down to the east. Bad decision. Nick looked behind him to check on Conner and stepped on a loose rock. Down he fell, frantically grabbing at shrubbery, but to no avail. As he slammed into a tree, he heard a snap in his left leg.

Ever so carefully, Conner made his way down the slope until he reached his dad.

"My leg is broken," he moaned, clutching it. "Can you find a straight stick to use as a splint?"

In seconds, Conner returned.

"Will this do, Dad?"

"Yes. Now, tear my shirt into strips."

Conner stabilized the leg by tying the stick to it.

"I won't be able to walk. Do you think you can get back to camp using the route we came up?"

"I—I think so, but it would be closer going on down this way," Conner protested.

"True, but it's too steep and we don't want to risk another accident. When you get to camp, empty your pack except for your water bottle. Put the map in and a compass. The trail follows the river—it's pretty obvious. There might be some people at the hot springs. If so, ask them for help. If not, continue to the Jeep at the trailhead and honk the horn three times in succession and then repeat."

"Okay, but I'm scared, Dad. What if I get lost?"

"I'm counting on you, Conner. You'll be okay. Remember, the trail follows the river, so you'll know you're on the right track. Tell anyone you see I'm on the steep slope due west of our camp, all right?"

"Got it," he said, hoping he could remember everything.

Hiking alone, Conner found the mountains scary, but he gained some confidence when he made it to the campsite. He put the items his dad requested into his pack and headed down the trail as fast as he could walk, jogging at times.

In his excitement, Conner didn't notice the trail had turned left. He went straight. Panic set in when he realized his mistake. Remembering his dad saying the path followed the river, he decided to follow its course.

As he picked his way, the bank of the river collapsed, undercut by the fast-flowing water. Carried swiftly downstream, he struggled to breathe. Several hundred feet farther along, it jogged to the left, pushing him to the right. He escaped in the shallows there.

Shaking from fear and the cold water, he sat to warm up and collect his thoughts. He realized he needed to get back to the other side, but how? Suddenly, a magpie flew in front of his face and landed on a large log 400 feet downstream. Curious, Conner approached. It spanned a narrow stretch of the river, creating a perfect bridge.

Glancing warily at the icy water below, Conner sat on the log and scooted forward until he reached the other side. Once there, he saw the trail and soon continued on his way.

Arriving at the hot springs, he saw two men and a boy soaking in pools.

"How did you get so wet?" one of the men asked.

Conner explained how his dad had broken his leg, and he had gone to get help but had fallen into the river.

The men and boy quickly got out of the pools and dressed, the somewhat bigger boy giving Conner some dry clothes. They had cell phones, but because there was no signal, they split up. One man and his son hurried up the trail with Conner to tend to Nick while the other jogged to the trailhead to contact Search and Rescue and ask for a Coast Guard helicopter to land on Boulder Peak.

An hour later, Conner's team reached the camp and quickly packed the scattered belongings. The man carried Nick's pack up Boulder Peak. After reaching the summit, Conner collapsed on the ground. Too exhausted to continue, he described his dad's location.

In the distance, the helicopter raced toward them. The man and two rescuers, one a paramedic, went down to Nick, replaced the splint Conner had put on, and, worked their way back to the helicopter, Nick in a Stokes litter.

When Nick saw his son, he broke down, telling him how proud he was of him.

Asked about his different clothes, Conner recounted how he had lost the trail and had fallen into the river. The rescuers loaded Nick into the chopper first.

"Hop in," the paramedic waved to Conner.

Despite his weariness, he jumped in, excited to have his first helicopter ride.

"Well, young man, you've had quite a day, going on your first backpack trip, falling in the river, saving your father, and now riding in a helicopter. You are very brave! What do you have to say?"

Beaming, Conner replied, "I'm pooped!"

The idea for this tale came from my youngest son's unbridled delight on his first backpacking trip. The setting is based on one of my solo backpacking trips. I went on the same route described herein and slid down the steep place mentioned in the story. I managed to make it back to camp via this route without injury. All place names are real.

Dark Mountains

Cursing, Scott Wainwright looked for his flashlight, the only thing missing from his backpack. After extensive searching, he found it where he'd least expect it—in the water heater closet. Irritated, he reached for it but knocked it on the floor, causing it to come apart. Picking it up, he noticed the metal piece that closed the circuit had fallen out. He put everything back together and checked to ensure it still worked. Since the light was slightly dim, he took an extra pair of batteries.

On the day of his departure, heavy rain pelted his Jeep Wrangler, challenging his windshield wipers. Because he had often been out in bad weather, he was unconcerned, especially considering that sun was forecast starting the second day of his trip. His employer required three-weeks' notice before a vacation, so he either went now or forfeited his trip. He enjoyed his job as a Seattle city planner but cherished the opportunity to leave the frenetic pace and politics of the city for the peace and quiet of mountains.

Driving on the highway, listening to music on the radio accompanied by the drumming of the rain, the steady beat of his windshield wipers—this was the life. Soon, his thoughts drifted to his wife Robin who was visiting her mother while he backpacked. As much as Scott enjoyed these trips, he always missed her. He mused about the time they went family camping and raccoons got into their dinners. Robin wouldn't touch any of the remaining food items, requiring them to pack up and leave. She refused all camping thereafter.

Scott thought about their son, Lance, a mediocre student in both high school and college. Since jobs were scarce for undergraduates in psychology, he obtained a master's degree but wasn't accepted into a Ph.D. program. After two years of unemployment, living with his parents, he spent three years in a second-rate doctoral program. Scott worried his son might never graduate even from that.

Turning onto the side road to his destination, he silenced the radio, now producing more static than music, and stopped. Picking up a stick on the side of the road, he probed several large waterholes, making sure they would be passable. An hour later, he arrived at the trailhead, pleased to find only two parked cars. That meant greater solitude for him.

Shouldering his pack, he started out on a trail inundated with water. Before long, his boots were saturated and his rain-proof jacket was as wet inside as out, whether from sweating or leaking, he didn't know.

Another hour took him to a log bridge covered in slick moss. The log had rotated, tilting the flat walking surface and making it unsafe. Fording the stream made him wetter and colder than ever.

With five miles to hike and 2000 feet of elevation to gain before his first camp, Scott swore. The trail, overgrown with dripping foliage, increased his misery. Shortly, he encountered a group of hikers fleeing the rain. He exchanged a few words with them before continuing.

Weary, he reached his intended camp and removed his pack. Standing water made all but one tent site unusable. Quickly pitching his tent, he tossed his sleeping bag inside, getting it wet in the process.

Clouds poured forth more rain as he deliberated his next step. Since he didn't bring a tarp for a cooking shelter, he ate one of his no-cook lunches.

Body heat generated from hiking gave way to shivering. He crawled into his tent and exchanged his wet clothes for dry ones. After thirty minutes in his sleeping bag, he had warmed enough to quell the shaking.

Soon, he found it pleasant listening to the rain pummeling his tent. By the time he had succumbed to sleep, he had regained enough humor to chuckle, knowing how much Robin would have hated this experience.

When daylight appeared, the rain had changed to a manageable drizzle. Shuddering at the prospect of putting on his cold, wet clothes, he dressed and prepared a breakfast of coffee and oatmeal. His spirits rose.

He shoved the sodden mass of his tent into its stuff sack and struck camp. Shouldering his pack, now heavier because of wet gear, he headed up the trail.

With no more waist-high shrubbery swiping at him, his clothes began to dry. He hiked contentedly in the light drizzle, the stress of his job far from his thoughts. Clouds precluded views, but not tranquility.

Shortly, the drizzle stopped, and patches of sunlight punctured the clouds. Scott ate his lunch, enjoying the views. Savoring the warmth of the sun, he lingered for an hour.

Heading toward a lake, he hiked cross-country, gaining 500 feet of elevation, up the cirque to the ridge where he planned to camp. What glorious views! The lake in one direction and snowcapped peaks in the other. A Camp Robber flew nearby, checking him out and looking for anything edible. Farther away, a marmot whistled. Looking down from the cliff, he saw a hawk riding a thermal, soon rising high above.

After pitching his tent, he donned dry clothes, luxuriating in relative comfort again. He readied his kitchen area and found a limb from which to hang his food. Giving up on his tent drying, he put in his sleeping bag, and other items he'd want in the night.

Next, he went to a nearby spring to refill his water bag. Returning to his camp, he lounged on his sleeping pad, basking in the warm sunlight. Shutting his eyes, he dozed, perfectly at peace.

Around 6:00 pm, he fired up his stove and prepared a meal consisting of soup and freeze-dried stew, garnished with butter. The warm meal hit the spot after his cold lunch the previous evening. After cleaning his dishes, he hung his food from a high branch and covered his pack in case rain returned. Slipping on his jacket, he relaxed on a log.

The sky cleared by 10:00 p.m., showing off a bright blanket of stars. He marveled at how the Milky Way lit up the sky at this elevation. In Seattle, light pollution made such sights impossible to see. The constellations were obvious, and a satellite streaked across the sky—one of the few instances human-made objects enhanced the beauty of nature. A shooting star and crescent moon rounded out the celestial panorama.

Scott entered his tent, tying back the rain fly so he could enjoy the stars from his sack. He put his wet clothes in the foot of his sleeping bag to dry and put his fleece jacket in a stuff sack to make a pillow. A small rockslide rumbled in the distance. The picture of contentment, he lay on his back staring at the sky until sleep overtook him.

At 2:45 am, he looked up. To the northeast, a clear sky provided a glorious stellar display. To the southwest, he saw nothing but total blackness. The clouds formed a straight line across the sky. The leading edge moved steadily toward him, as if someone were pulling a curtain across the sky. He watched the blackness devour the stars for a while before zipping the rain fly and going back asleep.

An hour later, the sound of gentle thumping awakened him. Assuming it was snow, not unusual at high elevations in the summer, he thought nothing of the exceptional darkness and resumed sleeping.

Several hours later, he awoke to pitch blackness. He felt for his flashlight and stared at his watch, shocked it was 8:15. After dressing, he unzipped the rain fly. A plume of fine dust swirled outward,

He closed the fly and lay back down to ponder the strange turn of events. He aimed his light on some of the dust. Gray and exceedingly fine, it rolled around in his hand like microscopic marbles. To avoid breathing it, he tore up a T-shirt to cover his face.

Grabbing his flashlight, he stepped outside, creating a whirlwind of dust. He stood transfixed by what he saw in the fading light. A layer of dust four or five inches deep covered the ground, burying his pack and cooking gear. Without his flashlight, the darkness would have been absolute. He went to his pack, brushed it off, and waited for the dust to settle. He was glad he had packed spare batteries.

After finding the batteries, he carefully laid them on a stuff sack in his pack. Then he used his knife to open the flashlight case. Next came the moment of truth—turning off the light, removing the old batteries, and installing new ones. After putting in the new batteries, he turned on the switch to make sure the light worked. It didn't. Feeling with his fingers, he discovered that a metal spring had popped out of the case. Without it, the light wouldn't work.

Scott carefully sifted through the dust on the ground for the missing part, creating a suffocating cloud that sent him into a coughing fit. He chided himself for not ditching the cheap flashlight in favor of an LED headlamp, but this light had served him so well for years.

Closing his pack, he felt his way back to his tent, dragging in dust that mingled with the moisture inside creating a slimy mess. He lay down on his bag to think things through. He did have matches, but only forty or so, and they wouldn't provide much light. A fire would provide pleasing relief, and he would welcome any Ranger who showed up to admonish him for building a fire at this elevation.

He returned to his pack to fetch the matches. He lit one to search for firewood but saw only a few small twigs and water-soaked fir cones. As the light flickered out, he thought better of using another.

Next, he searched for firewood under the tree where his food was hanging. He lit another match hoping to see the tree, but it was fifty feet away—too far for the flickering flame. Remembering the location of the tree relative to his tent, he started walking, not realizing the difficulty in traveling a straight line in total darkness, much less the danger. He felt he had gone far enough to reach the tree but didn't find it. Lighting another match did not help.

He tried again and again to no avail. When the weight of despair descended upon him, he collided with it, producing a lump on his forehead. Calming his nerves, he felt for the parachute cord and lowered his bag of food.

Turning his attention back to finding firewood, he tied one end of the cord to the tree. Holding onto the other end, he circled around, feeling for wood, gradually working his way farther and farther out. With only a few small wet branches, he returned to his tent, guided by a snag on the tree that pointed in the right direction.

Using the tether for safety, he trudged carefully through the darkness carrying his food bag and meager pile of firewood. When the cord grew taut, he tied the end to his food bag and set down his wood. Then, he traced the cord back to the tree. After untying it, he returned to his food bag, a bundle of nerves as he passed through the eerie blackness.

If he had gone in the proper direction, his tent should be less than one cord length away. Using the food bag as a fulcrum, he resumed walking in a direction he thought was well left of his tent, letting the cord slide through his hand until he reached its end. He thought briefly of the irony of being at the end of his rope in more ways than one.

With waning confidence, he held the end of the cord and moved to his right. Twice he felt the cord catch briefly, but he guessed it had only snagged on rocks. Minutes later, the cord again caught. Following it back, he nearly tripped over a tent stake. With a huge sigh of relief, he tied the cord to his tent and returned to retrieve his food bag and wood.

Brushing off the dust as best he could, he crawled into his tent. Exhausted and with burning lungs, his thoughts returned to the missing flashlight part. Light from a fire might enable him to find it.

Before leaving the relative comfort of his tent, he reached for his water bottle to rinse the dust from his mouth and realized another major problem: the improbability of finding water without a flashlight. The 2.5 quarts he had left had to last until the sky cleared. Freeze-dried food required a lot, which meant he'd have to balance eating and drinking.

The thought occurred to him that he might be able to use the stove to find the missing flashlight part. So, he lit the stove, which cast an eerie glow over the dusty campsite. After searching in vain for 35 minutes, he stopped to preserve the fuel.

At 3:13 pm, he realized he hadn't eaten since previous evening's meal, so he used a small amount of water to make oatmeal. The water boiled just as the stove sputtered out. Once again, he was engulfed in total darkness. He nearly wept.

The oatmeal brought back a semblance of normalcy to his abnormal situation. He had nothing to sit on, other than the ground, and he couldn't walk anywhere because he couldn't see. In the absence of visual cues, he found it difficult to maintain his balance and returned to his tent.

His thoughts turned to Robin, wondering if he would ever see her again. There were so many things he wanted to say—how much he loved and appreciated her, how he regretted arguing with her, how much he missed the warmth of her lips. He thought about the time when she backed up too far for a photograph in the Jardin de Tuileries and fell into the fountain. She hadn't appreciated his laughter at the time but later saw the humor of it all. Hopefully, she was safe at home. He imagined Seattle had the benefit of electricity and, therefore, lights, heating, and cooking.

Lance came to mind next. Scott had been critical of him because he didn't seem to have the ambition to finish his education and get a job. Although he had dragged out his college years, he was a good-hearted kid who never got in trouble and would go out of his way to help a friend in need. He wished he had praised Lance for all his good qualities rather than dwelling on his weaknesses. These thoughts and more flooded his mind until he fell asleep, momentarily escaping distress.

Scott awoke disoriented, with no idea how long he had been asleep—a few hours perhaps. To lessen his anxiety, he struck a match just so he could see something—anything, however briefly, but it soon flickered out.

He still wasn't sure what caused the darkness, but when he heard the scurrying of some animal outside his tent, he thought of dinosaurs. His sixth-grade teacher had explained that dinosaurs became extinct after an asteroid struck the earth causing a thick cloud of ash to block the sun for two million years. Had a similar event occurred?

Then, he remembered the 1980 eruption of Mt. St. Helens. He was living in Kentucky at the time and hadn't paid much attention to it, but he thought there had been a lot of ash from it. Had another volcano blown? Mt. Rainer? Such an eruption could easily produce a blackout that would last days or weeks. Could he survive under such circumstances?

Deciding to eat and looking forward to the scant light of his stove, he put on his makeshift mask and crawled from his tent into the dusty darkness. The familiar roar of the stove soothed his nerves. As he rummaged in his food bag, he discovered some critter had eaten part of his stew. Shaking his head, he prepared the remainder of the dinner. To conserve water, he left the pot unwashed.

He guessed he had 45 minutes of fuel left—more than enough to cook the rest of his food, assuming he had enough water—but he didn't. Therefore, he kept the stove lit to provide a few more minutes of solace. He searched for the lost flashlight part again, but with no luck. Attempts to light the wet firewood were unsuccessful.

When the breeze picked up, stirring the dust, Scott had no choice but to turn off the stove and crawl back into his tent. The tent flapped noisily as the wind grew stronger. Scott welcomed the sound—any sound—at the same time hoping the wind wouldn't last long. Lying on top of his bag, his thoughts once again turned to Robin. She would be worried sick knowing he was in the wilderness. Not having anything to do, he drifted off into a restless sleep, his conscious misery slipping into disturbing dreams.

The wind had died down by the time Scott awoke, but the oppressiveness of total silence and darkness remained. He no longer knew the time, or even the day. He tried to clear his foggy thoughts by concentrating on a problem from work, but he found it impossible. Lying there, he became aware of a body beside him. Startled, he pushed it away, but a hand grabbed onto him. Panicked, he jerked away and slammed his hand against his water bottle. As pain spread through his arm, the body evaporated into thin air. Scott held his hand, questioning his sanity.

Scott passed the next two hours between sleep and wakefulness, his mind wandering aimlessly. Rats with enormous heads appeared, floating overhead and gnashing vicious looking teeth at him. He flailed his arms to fend them off, but they only disappeared when he yelled. Had he been awake or dreaming?

Another day passed with constant darkness making him too disoriented to leave the tent. Flailing about and yelling stopped the hallucinations briefly, but he soon just gave up. At times, his mind seemed blank—incapable of any thought at all. He dozed again.

Awakening, he thought he was in the front yard of his Seattle home. Struggling to free himself of his tent and stand up, he started running.

"I'm here, Robin, I'm here. I'm coming home," he yelled as he reached the front door. The moment he opened it, he experienced the exhilarating feeling of floating, completely at peace.

* * *

Rick Swanson cursed the ash, coughing as he hiked along a trail in the Cascade Mountains. Rick, one of several rangers caught in the aftermath of the eruption of Mt. Rainer, was at his well-equipped station when it blew. Headquarters had informed him of the eruption by radio. Since he had plenty of food, water, and a lantern, his wait was only an inconvenience.

Once the ash settled, all rangers were told to leave the wilderness, keeping an eye out for others who might be in trouble. Fortunately, the heavy rain scared most hikers away, so he doubted he would encounter anyone. One thing rangers were not prepared for was fine ash, and the neckerchief he used as a filter only made breathing difficult.

After a few miles, he noticed a tent on a ridge above a lake. He knew he had to check it out. Slipping backwards in the ash, much as on a steep scree slope, he approached the tent. A couple of stakes had pulled loose, and the tent had partially collapsed with nothing inside but a sleeping bag, water bottle, and a few clothes. Noticing footsteps in the ash leading toward the cliff, he followed them to the edge where he discovered a body sprawled on a ledge 200 feet below.

On May 18, 1980, the sky in Pullman, Washington became pitch black. Ash rained down and the streetlights came on as my son and I frantically covered our car with plastic. Mt. Saint Helens had erupted. As an avid backpacker, I often thought about what would happen if such an event occurred while on a trip in the backcountry, especially if the blast were even more catastrophic. Research has shown that prolonged reduction of sensory stimulation would likely produce hallucinations.

Survival

Looking over a brochure of backpacking trails in the Selway-Bitterroot Wilderness area, Keith picked a route that would take him to several lakes and mountaintops. Although lacking experience in the backcountry, he was in good shape and confident he could handle it.

He asked two friends to join him, Jim, an accomplished backpacker, and Dave, a novice.

Looking over his equipment, he wondered if it would be adequate since it consisted of heavy, inexpensive items from an army surplus store. After loading his pack, he grimaced at the scale: 55 pounds. That didn't even include the hatchet, knife, and canteen he planned to wear on a pistol belt. Thinking it would be nice to sleep outdoors under the stars, he didn't include a tent. The weather was warm, so he saw no need for a jacket, either.

The three hikers left Pullman, Washington, in Keith's car. On the way, he had second thoughts about sleeping outdoors and stopped at an outdoor sports store to buy an inexpensive single-wall tent. Six more pounds to carry.

Arriving at Wilderness Gateway Campground, the adventurers shouldered their packs and set out on Trail 220, enjoying warm weather and sunny skies. The brutal route gained 4,600 feet of elevation before their arrival at Huckleberry Butte. Exhausted from the long, steep ascent, they rested, thankful that they'd be going downhill the rest of the day. However, they found the descent more difficult. Their knees protested as they dropped 600 feet to Lottie Lake, site of their first camp. Bushed, they struggled to set up camp on rubbery legs.

After pitching their tents and arranging their sleeping gear, they heated water for freeze-dried food in a coffee can placed on rocks next to the flames. Carrying his dinner, Keith tripped, spilling it on the ground. He scrounged in his pack for a few edibles and crawled into his sleeping bag, ignoring the lumpy ground beneath him.

The following morning, the three men followed Trail 220 up to Stanley Butte, gaining 1300 feet of elevation. Then they switched to Trail 206, a murderous, steep descent of 2,500 feet to Old Man Meadows, where they camped. That night, dark clouds rolled in and heavy rain pelted their tents, making Keith especially thankful for his enroute purchase.

On Day three, they continued two miles to Old Man Lake in a downpour, soon turning to snow. Gale-force wind whipped their ponchos as their boots splashed in puddles covered by the white stuff. Keith's and Dave's cotton pants soaked up rain like a sponge, increasing their misery.

With aching legs, the trekkers slogged upward in several inches of snow, tripping on hidden rocks and falling often.

Where was the junction with Trails 3 and 133? With ponchos flapping around their shoulders and their eyes blinded by glare, they scanned the area for signs of the route but saw only a white blanket.

Heading in what they thought was the right direction, they hiked for over an hour before realizing they were going deeper into the wilderness. The route they wanted followed a ridge whereas a sharp drop loomed ahead of them.

"Damn, we've been going in the wrong direction," Jim announced, fumbling with half-frozen fingers for his compass. "We'll have to backtrack. If only we could see more than four feet ahead."

"Do you think we'll make it out?" Dave asked, his voice quivering.

"It doesn't look promising," Jim replied. "Maybe Trail 133 is in that general direction." He pointed. "All we can do is head that way and hope to pick it up. With this poor visibility, it's hard to avoid going in circles."

Eventually, a faint depression in the snow indicated they were on a rutted footpath of some sort. Hoping it was the correct one and heaving sighs of relief, they followed it, still falling frequently. Getting back up became harder after each stumble, and their packs became heavier with sodden equipment and clothing. They passed several lakes but couldn't see them even though the trail went within a few feet of the water.

Shaking from the freezing temperature and wetness, they stumbled along until encountering a vacant horse camp. Overcome with exhaustion, they knew they couldn't go farther. With numb fingers, they struggled to set up the tents. After putting his soggy sleeping bag inside, Dave removed his boots and crawled in the tent, trying to avoid pools of water in the low spots. Then, he slid into his clammy bag, shaking too much to zip it up.

Jim's "tent" had no floor and only went to six inches from the ground—not much more than a tarp suspended in the middle by poles at each end. After getting in, he took off all his clothes and crawled into his sleeping bag. He packed newspapers, intended for starting fires, around himself in an attempt to get warm.

Hoping to dry boots and clothes, Keith stayed outside. Since the wind had died down, he just had to contend with heavy snow. However, the wet wood made it impossible to start a fire. Poking around the camp, he found a can of gasoline. Using it, he soon had a roaring blaze.

Placing Jim's and Dave's shoes by the flames, Keith watched steam rise from them until the leather in the toe of Jim's boots sunk in like melted butter. He grabbed the boots, but too late. The leather hardened and would cause Jim pain the remainder of the trip. Moreover, the boots weren't much drier than when first placed by the fire.

Since everyone was famished, Keith scrounged through the camp's boxes until he found some canned food. Their dinner that night consisted of a can, either of peaches or beans—very little, but they were too exhausted to care. Keith gave one can to Jim and took the other two cans to his tent to share with Dave. The cold food tasted like a banquet.

Before entering his tent, Keith extinguished the fire. He removed his boots and wet clothes and crawled into his sack. Since Dave's bag was wetter than Keith's, they both squeezed into his, which allowed them to share body heat. Still, they shivered all night and slept little.

In the morning, they poured water out of their boots and donned their frigid clothes that had been soggy for days. Their shirts were soaked, and Keith's cotton fatigue pants were so wet he could wring water out of them. Not wanting to carry the extra weight, he left them at the horse camp.

Wishing they had brought jackets, they fought the wind, which blew their ponchos unmercifully, exposing them to more dampness and bone-chilling cold.

Soon after starting out, they saw a sign indicating the trail had been re-routed. With sinking hearts, they tried without success to see the new path. There was no choice but to follow the closed one. Weary and hungry, they limped along on sore feet, wondering if the old trail would lead to the highway.

After several hours, with despair overtaking them, Jim stopped.

"Do you hear that?"

"What?" Keith and Dave responded in unison.

"It sounds like rushing water," Jim said excitedly.

They lumbered along until encountering a break in the trees.

"The Lochsa River!" Keith shouted. "And cars on the highway beyond." With renewed energy, they flew down the trail and crossed the river on a suspension bridge. The sun shone brightly, providing welcome warmth. However, looking back in the mountains, they could see nothing but black clouds and darkness. Relief, weariness, and hunger struck all at once. They nearly cried when a driver pulled over to offer them a ride to Keith's car.

They had cheated death.

This story is dramatized version of my second ever backpacking trip. All location and trail names are real, as are the events described. The actual hike took five days, but I shortened it to four in the tale. This narrative emphasizes the importance of preparation when entering the wilderness.

The Maid

As she drove up to the house, Hope turned off the ignition and surveyed the scene. A large Craftsman house, dormer windows, and a large porch with a swing appeared innocent enough. She reached for the car door, but just as quickly withdrew her hand and took a deep breath. She thought about driving off and not going through with it, but she had her reasons for wanting this particular job. She summoned her courage once again, left her Saab, and forced herself up the steps to knock.

A woman, around 50, hair in a bun, looking like she would be comfortable as a prison warden, opened the door.

"What do you want?"

Again, Hope thought about leaving.

"My name is Hope Langford. I'm responding to your ad for a maid."

"That so? I warn you—I won't tolerate loafing. I pay for work, not nonsense."

"I assure you I'm a good worker if you'll give me a chance to prove myself."

"Humph. Well, come in and we'll see how things go."

Amelia Bennett led her housekeeping prospect into a large living room with a grand piano set in a bay window and motioned for her to have a seat.

"I expect complete compliance with my rules. You will cook all my meals according to my wishes. You do cook, don't you?"

"Yes."

"Breakfast will be at 7:00, lunch at noon, and dinner at 6:00, not 5 minutes earlier or later, at those times exactly. I want the floors polished, and everything dusted every week. The bed should be made at 8:00 a.m. I will ring the bell for other needs. And no cell phones while working for me. Refer to me as Mrs. Bennett. Do you understand?"

"Yes Ma'am."

"Not 'Yes, Ma'am! Yes, Mrs. Bennett!"

"Sorry, yes, Mrs. Bennett."

"I pay $20.00 per hour. Do you think you can meet my needs?"

"Yes, Mrs. Bennett, I'd like to try."

"Try be damned. You will do it, or you'll find employment elsewhere."

So started Hope's new job. Although leery, she hoped Amelia's bark was worse than her bite.

While dusting on her first day, Hope accidentally knocked over a vase just as Amelia entered the room.

"You clumsy oaf! That vase cost $200. It's coming out of your pay."

"I'm sorry, Mrs. Bennett. It won't happen again."

Amelia gave Hope a list of what she wanted for dinner, duck á l'orange, string beans sauteed with mushrooms, sweet potatoes with honey-butter sauce, and green salad with blue cheese dressing, no croutons.

Taken aback by the elaborate menu, Hope set out to shop for the ingredients. While at the grocery store, she looked up a recipe for duck á l'orange.

Good Lord, surely all her meals won't be this elaborate!

Expecting the preparation to take hours, she began right after clearing lunch. Hours later, she felt satisfied the meal would be a success, and set the table.

Amelia sat down promptly at 6:00 and instantly complained.

"You stupid oaf! Don't you know the knife goes to the left of the spoons?"

"I'm sorry, Mrs. Bennett."

Later, Amelia went on a rampage about the green beans.

"I thought you could cook. These beans are over-done." She flung her plate, spilling its contents on the table and stormed out of the room. "Call me when you've reset the table."

Trying to hold back tears, Hope left for the kitchen to get a dustpan and wet rag.

She thought of quitting right then and there but decided to give the crabby woman more time.

The next day started off badly. Hope forgot to leave her phone in her car, and it rang during breakfast.

"I told you no cell phones while you work for me," Amelia shouted. "Don't you understand English?"

Apologizing, Hope took her phone to the car.

The rest of the day went better, with only minor grumblings. In general, the berating's decreased over the next couple of days, encouraging Hope they could get along. However, everything came to a head at dinner on the fourth day.

Amelia's menu for the evening called for salmon, brown rice, and roasted veggies.

Hope wanted to make the meal really special. She went to several markets until she found one with fresh-off-the-boat king salmon. Rather than preparing plain salmon with lemon wedges, she served the fish with savory-whipped cream on a bed of fresh baby spinach. Seasoned brown rice, honey roasted veggies, and fresh pecan pie rounded out the feast.

Beaming at the results, Hope took everything into the dining room and set the salmon plate down.

"You idiot, what have you done? I don't want my salmon on spinach." She then shoved the plate and food onto the floor. "Now clean up this mess!"

That was the final straw for Hope.

"Clean it up yourself, Mom!"

"Don't tell me…wait, what did you say? Mom?"

"Yes—Mom. You gave me up for adoption 25 years ago. I've been trying to find you ever since. Before telling you who I was, I wanted to see what you were like. Now I know. Goodbye."

As she strode from the room, Amelia called after her.

"Wait. Come back."

Without hesitation, she walked out the front door, relief and remorse battling for dominance.

"If nothing else, I can at least put this question to rest," she thought as she drove away.

Adopted children often wonder about their biological mothers. Those who eventually track them down are often disappointed. In this story, I tried a novel approach to finding out about one's parent.

The Gathering

"Hi, Hon. Both Brian and Claire are here. You'd be proud of how they turned out, much of it due to your nurturing. They brought their children too. It's been eight years since we've all been together," Ken said.

"Yes," Brian remarked. "Mom, you wouldn't believe how much Kim has grown since you last saw her. She wants to go to Stanford and hopes to become the next Jane Goodall. We aren't so sure about her choice, but we support her decision. Jeremy, about to finish his junior year in high school, wants to go to Princeton and major in math. However, we can't afford it unless he gets financial aid. The counselor thought it likely he'd get a scholarship given his grades and activities, so we're hoping."

"You didn't mention Jeremy was the point guard on the basketball team that nearly won the state championship," Claire shared.

"They lost by one point on a last-second buzzer beater—pretty amazing given their opponents were from a larger school with better funding," Casey added.

"Tell Mom about your new job, Claire."

"I left Microsoft for Boeing. I'm a bit overwhelmed, but it is getting better. I never realized testing wings for stress tolerance would be so complicated. Nathan, now in eighth grade, excels in music. He plays the piano well, but the trumpet is his first love. Wish you could attend his recital next month. Mom, you'd be so proud of Kaylee. She's the star of her third-grade class. All A's. Michael will be three in August. He's a ball of energy."

"I have a new firetruck," Michael added, holding it up. "It was a birthday present."

"Here's a picture I drew for you, grandma," Kaylee said.

"I love you so much," Ken said, tears running down his face. Claire gave him a hug and held his hand as they left the cemetery to return to their cars.

People go to cemeteries to leave tributes for their loved ones, sometimes expressing their love or telling the deceased about events in their lives. The idea for this story came from friends who regularly conduct such visits.

Nostalgia

Restless from sitting for hours, Larry and his dad were on their way to visit his grandmother who lived on a ranch in the sandhills of western Nebraska. Dust devils provided the only diversion from the monotony of hills covered in prairie grass. The August sun beat down unmercifully on their 1947 Plymouth. The gravel road was deserted except for hundreds of bugs splattering the windshield. Rivulets of sweat ran down their faces and shirts clung to their bodies. The wing windows diverted air, along with considerable dust, into the cabin and steam arose from the overheated radiator. The car needed to cool down and they needed to stretch their legs.

"I wish grandma lived closer to Omaha," Larry remarked. "What's that up ahead?"

"A tree," his dad replied, the first one in the last forty miles

"Look, Dad. There's a picnic table by it. Can we eat there? I'm really hungry."

"Sounds like a good idea, son."

The table was half covered with prairie grass which, when disturbed, sent hordes of grasshoppers flying. They scraped off layers of dirt and bird droppings, then covered everything with newspaper. One side had a broken bench, but the other seemed okay.

Larry placed the ice chest on the table, trying to keep it out of the sun's rays, while his dad opened the hood and removed the radiator cap. Water from melted ice had made the sandwiches soggy, but hunger is not particular, and they made the best of it.

"What are you looking at, Dad?"

"It looks like the tops of trees. Strange. Trees are rare in the sandhills."

He got up, stretched, and grabbed the water sack to fill the radiator while Larry drained the ice chest and stored the remaining food.

Reluctantly, they got into the car and went on their way, feeling better after having stopped. They soon arrived at a row of dying poplars on either side of a driveway leading 500 yards to an abandoned house.

"Why would someone build a house out here?" Larry asked.

"Probably someone who raised cattle. There's lots of grass for them to graze."

"Can we check it out?"

"Okay, but we shouldn't spend too long since grandma is expecting us."

After parking the car, they walked down the driveway, trampling waist-high grasses and watching insects take wing. The house was a plain, two-story structure. Most of the windows were broken and the paint long ago had lost its battle with the weather. A small porch led to a door hanging by a single hinge.

"Can we look inside, dad?"

"Sure, but watch out. You don't want to fall through the floor."

They walked to the door, being careful to step on joists. Brushing aside cobwebs, they entered the living room. Remnants of lace window coverings hung from the single window. Parts of a chair and an empty picture frame lay scattered on the floor. An ornate chandelier hung askance from the ceiling, its brass tarnished and green, a mere inkling of its former glory. Flowered wallpaper hanging in shreds and a rusty pot-bellied stove rounded out the room's contents.

They gingerly walked around a hole in the floor and entered the kitchen with its antique, wood-fired range. Larry opened the oven door, jumping back when a rat scampered out. Rusty remnants of stove pipe dangled on the stove's warming oven. A wood table missing two legs reclined in the center of the kitchen. The remaining legs were ornate, suggesting it had been a prized possession.

"Why would there be a table in the kitchen?" Larry asked.

"To serve meals," his father answered. "When this house was built, people couldn't afford the luxury of a separate dining room."

Larry's eyes strayed.

"Look at that stairway, dad. It sure is steep. Can we see what's upstairs?"

"I don't know if it's safe," his father answered, walking over to peer at the steps. Some treads were missing but it looked like they could step on the joists. "Let me go first."

Upstairs were three small rooms, each one having hooks on one wall to hang clothes. Two rooms were empty except for cobwebs, old newspapers on the floor, and fragments of green shades still covering the tiny windows. The third room, slightly larger, had a bedframe, the metal head and footboards with tarnished brass trim, fancy for its time. A badly dented bedpan rested in a corner. A tattered throw rug lay in a heap, dust concealing its design. Sunlight streamed in from holes in the ceiling—most of the shingles on the roof had succumbed to mother nature.

"Notice that there isn't any source of heat up here," his father commented. "In those days, the potbellied stove and the kitchen range provided the only heat. Houses were a lot more primitive back then. Lots of heavy blankets kept out the cold. Reminds me to be thankful for our central heating."

They went back downstairs. Larry went outdoors but his father remained inside.

"Are you coming, Dad?"

"In a bit," he replied.

He stood in the living room, imagining the chandelier in its glory and the scent of fresh-baked bread coming from the kitchen. He could almost see the family sitting around the pot-bellied stove on a cold winter night. His eyes moistened as he ran his fingers over the lace window coverings.

"Dad?" Larry said as he poked his head back through the door.

"It's so sad to think this was once someone's home," his father lamented, "full of life and dreams for the future. This was where their kids were born and grew up, where they enjoyed meals cooked on the wood range, where they sat around the pot-bellied stove in the winter and visited or played cards. Now it's only a ghost, dying like the poplars along the drive."

Returning to their car, they drove away, both caught up in silent thought.

Seeing a deserted farmhouse, it's driveway often bordered by dying poplars, has always been a moving experience for me. I would wonder at the events that took place there, the joys and sorrows, the hopes and fears. In this story, I attempted to portray my experience of such encounters.

The Letter

Anticipating a long-awaited letter, John found sleep difficult. It had been six weeks since he had heard from his 44-year-old daughter, Lynn. When he had called four days earlier, she hadn't been able to talk because she was driving her sons to a soccer game. She had promised she would write a long letter that evening. Normally, the letter would have already arrived, but surely it would come that day.

When not working as a realtor, Lynn kept busy chauffeuring two teenage sons to their various activities. She seldom had time to talk, preferring to write letters. Phone conversations were difficult for John because of hearing loss.

His wife of 47 years had died two years earlier, and John had deteriorated considerably, if anyone cared enough to notice. Years of farm labor had left him with arthritic joints. His hearing and eyesight had diminished. If he had to stop driving, he worried about getting groceries or going to doctor appointments. Complicating matters, congestive heart failure made him short of breath and produced pain that radiated down his arms.

After retiring, John moved to Colfax, Washington. He used to drive the 271-miles to visit Lynn and sons in Seattle. However, he could no longer manage such a long journey. Since Lynn was too busy to make the drive, letters were his only means of contact.

While sitting in his rocking chair, he savored her letters over and over. He kept a file of then and often read them in the evening to enjoy them anew. She had written every week after her mother died, but gradually, the interval between letters became longer and the letters shorter. Occasionally, they talked briefly on the telephone, but her busy schedule kept phone conversations brief. Although he enjoyed her calls, he found he could not remember much of what she said.

Thinking about a new letter made sleep impossible, so he dragged out of bed at 5:00 a.m. Despite the short night, he felt energetic. The pain in his arms gone. He showered and shaved, lamenting how old he looked. Although he felt like the same person he had always been, the image in the mirror argued otherwise.

After dressing, John ran his fingers over the carved music box his wife had loved so much. A lump rose in his throat. Some days, a pit in his stomach engulfed him in depression, but anticipation of the letter put him in a good mood. He went through the empty house to the kitchen and poured a bowl of cereal. Most of his life he had enjoyed reading the newspaper at breakfast, but now his small Social Security check did not permit such a luxury.

Lynn felt he had let his health and the house deteriorate after his wife died, but since he felt more energetic while expecting the letter, he decided to do chores he had let slide. He washed the pile of dishes in the sink, picked up his dirty clothes, emptied the wastebaskets, and vacuumed the house. The grandfather clock struck 10:00 a.m.

After resting a bit, he mowed his small back yard, stopping often to catch his breath. He started on the front yard at 11:30. At 11:45, he heard a vehicle approaching and looked up to see the mail truck. At last! Trembling with excitement, he pulled the mail from the box and scanned the return addresses—Medicare, electric bill, two charity solicitations, and an overdue notice of a library book.

John's shoulders drooped as he stared at the envelopes in his shaking hands. Then, he shuffled by the mower and into the house. He slumped into his chair, tears running down his cheeks, pain running down his arms.

After we leave home, often we tend to think of our parents as they had been, not realizing how age has age has changed them. It is easy to look at things from our point of view rather than theirs, and to overlook small things unimportant to us but of paramount importance to them.

It

A 62-year-old curmudgeon, gaunt, bald, slightly stooped, with thick, bushy eyebrows, a goatee, and always wearing a red flannel shirt, even in summer—that was Ben Murphy. Standing out as he did, many people knew of him, including those outside his usual Capitol Hill haunts. Often seen mumbling while walking, he stopped now and then to peer in shop windows or dumpsters, look under cars, or up at the clouds. Some tried to engage him in conversation, but soon learned the futility of such efforts.

I first encountered Ben in the summer of 1988 as he examined the contents of a dumpster.

"What are you looking for?" I asked.

"It," he grumped. Attempts to find out what "it" referred to were met with silence. After a bit, he moved on, as did I.

A few months later, a concerned young couple approached him as he twisted and turned, looking all around. They also asked what he was looking for, to which he replied, simply, "It." They volunteered to help him look, but he said nothing more.

A group of senior citizens walking in a park saw him looking under picnic benches and in trash cans. Thinking he must have lost something, one gentleman asked what he was looking for.

"It," he replied, menacing and scowling.

Taken aback, they rushed away, afraid he might lash out.

A store clerk, asking what the man was looking for, was told, "It." Always the same, always, "it."

Local residents became concerned about his behavior. They reported him to the police who said he wasn't breaking any laws, so there was nothing they could do.

Over the years, business owners worried that his bizarre behavior would scare away customers, but try as they may, they could do nothing.

Baffled social workers tried talking with him, hoping to get him into counseling. However, the only word they could get him to say was "it." Inevitably, they, too, gave up in frustration.

Many people had come to know of him, and speculation grew over what "it" could be. Some thought he searched for money, which seemed unlikely despite his disheveled appearance. People who encountered him in Volunteer Park thought he might have lost his dog, but he did not have a dog. Some hypotheses were metaphysical—searching for happiness, the meaning of life. All were wild guesses. No one had a definitive idea of what "it" might be.

In 2011, the local newspaper carried Ben's obituary and his search for "it." The article concluded the mystery followed him to his grave.

While in college, I enjoyed Samuel Beckett's play, Waiting for Godot, *in which the actors await some unknown event that never happens. In this brief story, Ben Murphy looks for something but never finds it. Each of us has probably experienced such a feeling at some time.*

Reunion

Answering the telephone, Bryan listened as his sister, Cindy, asked him to come to Seattle for a reunion with her and their brother, Matt.

"I don't think so, Sis," he replied.

"Come on, Bryan. We haven't been together since our parents died."

Bryan had reasons for not going, the least of them the distance from Miami to Seattle, but he didn't want to bring them up. He had always felt somewhat ill at ease around his siblings. Quiet and unassuming, Bryan's best friends had always been his books and studies. He had graduated at the top of his class at MIT and was an award-winning civil engineer.

In contrast, Cindy and Matt, close in age and temperament, visited frequently, either in Seattle or Bangor, Maine where Matt lived. A vivacious woman of 44 years with loads of friends, Cindy served as chair of the local school board. Matt's outgoing personality made him a successful real estate broker. Being several years younger, Bryan had never felt close to his siblings. Fourteen years had passed since he had last seen them.

Matt's call came next. He had begged Bryan, who in the end agreed to join them. The reunion was scheduled for the Labor Day weekend at Cindy's Seattle home. Matt, who had arrived a day earlier, went with Cindy to pick up Bryan at the airport.

"Sis, Matt," Bryan said in greeting while giving each a brief hug.

"I don't remember you looking so thin and tired," Cindy commented.

"It was a long flight," Bryan answered, smiling weakly.

On the ride to Cindy's home, he sat in the back seat and let his siblings do most of the talking. Then he dozed off.

Cindy had planned several activities she thought all would enjoy—a trip to the Seattle Art Museum, a walk in Discovery Park, and others—but Bryan encouraged them to go while he stayed behind to read a book.

The evening before their departure, Cindy prepared an elaborate meal of king salmon, truffles, roasted vegetables with garlic Dijon sauce, and pecan pie, paired with a 94-point Chardonnay. As usual, Cindy and Matt did most of the talking.

"What a wonderful meal," Matt exclaimed, "You are quite the chef."

"Thanks. Since the three of us rarely get together, I wanted it to be special."

"I had the most awful experience at Macy's, Cindy added. "While shopping for an evening dress, the saleswoman had the gall to say I should wear a looser dress because of my stomach. She said other insensitive things as well. I reported her to the management, although I doubt it did any good."

Agreeing, Matt described his shopping experience.

"I looked for a specific toy, forget what now, but couldn't find it. I went to the checkout counter where the clerk sat reading a comic book. After a few minutes, the guy still didn't look up. So, I said, 'excuse me.' He looked up but said nothing. After I asked if he had the toy, he brusquely replied 'no' and resumed reading his comic. I've never seen such rude service."

"That's terrible," Cindy agreed. "I don't blame you. It seems to be an epidemic. The passenger door on my Lexus didn't close properly, so I made an appointment for ten days out. I took it in at 8:00 a.m., but when I went to pick it up at 5:00, the service manager said they didn't have time to get to it and wanted me to make another appointment. I did, but with another shop."

The conversation continued in this manner for some time. Then Matt spoke up.

"Bryan, you've been awfully quiet. What have you been up to?"

"Putting my affairs in order."

"That sounds ominous. What on earth is going on?" Cindy asked.

"I have glioblastoma."

Cindy dropped her fork.

"Bryan, that's not something to joke about," She reprimanded, but her eyes begged for a denial.

"I'm not joking."

"Oh my God!" Cindy's eyes moistened.

"C-can it be treated?" Matt stumbled over his words, his lips quivering. "Surgery? What did the doctors actually say?"

"It's too far gone. They think I have a month or two."

"Why didn't you say something before?"

"I didn't want to ruin your fun."

Wide eyed and ashen, Cindy and Matt rushed to hug Brian, tears streaming down their faces.

Although my dad had eight siblings who lived in a small town, they never got together. In this story, I explored possible reasons some siblings are close and others aren't, and what can happen if we don't try to bridge our differences.

Waiting

Mary stopped drumming her fingers and rose when the surgeon arrived in the examination room.

"I'm afraid your constipation problems are the result of what we call a redundant colon. That simply means your colon is so long that its many kinks inhibit passage of fecal material."

"Can anything be done to remedy the problem?"

"Surgery. We have to remove a section to eliminate the kinks."

"Is the procedure dangerous?" Mary wrung her hands

"Any surgery is risky. However, I've performed dozens of these, and all turned out well."

"How much needs to be removed?"

The doctor pointed to a diagram of the intestinal tract.

"In your case, we'd cut the transverse colon here and attach it to the rectum."

Shaken, Mary returned home to tell her husband, Jason. He frowned as he listened to the verdict.

"Don't worry, honey," he reassured. "It'll be okay. You said the other people he operated on were fine and I'm sure you will be too."

Driving Mary to the hospital, Jason did his best to hide his concern, reminding her that she'd no longer be bothered by constipation. At the hospital, they were directed to a room where she was prepped. When a nurse came to take her to surgery, Jason kissed his wife and left for the dining room for breakfast.

The doctor had indicated the procedure would only take a couple of hours. After eating, he returned to wait.

The first hour, he tried reading, but the only magazines he could find were old copies of *Field and Stream* and *Golf Digest*, neither of which interested him. He glanced at the pictures briefly, then put them down. Leaning forward with his forearms on his thighs, he wondered how the surgery was going. His watch indicated it had been an hour and a half.

Only thirty more minutes. I hope she's alright.

Rising from his chair, he paced back and forth, stopping to look at the paintings on the wall and to get a drink from the water fountain. A nurse on her way to the cafeteria asked if he'd like some coffee. He declined.

At the end of two hours, he kept his eye on the door to the operating room, willing the surgeon to emerge. No one. After 2½ hours, a nurse came through the door.

At last!

He asked about his wife, but the nurse had no information. She was on her way to check on a patient in the recovery room. He put his hands to his face and chewed his lower lip.

By the three-hour mark, he resisted taking a trip to the restroom fearing he'd miss the doctor. Yet he found it impossible to sit, so he rose and shook his arms to release his nervous tension.

Something must have gone wrong.

At 3 ½ hours, he was desperate. Another nurse walked by, and he pleaded for information. She kindly entered the surgical unit to inquire about his wife. Returning, she told Jason that although they had encountered a few complications, everything was fine.

A few complications? What does that mean?

By this time, he couldn't delay a restroom trip any longer. He ran down the hall and back, hoping he hadn't missed anything. Four hours passed, then 4 ½. Still no word.

Finally, the surgeon appeared at the five-hour mark.

"Your wife is fine. The operation was successful. We had some difficulty stopping bleeders, but other than that, everything went as expected. You can see her after she's transferred to the recovery room."

Waves of relief flooded his body, and he put his head in his hands and cried.

Waiting for a loved-one's serious surgery is stressful, especially when the surgery is longer than expected. This story is loosely based on my experience awaiting news of my wife's colon procedure. On later visits, I became emotional whenever I walked through that part of the hospital.

My Journey with Alzheimer's

My life has changed so dramatically I am lost much of the time. In the 8th year of losing my identity, I can be with a caregiver all day. Seconds after she leaves, I have no recollection of anyone having been here. I get mixed up easily and often think it is bedtime in the afternoon. I have no idea who the president is, what day it is, what month it is, or even what year it is.

I generally know my husband and my main childhood friends, but I sometimes don't recognize my children. Occasionally, I've talked with my husband but thought he was someone else. At other times, I asked him what his name was. My children's families are a total mystery to me. I don't remember that my oldest son died, nor do I remember major events in my own life such as surgeries, getting married, or dating my husband in college. I think my mom is still alive although she died many years ago. Most of the time, I've reluctantly come to accept this new version of life, but I'm increasingly saddened at my shortcomings. I understand my brain is dying, but I have no comprehension of what the future holds. My feelings of helplessness and inability to do things can lead to tears.

I'm afraid of many things, including falling down. Because of my fear, I lean forward constantly, making walking more difficult. I'm afraid of riding in a car, especially when a road is bumpy, steep, or curvy. Whatever our speed, it always seems too fast. I don't know why I have such fears, but my husband thinks it may be because I live in a world where everything is new and there is no memory of what car rides are like. To me, riding in a car may be like riding in a rocket for the first time.

When my husband goes somewhere, I'm afraid he won't come back, and that scares me. He assures me he will always return, but I can't hide my tears of relief when he does. Even an hour away seems like an eternity. He's the only person I really know.

I hate showers and see no reason for them. My husband washes me while I whimper and cry. Washing hair is the worst part because I'm especially fearful of getting water on my face.

When it's dark, I'm uneasy. Looking out the window at night, I see many reflections I don't understand. My husband tries to explain what they are, but still, they often frighten me, as do sounds I cannot recognize, such as the wind.

Dressing requires extensive help. I have sometimes put my panties over my head or my shirt on my legs. At times, I'd like to put my shoes on before other things, but my husband insists on socks and pants first. Often, I don't understand what my husband is telling me to do, like pulling up my pants or lifting up my foot. Now and then, I express my frustration by telling my husband I am sick and tired of him and caregivers always telling me what to do. As for undressing, I see no need for it at all. Why not go to bed with my clothes on? As might be expected, dressing and undressing often makes me cry.

Toileting is especially challenging and can result in more weeping. Usually, I forget to take down my panties unless someone reminds me, and even then, I frequently don't know how. If I forget, shoes and pants need to be removed to change the soiled garment. I find sitting on the toilet difficult, generally needing reminders of how to use the grab bars. I go frequently, often one time right after another, possibly many times per hour. Besides, it gives me something to do. After going, I often require instruction on how to wash my hands.

Stools are another problem, since bowel movements can occur ten or more times daily. Because I sometimes use inappropriate things to wipe with, such as a handkerchief or towel, I now require help cleaning my bottom. Periodically, I have loose stools, and fecal matter gets all over my pubic area, leading to urinary infections. It would help if I drank more water, but I find it difficult to drink more than a few sips.

I have to wear diapers at night because I no longer wake up. I also wear diapers during car rides since restrooms might not be available when the urge hits. I have accepted this fairly well, but it does increase my feeling of helplessness.

My appetite varies greatly. Many times, I'll eat a bite or two and then push the food away and walk around before returning to the meal. Sometimes, I'll repeat this process several times per meal. I often eat standing and with the wrong utensil, such as using a knife to eat a sandwich. At times, I eat quite a bit, but at other times virtually nothing.

Perhaps the most disturbing thing is my inability to communicate. I can use many words easily, but the ones I need to express my thoughts escape me. I ask my husband questions all day long, but he usually can't decipher what I'm asking. For example, I might ask if he sees something, or if we're going to leave. I can't come up with the words to express what or where, despite repeated attempts. Now and then, I string sensible words together in a nonsensical fashion. It's so frustrating to want to say something without being able to do so.

I can't read, largely because I can't remember the content of the previous sentence. Writing is impossible. At times, I cry because I know my husband has a lot to do and I' like to help him, but carrying out a simple task, like putting my plate by the dishwasher or dusting a countertop, is beyond me.

My inability to do things makes me incredibly bored. In fact, boredom is probably the most difficult aspect of Alzheimer's for me. I like to go grocery shopping—the people are so friendly and I enjoy pushing the shopping cart. However, there are only so many times we can go there. My husband puts on music for me. All my life I've loved classical music, and I still do. However, sometimes the music makes me sad and I sob. After fifteen or twenty minutes, I feel overwhelmed, which I'm told is common for people with Alzheimer's. I especially like songs from the 1940s, but after a while, I leave the room, feeling lost.

The simplest games are impossible. My husband has tried to interest me in various objects such as seashells, rhinestones, beads, and things of different shapes, textures, and colors, but I'm not interested in them.

I want to be wherever my husband is, even when caregivers are here, but much of the time, I just sit and look at him. We try talking, but that's difficult for me and doesn't work well. I think I'm fixated on going somewhere—anywhere—just to have something to do. My best time is probably after dinner when we watch a movie. Sometimes I doze, but if it's engaging and easy for me to follow, I can stay awake until the end even though I don't understand it.

Many tasks are beyond me. If I have pain, I can't tell anyone where it is or what type of pain I'm having. I require help brushing my teeth because I can't remember where I have brushed and where I haven't. I can't handle teeth flossing, so my husband does that, as well as putting lotion on my legs, antifungal cream on my toenails, rosacea ointment on my cheeks, saline gel on my nose, and drops in my eyes. I misplace my handkerchief many times per day. Occasionally, I've started to drink liquid soap but quickly realized it tasted horrible and spit it out. I also put objects in strange places.

Despite my limitations, we do have many good belly laughs. My husband makes up silly songs that make me laugh. He also does "buttal checks" that crack me up. They involve us hugging and my husband feeling my bottom. Once in a while, I say something that doesn't make sense and realize it, which makes us both laugh. I have lots of gas and that, too, can be a source of merriment. After putting me in bed, my husband says, "Good night, my pretty." I like that and reply, "Thank you. That's nice."

> *Anyone who has a loved one suffering from Alzheimer's knows the heartache and challenge involved. But how many of us have ever considered Alzheimer's from the point of view of its victims? After my wife of 62 years developed Alzheimer's, I imagined what might have been going on in her mind during her decline. All of the described incidents actually occurred. My hope in writing this story is to give readers compassion and understanding in dealing with family or friends afflicted with this horrible disease.*

Voices

"Is that you John?" Abby asked when the back door slammed. John walked into the kitchen.

"What did ya say?"

"Nothin.' Just wondering who it was. Did you get all the hay baled?"

"Not quite. Still have about twenty acres on the north forty. Hopefully we can finish tomorrow mornin' if the weather holds."

Hay baling with a '46 Case NCM was a noisy, dirty job. It required three people, one to drive the tractor pulling the baler, a second to thread wires through needles to a third man who grabbed the wires and fed them back to be tied. The ram compacting the hay into bales produced a lot of dust, covering John's body in thick layers of itchy debris. He had his eye on a '52 New Holland 66 baler which needed only one man to operate it. But, money was tight since hail had destroyed most of their wheat crop.

Removing his shirt, John went over to the kitchen sink to wash up. He pushed the pump handle several times until water cascaded over his head and arms, removing some of the grime. He dried off and walked wearily to the kitchen table where supper awaited. He ate heartily of chicken, mashed potatoes with gravy, fresh baked bread, and peas, topping it off with a huge slice of cherry pie and ice cream.

At 8:30, he milked the cows and fed the hogs. Abby had already taken care of the chickens. Before the war, he had a hired hand, but the draft took him. Since he was a D-day casualty, John now had to do all the work himself.

Returning to the kitchen, he picked up the paper to check the latest prices for livestock and grain.

"John, are ya thinkin' of takin' the steers to market?"

He didn't reply. Abby repeated her question, only louder. Noisy farm machinery had taken its toll on her husband's hearing.

"I believe prices will continue to rise for a while longer. I think we should wait."

"John, ya really need to check into your hearin'."

"I don't want no damn hearin' aids. Have ya seen how big those things are?"

"May Hansen said Claude got some. He didn't want none either but now he really likes 'em. His have somethin' called a printed circuit board, much smaller than the old style. It's called Solo somethin' or other."

John dismissed the idea. Several days later, he went to the bank to see about a $2100 loan for a new corn picker. Since he had difficulty hearing the loan officer, he had to ask him what he said several times.

The same afternoon, he went to the sale barn, hoping to get a boar. He had difficulty understanding the auctioneer and missed out on the animal he wanted. That was the final straw. He decided he would at least talk with Manford, who had the hearing-aid store on Main Street.

"Maybe you're right about my hearin'," he admitted to Abby. "I'll check into it after the hay's in. Give Manford a ring tomorrow and find out when I could see 'im." As the town's only policeman, Manford's business had irregular hours, opening only as needed.

Tired of shouting at John and hearing the radio blare so loud it hurt her ears, Abby had been after John to do something about his hearing for a couple of years. At supper the next day, she told him Manford could see him the following Thursday at 11:00 a.m.

Thursday came, and John drove into town after his chores. Manford conducted some tests, asking him to tap his finger whenever he heard a tone. After the test, Manford showed him the results.

"You have a lot of hearin' loss. No wonder you have difficulty hearin' people. With your situation, I'd recommend the Solo-Pak. It's the first aid to have a printed circuit board with three small vacuum tubes, makin' it more compact than the others. It costs a bit more but works better. I could set you up for about $175. Whadaya think?"

"I think that's a lot of dough. Don't you have anything cheaper?"

"Sure, but it would have over 160 wires, each of which has to be soldered and each of which might end up with a bad connection later. It's not so reliable, doesn't work so well, and would be a lot bulkier. The Solo-Pak has no wires and fits easily in a shirt pocket. Believe me, John, the Solo-Pak would change your life. Tell you what. Try 'em out for a couple weeks and if you don't like 'em I'll give your money back."

"Well, I'll think on it. I'd better be runnin' along. I'll be in touch."

Manford shook his hand.

John jumped into his truck, got some gas, and headed home. He pulled up just as Abby approached the house with a basket of eggs.

"Well, what did Manford say?"

"He wanted me to get hearin' aids—said they would change my life. Maybe he's right, but they'd put us in the poor house. I'm not goin' to spend $175 for no damn hearin' aids."

Abby knew better than to press the point when her husband was so riled up. She bided her time until the day Claude Hanson brought his bull over to service a cow in heat. Claude knocked on the kitchen door.

"Hi Claude, good to see you." As she hoped, he wore his hearing aids. "How are those hearin' aids workin' out?"

"They're somewhat of a nuisance, but they're a damned site better than not hearin'."

"John's cleanin' stalls in the barn. I'd sure be obliged if you'd mention you like the aids. John's hearin' is horrible, but he's dragging his feet about doin' anything."

"Be glad to, Abby. John's just like me—we don't like to change unless we absolutely have to."

Claude made his way to the barn and found John. After talking about the price of steers and the lack of rain, Claude brought up the purpose of his visit.

"Where's your cow that's hankerin' for my bull?"

"Just back up to the pen yonder. I'll pull my ramp over there to unload 'im."

After putting the bull in the pen with the cow, they waited for the action to begin, giving Claude the opportunity to bring up hearing aids.

"I hear you've given some thought to gettin' hearin' aids. I'll tell you, these Solo-Paks sure help me a lot. I had no idea what I was missin'. Think you'll take the plunge?"

"I don't know, Claude. They cost a fortune."

"True, but we ain't no spring chickens and our hearin' jus' keeps gettin' worse. I decided I missed out on more than I wanted. I got to the place where I couldn't even listen to Jack Benny on the radio. And I had all sorts of trouble understandin' my kids. Hell, life is too damned short to miss out on them things. Did Manford offer to give your money back if you didn't like 'em?"

"Yep, but I'd hate to make 'im eat 'em if I didn't like 'em."

"Well, I'm not a bettin' man, but I'd wager you wouldn't want to return 'em. You needn't worry about Manford, anyway. He does okay with his police pay and hearin' aid income. He also gets income from sharecroppin' 60 acres."

John glanced at the pen with the bull and his cow.

"Well, I'll be damned! Look at that, wouldja? They're getting' it on already! Looks like you won't have to leave your bull overnight."

John returned to the house after loading the bull.

"I noticed Claude took 'is bull home. He did 'is job?" Abby asked at dinnertime.

"Yep, and didn't waste no time neither."

"Did Claude say anything about his hearin' aids?"

"He seemed to like 'em."

"Have you given more thought to gettin' some?" she asked.

"I don't know. I suppose it might be okay. But we'd have to sell a steer to pay for the damned things."

She didn't push the idea for fear of arousing his resistance, knowing it was better to let him make up his own mind.

"Well, a couple steers are ready for market. If ya sold one now, we'd still have another to fall back on if the need arose. We could hold off on gettin' an indoor toilet, too."

John was impressed Abby would be willing to wait for an indoor toilet. She had asked for one for a couple of years.

A few days later, John saw Manford having coffee at the Silver Café.

"Manford, I guess I'll get them hearin' aids, but I wonder if you'd let me pay for 'em in a few weeks, after I get a chance to sell a steer."

"No problem, John. I'll get right on it. It'll take a couple weeks before they come in, anyway."

John finished haying and cultivating the corn by the time Manford called to say the aids had arrived. A couple of days later, John picked them up and got briefed on their use.

"These feel damned funny," he exclaimed.

"You'll soon get used to 'em," Manford replied. "Give 'em a good try and, if you don't like 'em, I'll take 'em back."

John found the aids bothersome, but he got used to them. He wore them when not working in the field and had to admit he could hear better. He understood the pastor better at Sunday service, although he didn't consider that much of an advantage. He could hear Abby better and she didn't have to shout. All in all, he couldn't help but admit the aids were worth the trouble and expense.

The summer went by and fall rains began, which meant John had more time on his hands. He still had the livestock to tend, machinery to repair, and fences to mend, but there were no more sixteen-hour days.

As he checked grain prices one day, he heard a voice. He looked around, but nobody was there.

"John, do you know what Abby is thinking? Can you trust her?" Again, he scanned the room. No one.

What in hell is goin' on?

He shook his head and got up to get a drink of water, dismissing the warnings. After all, they had been married 21 years and had worked together to make the farm a success. It hadn't been easy, but they seldom argued, and he trusted her completely.

As time went on, he continued to hear voices. After a couple months, he heard a voice telling him to sell his hogs. He ignored it at first but eventually became convinced it made sense despite the price plummeting the previous month. Abby protested, but John would not be swayed.

The following week, he heard a voice again as he ate dinner.

"Do the mashed potatoes taste strange? Is something in them?" He paused—they did seem strange.

"What didja do to the potatoes? They taste funny," he commented.

"I made 'em same as always," Abby replied.

"Did you see the way she looked at you?" the voice said. John shoved the potatoes away, claiming to be full.

As the voices became more frequent and alarming, John became more upset. He ate less than usual, had difficulty sleeping, was more irritable, and got into frequent arguments with Abby. The change alarmed Abby who encouraged him to see his doctor.

"Hell no, I don't need no damn fool doctor," he'd reply.

The voices came many times a day by that time. John became convinced Abby intended to do him in. He ate very little and refused to listen to the radio, fearing Abby used it to control his mind. He also neglected the farm, leaving Abby to do whatever she could to keep it going.

Abby was at her wits end when Elias Andersson, a neighbor who lived a mile east, stopped by to see if John would help him erect a new barn. As soon as Elias started to speak, she broke into tears.

"Why Abby, what on earth is wrong?"

Struggling to control her emotions, she answered, her voice shaky.

"I don't know what's wrong with John. He's just not himself." She went on to describe his strange behavior and how he had neglected the farm.

"I'm sorry, Abby. That's got to be very upsettin'. Have you suggested he see Doc?"

"He won't do it. He'll hardly speak to me. Frankly, I'm scared of 'im now."

Elias thought a moment.

"I have an idea. I think I can get 'im to go into town with me. I'll set things up with Doc Baer to be in the Silver Café. John and I'll drop by to have a cup of coffee and see Doc there, so John won't be suspicious. Doc can get an idea of what's goin' on and recommend what to do."

Elias made the arrangements and convinced John to go to town with him. It took some doing, but Elias got him to go into the café for a cup of coffee. As they walked in, Doc Baer motioned for them to join him. John, suspicious, reluctantly sat down.

"I haven't seen you for a while. How are things going, John?" Doc asked.

John looked around suspiciously.

"She's tryin' to poison me," he whispered.

"Who is?"

"Abby."

"Why would she do that?"

"Because of the radio."

The talk continued a bit before Doc excused himself and motioned for Elias to join him.

"Elias, this isn't my area, but I'd say John is showing signs of schizophrenia. I suggest Abby have him committed to Mercy Psychiatric Hospital in Des Moines. I'll take care of the paperwork, but Abby will have to sign."

"He's not goin' to take kindly to that. How can we get him to go along with the idea?" Elias asked.

"Well, if he resists, and I suspect he will, we'll have to be firm. I'll contact Mercy and they can pick him up at the farm—forcibly if need be."

The arrangements made, Mercy orderlies took John to the hospital. After putting him in an examination room, they asked him to remove his clothes and put on hospital garb. He put his hearing aids and clothing on a table. After dressing, they took him, protesting, to a waiting area to be seen by a psychiatrist.

An orderly collecting John's clothes heard faint whispers. Picking up his clothes, he discovered they came from the patient's hearing aids.

What if the voices schizophrenics hear really exist? Would that diagnosis still be correct? This story is based my training as a psychologist and my farming experiences as a youth in the 1950's.

Desdemona

On her daily walk in Lincoln Park, only four blocks from home, Desdemona was enjoying the bright, sunny day. Trees had assumed their fall colors of crimson and yellow and the crisp air bit at her ears and nose. Worries about an argument with her husband were far from her mind.

As she approached a playground, the sun disappeared behind dark clouds. Her bonnet flew off and she shivered in the wind. A murder of crows perched in nearby trees took flight and dove at a group of children playing soccer, ramming their heads and pecking their eyes. A clear liquid mixed with blood ran down their faces. Screaming, the blinded children ran in all directions, colliding with one another and falling to the ground. Desdemona went to pick up one child and saw he had no face, just eyes dripping a cocktail of blood and eye fluid.

Screaming, Desdemona ran all the way home, her chest heaving and her whole body shaking. She slammed the door and collapsed into a chair. Her short-rapid breaths soon led to a fainting spell.

The mother of two grown daughters, Desdemona, 47, a former cheerleader in high school, prided herself on her looks, though age had left its marks. Her husband, a professor at the local college, found his wife a mess.

"Honey, what on earth is the matter?"

"Nothing, just not feeling the best," she lied.

What could I say? That I saw crows pecking the eyes out of faceless boys? Who would believe that? It seemed so real, but I must have imagined the whole thing.

Although reluctant to return to the park, she loved walking on the curving paths among old growth trees with fall leaves raining down in the breeze. Convinced she had imagined the crow episode, she went back.

As she walked by Heart Lake, she noticed a woman sitting on a park bench with a baby in a stroller. An alligator sprang from the water, its steely eyes gazing at the woman. She removed the screaming baby from the stroller and placed it on the ground. The animal waddled over, its head moving from side to side, and then swallowed the screaming infant in one gulp. Turning its ugly head toward Desdemona, it started toward her.

Once again, Desdemona ran for her life.

What is going on? Am I cracking up? There're no alligators in this area.

Once home, she plopped on the bed, shaking with fear. She was still in bed when her husband arrived home from work.

"Honey, I'm home." He received no answer. Looking in the kitchen, he saw no evidence of dinner preparation. Calling her name, he looked downstairs first and then upstairs where he saw her lying on the bed, mouth gaping, eyes wide open, staring blankly at the ceiling.

"Des, are you okay?" he asked,

No answer. He shook her shoulder.

"Des...Des, what's going on. Look at me."

Slowly, she turned her head toward his face, still expressionless and pale. Suddenly, she sat up and grabbed him, hugging him in a fierce embrace and crying.

"I don't know what's happening—I see frightening things, terrible things. Sometimes I think I'm losing it." She still couldn't bring herself to tell him *what* she saw—it was just too preposterous.

"There, there, don't worry. You're probably just stressed out trying to keep up with your studies and the house. Tell you what. Get dressed and we'll go out for dinner. The change would do you good." She didn't see the smirk on his face as he hugged her.

Desdemona had no more scary episodes for three days. Then it happened again. As she was preparing dinner, she experienced a vision of an old man with grotesque features picking up a pot of boiling soup and pouring it on a growling bulldog. The dog's head metamorphosed into that of an old woman who let out a blood-curdling scream.

Dropping her spoon, Desdemona slowly backed away, then sprinted for the stairs and the sanctuary of her bedroom. Again, she flopped face down on the bed and pulled a pillow over her head. After her body stopped shaking, she sat up.

Why do I see these horrible things?

Determined not to let the images disrupt her life, she went downstairs to finish dinner preparation. Although still trembling, she managed to set the table. Her husband noticed her nervousness and addressed her.

"Are you still seeing troubling things?"

Despite her vow not to let the images get her down, she ran to him, sobbing and holding him tightly. Frowning at the sticky moisture from her tears, he grabbed his handkerchief to dry his cheek.

"Des, get ahold of yourself. You have to realize these things you see aren't real. Don't let them get to you," he said, kissing her neck.

"I...know...and...I'm...trying," she said between sobs.

Desdemona stayed in her bedroom for five days, afraid to venture out of her safe haven, the only place she could relax. Nevertheless, it happened again. She awoke to a room filled with snakes slithering under the blankets, up the walls, on the furniture, even on the ceiling. The same sinking feeling of days earlier threatened to overtake her. She shrieked, then passed out.

Hearing the scream, her husband came running. She soon revived, but her stare was blank, and she could say nothing—limp, mute, ashen.

"I'm taking you to someone who can help," said her husband, carrying her down the stairs. He put her in the back seat and drove several miles before stopping at a bungalow on a narrow street. Wife in arms, he entered the door without knocking and went directly to a woman in a back room. The two engaged in a few moments of whispered conversation.

"Des, this woman is a therapist who can help you. You can stay with her until you're better."

"You know what to do," he said to the therapist in parting.

The therapist took Desdemona to a small room with flowered wallpaper, a bed, and a small window looking out at a fence. Two days later, Desdemona experienced three episodes of frightening scenes and became catatonic. At that point, her husband committed her to Hope Psychiatric Hospital.

The following day, the "therapist" drove to Desdemona's home, walking in without bothering to knock. Roy was in the kitchen.

"Our post-hypnotic suggestions worked just as you said they would," she said, running to embrace him. Together, they laughed at how easy it had been for them to get rid of Desdemona. Then he lifted her in his arms and happily took her to the bedroom.

As an undergraduate student, I wrote a term paper on hypnosis and post-hypnotic suggestions. That gave me the idea for a tale about using such suggestions for nefarious purposes. A few weeks after writing this story, I saw a movie along the same lines.

My Son Pete

On a cold, dark day in February, Clarence Welch, the local coroner, asked his friend, Dr. Ray Higgins, a clinical psychologist, to read a notebook found among the possessions of John Mathiason. Clarence had done an autopsy on John and wanted Ray's opinion of John's mental state. Ray agreed, reluctant to refuse his good friend. That evening, he started reading and, to his surprise, found it captivating.

John Mathiason, Seattle, Washington

Today I walked along Terminal Street in a part of town I had not before encountered. I felt compelled to enter a small bookstore, unusual since I seldom read. The store specialized in used books, well-used in most instances. I spied a large black volume on the top shelf with *My Son Pete* embossed on the cover. Thumbing through a few pages, I found it strange that the book was handwritten, some letters slanting to the left and others to the right.

I purchased it and left. That evening I commenced reading. It was obvious that Pete's father wrote the book. The story began with an account of a difficult birth during which Pete's mother died. There were accounts of his first steps, trips to the park with his father as a toddler, his first day of school, his dislike of his seventh-grade teacher, his apprehension about entering high school, and his thoughts on religion. There were also accounts of illnesses, aspirations, and disappointments. Pete appeared to be an average boy doing average things, but these events seemed oddly intriguing to me, and I did not put the book down until I had read 147 pages.

The next day, I left work early, claiming to have a headache. In truth, I wanted to resume reading about Pete. I poured a glass of Merlot and began. He had been a good athlete but suffered from a lack of self-confidence. Although a top student in high school and college, teachers and family members felt he underachieved, contributing to his low self-esteem.

As I read, I became more and more fond of him, perhaps because of the similarities to myself. One passage described Pete's disastrous dating experiences. Like him, I never married and long ago gave up on finding a soul mate.

The book's peculiar penmanship gnawed on me. It seemed to me I had read something else with some letters slanting to the left and others to the right.

I stopped reading to do some chores, the first of which was to repair my dresser which was falling apart. The top three drawers were easily fixed with glue and clamping. However, the bottom drawer had been stuck for years. Using a pry bar and lots of pulling, it finally popped out. It contained personal effects I had received after my father died. I was 42 at the time, and still recovering from a serious automobile accident two months earlier. I put everything in my bottom drawer thinking I would go over the items once I recuperated. However, when I tried to open the drawer, it was stuck and I forgot about it. With it now open, I saw a pocket watch with a closed face, some tie clasps, a small brass baseball inscribed "Metro League Champions," a few items of clothing, and a letter from my father written a few days before his death. I opened the letter and read the following.

* * *

"Dear Son,
I realize you do not remember me as your father ever since your car accident which resulted in your amnesia. I want you to know how much I appreciate your willingness to get to know me anew and to try to think of me as your father. That had to be difficult for you, and your devotion is appreciated more than you can ever know. In a way, I feel I've had two wonderful sons.

I also want to tell you how proud I am of you and how lucky I feel to be your father. I will always cherish our times together at the park, watching you learn to ride a bike, reading stories to you, and later listening as you read them to me—so many things. I recall the pride I felt at your piano recitals and athletic events. And to think you were valedictorian—amazing. I only wish your mother could have watched you grow up. She would have been so pleased!

I could not have asked for more in life than to have you for a son. I will cherish you always.

Love,

Dad"

* * *

Tears came to my eyes. The shaky handwriting suggested it was difficult to write, both physically and emotionally. Then something else caught my attention—something the shaky handwriting had nearly obscured. Some letters were slanted left and others right!

Trembling with excitement, I compared the writing in the letter with that in the book. They were the same, indicating my father had written the book. But why call it My Son Pete? Who was Pete? So far as I knew, I had no brothers or sisters.

Over the following days, I reread portions of the book. Gradually, I remembered Pete had been a name my father called me in my youth. I never knew how he came up with it, or why he didn't call me John, as everyone else did. Perhaps he wanted something just between us. In any event, I now had more reason than ever to read the book. I started again at the beginning and savored every word. The more I read, the more memory I recovered. How wonderful to read about forgotten events and to recover partially from my amnesia.

How did the book end up in the bookstore? It seemed unlikely Dad or anyone else would have taken it there. Perhaps the proprietor could tell me. I walked to the store, or rather where the store had been. The building was empty and boarded up. I looked where the sign 'Terminal Street Books' had been. However, the sign now read, 'Gifts From The Heart,' and looked like it had been there for years.

I asked an elderly couple sitting on a bench across the street about the bookstore, but they had not heard of it. In fact, they said all stores in the block had been closed for at least a couple of years. Perplexed, I returned to the store and peered between the sheets of plywood, seeing nothing but broken shelves, dust, and cobwebs. I left disappointed. Subsequent inquiries produced no more enlightenment.

Back home, I opened the book to read about events right before my accident. With my memory nearly complete, I was overjoyed to be reminded of many episodes in my younger days. Some things were unpleasant, particularly my love affair with a woman who had left me for a handsome drug addict. However, disagreeable events were countered by the satisfaction of recovering episodes that amnesia had taken from me. I wondered how Dad had obtained so much information, and what had prompted him to write the book.

The names of several friends were mentioned. Searching the phone directory, I only found the number for one—Jeff Jacobson. Jeff and I had been close, and I looked forward to seeing him again. We talked on the phone for an hour or so—more than sufficient time to realize how far apart we had grown.

I resumed reading. There were accounts of my life after the accident, especially my addiction to antidepressants. By the time I kicked the habit, my physical injuries had healed.

The book ended abruptly with an account of my visit with Dad about one month before his death. The book mentioned things we had talked about and how much he enjoyed the visit. Blank pages at the end suggested he would have written more had he lived longer. I put the book down and fell asleep in my chair.

Reading the book consumed so much time I fell behind at work and my dishes piled up. For a few days, I tried to forget about it, but as time passed, I found myself thinking about it more and more. Finally, I could resist no longer and re-read the last few pages—the only ones I had not read several times. Astonishingly, there were several new pages. Events were described occurring after my father's death. Confounding the issue further, the handwriting appeared the same. How could that be?

I read about attending my father's funeral, and, while definitely sad, I was less emotional because of my amnesia. I thought of him as a wonderful friend rather than a father. I felt badly he did not have the emotional support a son without amnesia would have provided.

The book continued with accounts of my life up to and including the last few days. Shivers went down my spine as I contemplated many questions. How could these pages have been written with the book in my possession the entire time? Who could have written them? How could the writing be identical to my father's? Trembling, I lay down, but found sleep impossible.

Eventually, I got out of bed and made some coffee to ease the extreme tiredness pervading my body. Fortunately, it was Sunday so I did not have to go to work. I immediately got out the book to re-examine the pages that had so puzzled and upset me the previous day. Gasping, I saw several new pages describing the distress I had felt only a day earlier. The text continued with descriptions of events I had not yet experienced. Could this be describing my future?

At one point, I returned to a previous page, shocked to find it blank. As time wore on, the writing vanished soon after I read it—so quickly, in fact, I had to read faster and faster. Trembling so badly I could scarcely hold the book, I read I would lose my job and be overwhelmingly depressed. There were accounts of financial troubles and of losing my house because of my inability to make mortgage payments.

*   *   *

At this point, the writing became so illegible and nonsensical, Dr. Higgins could only get general impressions of its contents. John became increasingly obsessed with learning about his future and how his life would turn out. He learned he was destined to live in his car and either beg for food or live out of dumpsters. Eventually, the writing stopped.

At the end of the notes, Clarence had inserted a newspaper clipping about John Mathieson. The clipping indicated a citizen had reported an abandoned car parked on Terminal Street. The police officer sent to check it out had found a man, later determined to be John, lying dead on the front seat of a clutter-filled car. An autopsy revealed he had died of heart failure. Dr. Higgins felt shivers run down his spine as he contemplated the cause of his demise. He went to the police station to ask if a book titled *My Son Pete*, was found among John's belongings. Several others were discovered, but not *My Son Pete*.

Have you ever lay in bed with your mind running wild? Such was the case with this story. Thoughts come easier in the dark without the interruptions of visual and auditory stimulation. The boundary between real and imagined events becomes blurred freeing one to be more creative. In this story, I show the tricks the mind can play on the mentally disturbed.

Encounters in the Fog

A loud sound startled George from a deep sleep. Groaning, he turned over, tapped the nightstand until he found his phone and put it to his ear.

"Yeah?" he croaked.

"Is this George Ellison?"

"Yeah."

"This is Dr. Lindley calling from Rockwell Regional Hospital in Ashville. Your father was brought here at 1:15 a.m. after having a severe heart attack. I'm sorry, but I think he won't last long, probably not more than 24 hours. We're doing all we can to keep him as comfortable as possible."

"My God! Is anyone with him?" George asked, jumping out of bed.

"His neighbor—I believe he said his name was Al Peterson or Patterson."

"Patterson—he's a good friend. Could I speak with Al?" He heard muffled speech, then Al's voice.

"Hello, George," Hearing nothing but muted sobbing, he continued. "I'm so sorry. Your father and I were enjoying a few beers after our weekly poker game when he grabbed his chest and collapsed. I called 911 and went with him to the hospital."

"Thank you, Al. Is Dad awake?" George asked haltingly.

"Yes, he has asked for you."

"Would you tell him I'll be there as soon as I can? It's a six-hour drive. I can be on the road in ten minutes."

George's mind raced as he pulled jeans over his portly belly and grabbed a flannel shirt. He thought of his father lying in a hospital bed. What would it be like to know you only had hours to live? What should he say to him? He had always been close to his dad, unlike his two estranged brothers—drug addicts who had disappeared years earlier.

Please let me see him before he dies!

He ran to his car, struggling to put on his coat.

While searching for an open gas station, his mind flitted about, wishing he had visited his dad instead of going on the five-day fishing trip he had taken three months earlier. Concerned about snow on Golden Pass, he checked his phone, relieved to find it open.

He made good time for the first 200 miles, but then encountered fog so thick he had to slow to thirty miles per hour. Cursing, he struggled to see through the murky mist. The higher he drove, the denser it became. He looked at his speedometer. Fourteen mph. He slammed his fist on the steering wheel.

Will I make it?

The hypnotic thumping of his windshield wipers made focusing on the road a struggle. After driving five hours straight, pain radiated down his back and his right leg was cramping. Squirming in his seat, he realized he had to stretch his legs, but the thick fog made stopping dangerous. Thankfully, he hadn't seen another vehicle for over an hour.

Approaching the summit, he spied a short spur leading to a shed. He parked beside the structure and looked for an entrance to get out of the cold and fog.

The building looked like it hadn't been used for a long time. Weeds, beer bottles, and other litter were scattered around it. He noticed two small windows but no entrance. Walking around the structure, he found a side door. It creaked loudly as he pulled it open.

Once his eyes adjusted to the dim illumination, he saw that the shed, about twenty by thirty feet, had a dirt floor. To his left were two shelves, each with various items, including an old baseball with frayed stitching, a toy soldier, several tattered books, a rusty pocketknife, and a teddy bear missing one ear. Thick layers of dust covered everything. Each item had a tag with a hand-written price ranging from $.05 to $1.00.

When he saw the baseball, he thought of his dad—playing catch, Little League games coached by him—such great times. The other items also seemed strangely familiar.

The squeaking of a door startled him. Turning, he spied a small room at the opposite end. A tall, gaunt, bearded man, about 45 years of age, emerged from the darkness and stood silently, staring at George. He was dressed in well-worn overalls and a tattered blue flannel shirt with sleeves rolled up. George blanched. Trying to act normally, he greeted the man, indicating he stopped to stretch his legs and find shelter from the weather. The gaunt man said nothing but extended his hand toward George, the corners of his mouth turned down and his eyes misty. George backed away.

As he pondered his next move, another man emerged from the shadows, shorter and even more gaunt than the first, with scraggly hair covering his shoulders. He also held his hand out. George panicked. He started for the door, but with alarming quickness, the tall man blocked his passage, his arm still extended.

Drug addicts, mental cases, escaped prisoners? How can I assure them I mean no harm?

Looking uneasily around the room, he again spied the items with price tags.

Perhaps these men think they're shopkeepers. Maybe buying something would pacify them.

Walking over to the shelves, George picked up the baseball priced at $.75. He walked slowly over to the tall man and held out a dollar bill. The man shook his head and again offered his hand.

He wants to shake hands?

When the tall man moved away from the door, George started to leave but noted the short man was nowhere to be seen.

Is he waiting just outside the door to attack?

In a cold sweat, George forced himself out the door. With the tall man at his heels, he was jogging toward his vehicle when the short man stepped from behind the corner, blocking his way. The men stood unmoving, one in front and the other behind, holding out their hands. With the fog clearing rapidly, George knew he had to get to his car at all costs. Although these men had done nothing, they looked menacing enough to harm him if he made a wrong move. Therefore, he bolted past the short man to his vehicle.

He got into the car, slammed the door locks, and started the engine. He shifted into drive and looked up. The two men stood directly in front of his car. He backed up in wild fashion right onto the highway. The men chased after him with outstretched arms. He shifted into drive and shivered as they disappeared in his rearview mirror.

Breathing a sigh of relief, George pulled over a mile down the highway to calm himself. He remembered his dying father and realized he needed to put his narrow escape aside and get underway. Nevertheless, his mind raced as he kept trying to make sense of his ordeal. He didn't even notice that his back and legs no longer hurt.

A sharp switchback sent him in the direction from which he had come and afforded a last view of the shed. Looking up, he gasped. The shed…gone? Unnerved, he told himself he had to keep going. Only one more hour.

Arriving at the hospital at 10:15 a.m., he rushed to the information desk to get the room number for his father.

"Hello son," his father said, his voice weak.

I made it.

Finally at his bedside, he embraced his dad for several long minutes. They talked until his father's eyes closed for the last time. George cried, kissed his cheek, and held his hand for close to an hour, never lifting his head from his father's chest.

Days later, George sat in his living room, pondering his strange experience on Golden Pass. It dawned on him the objects he saw in the shed were all childhood gifts from his father. The two men? Emaciated versions of his estranged brothers, both drug addicts the family hadn't seen for years. He decided the stress he was under, his dying father, the thick fog, led him to imagine the entire incident.

But it seemed so real.

Suddenly, the baseball he had bought and placed on the passenger seat came to mind. Checking his vehicle, he looked at the seat. Empty. He sighed with relief. But as he was shutting the door, he glanced at the floor and gasped. The ball with frayed stitching had rolled off the seat.

Under normal conditions, driving to a funeral can be stressful, especially if the deceased is a family member. Add bad weather to the mix, the stress would be increased. This story is a product of a trip home for my father's funeral in bad weather interwoven with psychological aspects.

The Chamber

Bolting up, I cracked my head against something in the dark. My head throbbed with pain as blood trickled down my forehead. I was in some sort of chamber only thirty inches high and fifty inches wide. I could not tell its composition, but pounding my fists against the walls produced little sound, suggesting thick steel. All surfaces felt smooth and comfortably warm. There were no seams or cracks and no door. How could I have gotten inside? More importantly, how could I get out? A faint glow from the ceiling provided enough light for me to see the outline of my hand. Pushing against the walls with my hands and feet produced nothing but frustration and wasted energy. Since I couldn't sit up, I had no choice but to recline and contemplate my fate.

Had someone put me here? Was this a sadistic prank? Did someone want revenge from a past affront? That seemed implausible since I got along well with everyone at work. I was even known for diffusing office conflicts. I simply didn't have any enemies—at least, none I knew about.

To keep panic in check, I passed the time thinking about pleasant events in my life: playing games with friends, swimming in Heart Lake, riding my first bicycle, driving a car for the first time, and meeting my wife, Robin, and all our adventures together. Hours must have passed, but since I had no watch, I couldn't be certain.

Because my back ached from my cramped position, I especially wished for a chance to sit upright and for more light. They wouldn't help me escape my prison, but they would relieve my despair. With nothing to do, I eventually fell into a fitful sleep.

When I awoke, my circumstances had improved. The ceiling was higher enabling me to sit upright. Moreover, there was more illumination, and I could see the walls clearly. Such a relief! Only then did I realize I had neither food nor water. I couldn't last long without them. Even bread and water would have seemed wonderful in my present predicament.

Looking up, I wondered whether the ceiling had risen or the floor fallen. It didn't matter, but it helped occupy my mind. Grabbing a pencil from my shirt pocket, I marked where the walls met the floor and ceiling so I could determine which had occurred. I shuddered to think what would happen if the height were to decrease rather than increase.

Tired of sitting, I lay down again. I knew Robin would be beside herself at my disappearance. However, I could do nothing to allay her fears—or my own, for that matter. I fell into another fitful sleep.

When I awoke, I had more light, and the chamber was taller. An alcove in the walls contained a glass with a clear liquid and a plate with slices of bread. Although thirsty, I was suspicious of the liquid. Could it be poisoned? I detected no odor, so I took a sip, holding it in my mouth for a few seconds. Noticing no burning, I assumed it was safe and drank the rest. How refreshing! I sniffed the bread—nothing suspicious. So, I ate it, marveling at how good plain bread could taste. Still, I longed for more substantial fare.

Momentarily satisfied, my attention shifted to the chamber. Standing for the first time, I flexed my legs to get the kinks out. Then I looked for my pencil marks on the wall. The one by the floor, now at eye level, indicated the floor had dropped. The other mark—still by the ceiling.

By this time, my fears had metamorphosed into an intellectual curiosity about my situation. Clearly, my position was less threatening. I had food and water, and the increased chamber height enabled me to stand.

The illumination had increased, permitting me to examine the chamber more closely. Although the height had changed appreciably, its breadth had remained the same. The walls and floor were glassy smooth and totally void of any markings. I wished for a pry bar or rope, but then I realized they'd be of no use.

I quit thinking about escape and passed the time as best I could. I had no idea how many hours elapsed before I once again dozed off, nor did I know how long I had been asleep. By the time I awoke, the floor had dropped several more feet, revealing another alcove containing a plate of tantalizing food, a carafe of red wine, a pry bar, and a rope.

Overjoyed, I hurriedly removed all the items. In the process, I spilled wine on my shirt, creating three red splotches. I cursed. There didn't seem to be any use for the tools, but I put them in a corner in case a use arose. Then, I enjoyed my first real meal since my ordeal began: a tossed salad, a juicy slice of prime rib roast, string beans, and a baked potato with sour cream and chives. The wine, particularly delightful, almost made me forget my hopeless predicament.

Looking around, I saw writing on a wall near the floor. Although the bottoms of the words were cut off by the floor, I could make out: *"Notice: Next appearing will be...."* Another line would surely be revealed as the floor dropped. But, with the slow rate of descent, I turned my attention to the tools.

The pry bar couldn't be inserted between the wall and the floor, and hitting the walls as hard as I could made no mark of any kind. I ignored the rope. Since there was a way of getting into the chamber, there had to be some way of getting out. Even if there were a door, what would be outside the chamber? Would an opening just lead to empty space? My spirits fell in a tailspin.

Much later, the floor's descent revealed the entire message: *"Notice: Next appearing will be an exit. Be vigilant."* I could scarcely contain my excitement. Could I finally escape this prison? I looked at the writing again and again, monitoring the floor's descent. But after what seemed like hours, no exit appeared.

I turned in circles, counted backwards by sevens—anything to stay awake. Hours passed and still no exit. Fearful that the exit might pass me by, I fought against my fatigue with more useless circles and mental exercises. Eventually, I lost the battle and fell into a deep sleep.

When I awoke, I saw a door well above my head and out of reach. I hurriedly piled up the rope and stood on it to gain a few inches, but it wasn't enough. Grabbing the pry bar, I held onto one end and hooked the other on the doorsill. Pulling myself up, I grasped the sill with my hands, but its surface was too smooth. I slipped, falling to the floor with a thud.

Looking around in confusion, I saw no signs of a chamber nor any of the items that had been in it. It took some time for me to realize I was on the floor beside my bed. I glanced at Robin, still sleeping soundly, unbothered by the commotion. I decided I must have had a disturbing dream.

Picking myself up, I went into the bathroom, still shaken. When I glanced in the mirror, chills went down my spine. There were three red splotches on my pajama shirt.

Have you ever awakened from an interesting dream you'd like to remember but found it gone in the morning? Afraid that would happen, I jotted down my dream in the middle of the night, finding sleep difficult thereafter. Ideas often come to me at night, a fact that often disrupts my rest.

Peril on the farm

The headline on the front page of the local paper read, *Blizzard to bring several feet of snow.* As he read the article, Jason worried about his upcoming trip home with his friend, Frank.

By leaving at 8:00 in the morning, we should miss the worst of the storm. I'd hate to be stuck on an empty campus during Christmas break.

Though he had informed his friend of the departure time, Frank forgot to set an alarm. Jason awakened him by repeated pounding on his door. It was 10:30 by the time Frank had dressed and packed his suitcase. By then, the weather had already become treacherous. The wind tore at Jason's coat as he put the suitcases in the trunk. His brow wrinkled as he pulled onto the already snowy highway.

Jason struggled to see the road, even though the windshield wipers drummed away at top speed. With visibility worsening, he slowed to 25 miles per hour.

"Do you think we should turn back?" Frank asked. "It's getting dangerous."

"I don't know about you, but I sure don't want to spend the holidays in a deserted dorm," Jason replied. "We'll be okay." However, thirty minutes later, the wind-whipped snow made it impossible to see through the windshield.

"We'd better turn back. I can't make out a thing." Frank implored.

"We're over halfway. Returning would be just as bad. Roll down your window and watch the side of the highway. Holler if I get too close to the ditch." Only able to go ten miles per hour, they continued, with wind and snow blowing in the open windows, stinging their faces. They forged ahead for another half hour.

"Watch out," Frank screamed as they descended a hill. "I think there's something in the road."

Their car crunched into several others, but with minimal damage since they had been traveling so slowly.

Looking out the open window, they barely made out an eighteen-wheeler jack-knifed in the road ahead with a number of other vehicles piled up behind it.

"What'll we do now, Jason?"

"We can't stay in the car. We'd freeze," Jason lamented. "There's a farmhouse over there. Let's head to it." He opened his door only to have it ripped from his hand.

"Damn," Frank said as the ferocious wind sent his cap flying into the distance. Wading through snow up to their knees, they fought their way to the house. A man in overalls answered their knock, gripping the door firmly to prevent it from being torn off its hinges.

"Mildred, we have two more. Come on in, boys. You can warm up by the fireplace over there."

Entering, they saw a living room filled with people, some sitting on the floor.

"Make yourselves at home. You're fortunate to land here. You could've died had you gotten stuck where there wasn't a house."

Shaking snow off their clothes, he and Frank rushed to the fire. Mildred brought hot coco, helping to warm their numb fingers.

Jason noticed Reinhardt and Mildred whispering and glancing at their visitors now and then.

An hour later, Reinhardt asked one of them to help him with his chores. A man with farm experience volunteered and they left for the barn. An hour later, Reinhardt returned—by himself.

"Frank, did that man who helped Reinhardt come back?" Jason asked.

"I didn't notice," Frank replied. "There are so many people here, it's hard to keep track of them."

Soon everyone lined up to get plates of spaghetti.

"This food has a strange taste," Frank muttered, pushing his half-finished plate aside.

"You can say that again," Jason replied, his speech muddled. Soon they and all the other guests were sound asleep on the floor.

The following morning, the stranded visitors awoke in a daze. They walked haltingly, with eyelids half closed, muttering to themselves.

The storm still raged with three feet of snow and more accumulating. Power had gone out in the night. Mildred placed candles here and there, but most of the light came from the fireplace.

"Frank...I...think...the...meals...are...drugged...don't...eat."

"O...kay."

After breakfast, Reinhardt picked another man to accompany him to the barn. Again, Reinhardt returned—alone.

"This time I'm sure Reinhardt came back by himself," Jason remarked, his speech still slurred.

"I agree. Should we ask Reinhardt about it?"

"Let's wait. Maybe the man will return in a bit."

An hour later, the person still was missing. When Jason asked Reinhardt about the missing volunteer, he sneered and denied anyone had gone with him.

"Now this is getting creepy," Jason remarked when they got a moment alone. "Let's get out of here once the blizzard lets up so that a wrecker can untangle the vehicles."

Mildred served sandwiches for lunch. In a stupor, the other visitors accepted them. Jason and Frank demurred, feigning sickness.

"But you need to eat," Mildred frowned. She went to her husband and whispered in his ear.

By evening, their stupor had completely worn off, although they acted as though it hadn't. Again, Reinhardt picked someone to go to the barn with him. Determined to solve the mystery of the missing helpers, Jason and Frank followed, despite Reinhardt's attempt to keep them from going.

"Jason and Frank, you can collect the eggs and fill the chicken feeders while this man and I milk the cows."

"We'll go with you. I've never seen cows milked," Jason insisted, not wanting to leave the volunteer alone with Reinhardt.

Squirming, Reinhardt frowned at the rejection of his suggestion. After helping to milk the cows, Jason asked about feeding the hogs. Reinhardt's fidgeting increased.

"There's no need for that. They have an automatic feeder," he replied.

On the way back to the house, Jason was curious about all the grunting and squealing of the pigs and stopped to peek through a crack in the door leading to their pen. He spied one of them chewing on…a human leg.

"Frank," Jason whispered. "Is that what I think it is?"

"My god, how sickening!" Looking closer, he saw other hogs feeding on various body parts.

Creeping slowly from behind, Reinhart raised an axe.

"Watch out, Frank!"

Frank ducked, and Jason grabbed a nearby pitchfork, keeping Reinhardt at bay with its long handle. Reinhardt bared his teeth and put the axe down, as if daring them to tell the other guests. He led them back to the house. Once inside, Jason described the horrors they had witnessed in the barn, but the other individuals, still drugged, merely chuckled, refusing to believe such an outlandish tale. Reinhardt sported a garish grin. That evening, Jason suggested they take turns keeping watch in case Reinhardt tried anything while others slept.

The blizzard abated the following morning. By afternoon, a snowplow had opened the road. Once the truck was cleared, Jason and Frank resumed their trip home, wondering what they should do about their harrowing experience at the farm.

When they stopped for gas, Jason saw a newspaper vending machine. Putting in some quarters, he pulled out a paper and saw the bold headline, "Crazed serial killers on the loose."

"My God, Frank. This article says that Reinhardt Mahler and Mildred Bates escaped from an institution for the legally insane."

The idea for this story originated from a trip a college friend and I took in a blizzard. The part up to arrival at the farm is a quite accurate description of actual events, except there was only one car besides the jackknifed truck. The rest is fiction.

The Gift

Watching professional wrestling on TV, Seth got up to get his sixth beer just as Emily returned carrying two bags of groceries.

"Where the hell have you been, Emily?" he shouted. "It doesn't take over three hours to get groceries."

"I saw some friends who asked me to have coffee."

"You expect me to believe that? I'll teach you to step out on me."

He grabbed her arm, spinning her around and causing her to drop her purchases. Then he slapped her face. When she whimpered, he struck her again.

"No, please stop," Emily begged as he hit her so hard she fell. Her daughter, Caitlyn, cowered in the corner, crying.

"You slut. Pick up those things," he replied, flinging a chair to the floor as he stormed from the room with his beer.

Sobbing, Caitlyn ran to her mother and held her tightly.

"There, there, honey. It's alright," Emily said to sooth her daughter.

"Mommy, why does he always hit you?"

"It was my fault. I should have come right home after shopping and not gone to the coffee shop."

"I hate him," Caitlyn replied.

"Don't say that, honey. He loves us. I had it coming."

Despite her mother's excuses, Caitlyn wished her stepfather would leave. Her biological father, who died in an automobile accident, had been affectionate and never once raised his voice. In contrast, Seth constantly reprimanded her. That evening at dinner, he spanked her for spilling milk and made her go to her room without food.

The following morning, Seth was apologetic.

"I'm sorry, Emily. I shouldn't have hit you. It was the beer. It won't happen again."

Two days later, Seth and Emily went to the bank to apply for a loan. Upon their return, Seth got angry.

"I saw the way you looked at that loan officer. You are nothing but a slut," he shrieked, slapping her. He slammed on the brakes in the driveway and yanked his wife out of the car, heedless of the neighbors. On his way to the living room, he yelled, "Bring me a beer."

Looking for her doll a few days later, Caitlyn entered the living room to the thundering sound of race cars on the TV. Several empty beer bottles littered the coffee table and floor.

"Get the hell out of here, you stupid brat," Seth yelled. "You know better than to bug me when I'm watching TV."

Caitlyn ran to her room and threw herself on the bed, sobbing.

The following week, Emily had a doctor appointment to check on a urinary infection. While there, the doctor asked about the bruises on her face and arms.

"I tripped and fell," she lied, quickly pulling her blouse sleeves down to cover the purple marks.

"Those don't look like bruises you'd get from a fall," the doctor replied. If I see this again, I'll have to report it."

Upon her return, Seth met her at the door, beer in hand.

"Where in hell have you been?"

"I had an appointment for my urinary infection. The doctor had an emergency. He was seventy minutes late."

"Is that the best excuse you can come up with?" he said, shoving her against the wall. "You were probably making out. I can't believe you'd do this to me."

Again and again, Emily did her best to disguise her bruises with makeup and to protect Caitlyn. Despite his beatings, she loved Seth and knew his outbursts were her fault. The thought of life without him frightened her. Her only option was to minimize the abuse by trying not to aggravate him. He always apologized, usually blaming the beer for his rants, so she was convinced he loved her. Deep down, she knew he was a good man.

One day, Caitlyn received a mysterious package in the mail. Opening it, she found the most beautiful box she had ever seen. Carved from marble, all surfaces were decorated with bas relief of young girls and animals romping in a forest. When she opened the lid, a ballerina twirled to the tune of Beethoven's Für Elise. It was exactly what she needed to hear after all the trauma she had suffered. She looked for a note indicating who sent the box but found none.

Excited, Caitlyn ran to show the music box to Emily.

"Look what I got, Mom. It came in the mail."

"My, what a pretty box. What's it for?"

"It's a music box—listen." She lifted the lid, this time hearing Beethoven's Moonlight Sonata.

Emily leaned back in her chair and closed her eyes, finding the music soothing, a salve to counter Seth's abuse.

Returning to her room, Caitlyn carefully placed the box in a prime spot on her dresser. She played it often, especially after encounters with her stepfather. Each time, it played a different tune that seemed to fit the occasion.

One evening as Caitlyn sat on her bed listening to the music box, her stepfather walked by her door. Hearing the music, he entered to investigate.

"Where'd you get that?" he asked, frowning.

"It came in the mail," she mumbled.

"Who sent it to you?"

"I don't know. There wasn't any name."

"Don't lie to me, young lady."

"Honest, Dad, there was no name."

"Let me see it," he said, grabbing it and looking it over. "This could bring a nice price at a pawn shop."

"Please give it back. It's mine."

Smirking, he handed her the box and left the room. Knowing that he had taken other things of hers, she hid it in the bottom of her toy chest.

After she left for school, Seth looked for the box but couldn't find it. He tried again the following day, this time searching among her toys. Tossing them aside, he dug deeper and deeper, eventually spying it.

"Ah hah, this ought to bring enough for several six packs," he proclaimed triumphantly.

He set the box on her dresser and opened the lid to hear it play. Rather than beautiful music, he heard the Funeral Dirge by Michael Ibrahim. The ballerina moved jerkily and had an evil smile.

"What in hell is going on? I can't pawn this."

At first, he fiddled with the box, closing and opening the lid. Each time the same menacing tune began. He scratched his head but let it play while he thought about the situation. Soon, his eyes turned glassy, and he couldn't move. The ominous music grew louder and louder until it reached an ear-splitting climax, Seth collapsed on the floor, unable to move or breathe.

When Emily returned from work, she called for Seth, excited to tell him she had gotten a raise. She searched in the kitchen and living room. No one. She went upstairs to their bedroom, but he wasn't there either. As she turned to go back downstairs, she glanced through the open door of Caitlyn's room and screamed.

"Oh my god, what happened?' she sobbed, rushing to his lifeless body. Fumbling for her phone, she dialed 911, then tried to revive her husband until the paramedics arrived fifteen minutes later.

The EMTs soon pronounced him dead.

"Do you know how this could have happened?" they asked.

"I...don't...know," she cried, barely able to talk. "He...he... was...fine...when I...left for work."

"We'll take him to the medical examiner. He should have the results by tomorrow afternoon.

The following day, Emily sat in her home, numb from the events of the previous day. Late in the afternoon, she received the long-awaited call from the medical examiner.

"Did you discover why he died?" she asked.

"Well, since the standard tests didn't reveal anything conclusive, I performed an experimental procedure to determine neuron functionality," he explained. "Normally, stimulation of individual neurons with electrical current would generate an impulse. It didn't. So, I examined individual neurons under an electron microscope. When stimulated, openings normally appear in the cell membrane letting sodium ions enter, thus creating a nerve impulse. However, in Seth's case, openings failed to appear, so his nerves couldn't fire. Hence, breathing, heartrate, and all other bodily functions stopped, resulting in his death."

"What could have caused that?"

"I have no idea," the M.E. replied. "I've never seen anything like this before."

Overhearing the conversation, Caitlyn went to her room and plopped on the bed. Glancing at her dresser, she noticed the music box there rather than in its hiding place. Puzzled, she got up to examine it. When she opened the lid, Beethoven's Symphony Number 9, Ode to Joy, rang triumphantly throughout the house.

I knew two abused women who confided their miseries to me. Their experiences provided the basis for this story. Except for playing only one song, Für Elise, the music box is similar to one I found in an antique store and gave to one of my granddaughters.

The Visitor

Every night Roger Smith and his wife, Meg, watched *Wheel of Fortune*, doing their best to solve the puzzles but seldom meeting with success. In their 70s, they were retired, Roger from Ford Motor Company and Meg from a legal firm.

They lived in the suburbs where no two houses were alike yet all looked the same—pastel colors, multi-angled roofs, and more rooms than two families needed. Most, including the Smiths, had three-car garages, largely filled with furniture and junk. Restrictive covenants eliminated any threat of originality. Even the landscapes were similar, with shrubs around the foundation and matching trees in front. It was a highly coveted place to live, at least for those desiring homogeny.

Since retirement, Meg and Roger had fallen into a satisfying routine. They went to bed at 10:00 and awoke at 7:00, taking their meals at 7:30, 12:30, and 5:30. Their dinnertime enabled them to be finished with the meal and dishes by 7:00, at which time they watched television. On constantly, the TV was generally ignored except for their favorite programs. One evening, as they were looking forward to watching the movie, *Peyton Place,* they discovered it went thirty minutes past their bedtime. So, they had the disconcerting task of picking another show.

The Smiths enjoyed the local newspaper and *Modern Maturity*, which they read cover to cover. They shopped for groceries on Thursday so they could take advantage of the specials. On Sunday, they went to church. On other days, they worked on separate activities, Roger in his wood shop and Meg on her quilts. In short, they were busy and contented with their lot in life.

At 7:17 on a rainy Wednesday evening, the doorbell rang as the Smiths awaited the bonus round on *Wheel of Fortune*. Frowning, Roger arose from his recliner. Opening the door, he faced a woman so disheveled that he retreated a step. Her hair hung from her head like a string mop, water dripping from the ends, her clothes soaking wet.

"Please help me," she said in a soft voice barely audible above the rain. "I ran out of gas, and no one will help me."

Looking her up and down and wanting to get back to his TV program, Roger thought of telling her he couldn't help, but instead said he would call a gas station to bring her some gas.

At this point, the woman started sobbing uncontrollably, increasing his discomfort. Asking her what was wrong, he had to wait for her weeping to subside before getting an answer.

"After I ran out of gas, a man stopped to help—or at least I thought he stopped to help. He said he knew that the people living in a house about 200 feet away kept a spare can of gas. I went there but they slammed the door in my face. I started to return to my car only to find it was gone. That man must have put gas in it and driven away. Soaking wet, I couldn't find anyone to help me—unless you will, that is."

Fidgeting, Roger eyed her with suspicion, but his conscience wouldn't let him turn the woman away.

"Did you report the theft to the police?" he asked, inviting her in.

"No, I left my phone in the car. May I borrow yours?"

After calling, the woman told Roger the desk sergeant would send someone to get her statement.

Roger led her to the bathroom and handed her a towel.

"Here, get out of those wet clothes and put these on," he said, handing her one of his wife's sweat suits. "It's probably too big but should do until your clothes are dry."

Roger hurried back to his wife in the living room and filled her in on the details.

"What were you thinking?" Meg exclaimed, jumping from her seat. "What if she robs us, or worse, what if she's a murderer?"

"I couldn't leave her out in the rain with no car and no help," Roger argued. "What if our daughter were in that situation? Not everyone who gets in trouble is a thief or murderer. She's more likely a victim of circumstance. Also, the police are coming to take her statement about the theft of her car. She wouldn't have called the police if she were a thief or murderer."

After twenty minutes, the woman came out of the bathroom dressed in Meg's sweats.

All three stood, assessing one another, when Roger broke the silence.

"I guess we haven't introduced ourselves. I'm Roger, and this is Meg," he said, nodding in the direction of his wife. "What's your name?"

"Joy Wilson," she replied. Hesitating briefly, she added, "Thank you so much for helping me. I didn't know where to go or what to do."

"Would you like to call a family member?" Roger asked. Joy started crying again, prompting him to direct her to a chair.

"I have no family, no parents, no sisters, no brothers, nobody," she said. "I lost my job at Boeing and have been living out of my car. Now I don't even have a car."

"Surely there's a friend or someone who knows you," Roger countered. Her sobbing reached a new intensity, making him regret pursuing the issue.

Meg put her arm around Joy's shoulders, but Roger had no idea what to say, so he said nothing. Eventually, the crying ceased and, after a moment of embarrassing silence, Joy said she grew up in an orphanage. She had a good job at Boeing but lost it because of downsizing. Without a job, she also lost her apartment and had lived out of her car the last six months. What money and belongings she had were in her car, including her purse and cell phone.

"Do you know the penalty for writing a bad check?" she asked out of the blue. "Perhaps I shouldn't have called the police."

Roger's brow furrowed.

"Why do you ask? Have you written bad checks?"

Joy hesitated.

"I bought my auto from a used-car salesman who said it was in good shape. I paid him the $795 asking price in cash, wiping out the last of my savings. Then, the swindler informed me the tie rods were bad and he couldn't let me drive the car off the lot unless they were repaired. He wouldn't return my money, and I didn't have enough to pay for the repair, so, in desperation, I wrote a check for $276 on a checking account I had just closed. I know I shouldn't have done it, but he cheated me!"

A smile crept onto Roger's lips, for he had little regard for used-car salesmen and had to admire her guts for putting one over on the cheat. On the other hand, something bothered him about her story. Could it be a lie? Nevertheless, he felt obliged to help.

"When the police come, wait to see if anything is mentioned about a bad check. The salesman may not have reported it."

Shortly, the doorbell rang. A heavyset policeman showed his badge.

"I'm here to speak with a Joy Wilson. May I come in?" the policeman asked.

"Certainly."

The policeman took Joy's statement and description of the man.

"This sounds like a guy we've been after for some time but haven't been able to pin anything on him. What's your phone number? I'll let you know if we find your car."

Joy explained her phone was in the stolen car. Since the policeman made no mention of a bad check, Roger assumed the salesperson hadn't tried to cash it yet.

Once the officer left, Roger glanced at his wife, and then addressed their guest.

"Have you had dinner?"

"I had a couple candy bars. I didn't want to spend much money for meals since I needed to use what I had to find a job."

Roger and Meg went to the kitchen to prepare her something to eat. There they had a hushed but spirited discussion about the visitor. Roger finally convinced Meg they should see where things led after the meal.

Clearly starved, Joy quickly devoured a chicken sandwich, salad, milk, and leftover beans. For the first time, Roger noticed her striking beauty, despite the baggy sweats and still damp hair. How could such an attractive woman be so alone in the world?

Meg cleared the dishes while Roger retrieved Joy's clothes from the dryer. They all sat in the living room, vacantly staring at reruns of *Three's Company* on television. Roger finally broke the silence by asking Joy where she had planned to stay while looking for a job. Fighting back tears, she said she didn't know; the car was her home.

"You have no place to stay, then?" he asked.

"No," she stated simply.

"And no money?" he said, immediately regretting asking a question to which he already knew the answer. She hung her head in reply but said nothing. Roger looked at Meg, searching for some way to avoid inviting Joy to stay in their home.

"I'll make up the guest room and you can stay here tonight. Tomorrow, we'll figure something out," Meg said, getting up from her chair.

"Thanks a lot. People generally don't want to help me," Meg replied.

Roger wondered if she had been in other similar situations.

"If you don't mind, I'm really tired and would like to go to bed," Joy said at 8:30.

Meg took her to the guest room. At 8:45 p.m., Roger sat in front of the television, not knowing what to do. He felt they ought to help Joy so long as no trouble ensued. Realizing it was too late to watch a movie but too early to go to bed, he tuned in an episode of *Survivor*.

As they got ready for bed, they talked briefly about Joy. Roger convinced Meg to let her stay with them while she looked for a job. After turning off the lights, he thought about the visitor until sleep overtook him.

At 6:15 a.m., the Smiths were awakened by loud music. Joy had tuned in rock music on the clock radio in the room. Although accustomed to rising at 7:00, they couldn't sleep. So, they got out of bed. Once downstairs, they discovered Joy frying eggs in their Teflon skillet using a metal spatula. Roger's blood boiled, but he refrained from reacting.

"Morning," Joy said. "Hope you don't mind me cooking breakfast. I'm famished and heard you up, so I put some eggs on. I saw you had a couple of egg cartons, so I figured you ate them. Here you go," she said dishing them onto plates.

Seeing Meg's wrinkled brow, Roger knew his wife was appalled this stranger had just helped herself to the kitchen. Besides, they never ate fried eggs, preferring poached or hard boiled. However, not wanting to waste food, they sat down and ate.

Joy seemed to be a totally different person from the bedraggled, downtrodden individual who had come to their door the previous evening. Cheery, even bubbly, she prattled incessantly. After breakfast, she placed the dishes in the dishwasher. Roger saw Meg wince at the way they were loaded and knew she would rearrange them.

"We can take you to look for a job later. What type of employment do you want?" Roger asked, thumbing through the classified ads,

Joy demurred, saying she couldn't go job-hunting in the worn-out clothes she had been wearing upon her arrival at the Smiths.

"Say, could you loan me enough to buy some new ones? I can pay you back when I get my first paycheck."

Roger looked at Meg, hoping she would say something to rescue them from having to finance Joy's wardrobe, but she remained silent.

"I guess we can help you out. How much do you need?" Roger replied, hesitantly

"$100 should be enough to get an outfit good enough for job hunting. I don't need anything fancy." Neither of them had much cash, so Roger suggested she charge things to their Penny's account.

Dropping Joy off at the department store, he made arrangements for credit payment, and then told her he'd pick her up in 1½ hours. It was Thursday, their day to get groceries, and he wanted to get to Safeway early before the specials sold out.

They returned to Penny's, only to find Joy waiting by the door with several large bags.

"I hope you don't mind. I found some great things on sale I couldn't pass up, so I ran a bit over $100."

"How much over?" Roger bit his lip.

"Here's the receipt."

Examining the total, $278.37, Roger's face turned crimson.

"What did you think you were doing? You have to return most of those things," he spat.

"These are clearance items, and all sales are final. Nothing can be returned. Don't worry, I'm sure I'll find a job and pay you back soon," she replied with a bubbly smile.

Roger looked at the sign in the window. *All sales final on clearance items*. No one spoke on the trip home.

Joy spent the rest of the day washing and ironing her new clothes, preventing Meg from her usual Thursday ironing. Joy took her new clothes to the guest room and turned the radio to rock music.

At 4:30, Meg went to work on dinner, finishing at 5:30. She asked Roger to call Joy. Since the music drowned out his voice, he went upstairs to her room.

Looking through the open door, he saw Joy lying nude on the bed. He immediately turned away, but the sight had been so mesmerizing he found himself slowly turning back around despite his best efforts not to do so. She was incredibly beautiful, with a perfectly proportioned body and an air of nonchalance inviting his attention.

"Hi, come on in," Joy said casually.

He entered the room, as though in a trance. She sat on the bed, making no attempt to cover herself, and motioned to a chair, asking him to be seated. Stunned, he recovered enough to tell her dinner was ready.

"I'll throw on some clothes and be right down," she said.

Roger returned to the dining room, confused and shaken. Shortly, Joy joined them, wearing a miniskirt that showed off her legs. She dominated the dinner conversation with talk about the time she hitchhiked to California. Meg got a few words in, but Roger was silent.

After dinner, Roger turned the television to Wheel of Fortune. Joy, looking at the program guide, suddenly squealed.

"I can't believe it! The Matrix is just starting. I've always wanted to see it but never had the chance. Do you mind?" Not waiting for an answer, she changed the channel.

Stunned by her audacity, Roger could offer no hint of protest. He and Meg had started watching the Matrix once, but they couldn't make anything of it and turned to something else. Noticing Meg's wrinkled brow, Roger realized she was as incensed as he was. When it ended, Joy went to the kitchen to get a bedtime snack, taking the last piece of pecan pie. Roger burned internally, knowing how much that meant to Meg; she only made it once a year.

As usual, Roger and Meg went to bed at 10:00 leaving Joy alone with the television. Joy mumbled something about the news, but they didn't really hear what she said. By the time they turned out the light, the TV still blared.

"The least she could do is turn the volume down," huffed Meg.

"I'd like to ram the remote down her throat," Roger contributed.

They complained about Joy for another 45 minutes until their guest turned off the TV.

"Tomorrow, we have to take her to find a job," Roger fumed, just as his wife's breathing became slow and heavy. Another hour passed before Roger calmed down enough to sleep.

Friday morning dawned too soon to suit the Smiths. Once again, they were awakened by the sound of rock music emanating from the guest room. As before, Joy helped herself to the kitchen. This time she broiled some steaks, spattering the oven with grease.

"I wish you wouldn't prepare breakfast. We are quite capable of doing it ourselves. Also, don't use our food without checking with us first," Roger said, hitting the table with his fist.

"Oh, I don't mind at all," Joy replied simply. "Do sit down and enjoy your steak." Either she didn't hear what he had said or chose to ignore it.

Cooked to perfection, the meal tasted surprisingly good.

Roger grabbed the newspaper to examine the job listings, mentioning several to Joy. For one reason or another, she nixed all of them. Frustrated, he asked what type of job she wanted.

"Whatever it is, it has to be something I really enjoy. I'm not going to waste my life flipping burgers or clerking in a store. I'd like to do something to bring pleasure to people, perhaps being a ballerina, architect, actress, or artist. Those occupations would be very rewarding."

"Do you have training in any of those professions?" Roger asked.

"No, but I think I'd be good at any of them," she replied.

"Well, you can't just get a job in those fields without training," he said, more than a little exasperated.

"We'll see," she said simply.

After an extended discussion, Joy agreed to look for employment and Roger offered to take her downtown. Joy didn't say what type of work she'd seek, and Roger knew better than to ask. Joy dressed in one of her new outfits, looking radiant and happy. Roger didn't think miniskirts appropriate attire for job hunting but had to admit she looked ravishing.

Roger dropped Joy off at the Museum of Fine Art as she requested and arranged to pick her up at 4:00 p.m. He then returned home to find Meg working on a quilt. They talked about how badly Joy had disrupted their lives and tried to come up with a plan to get rid of her. However, all ideas came to naught because they couldn't bring themselves to toss her out in the street. After a bit, Roger went to his shop to work on a wooden chest he had started to build weeks earlier. He had no idea what he'd would do with it, but he had seen the plans in a magazine and thought it would be fun to make.

At 3:30, Roger left to pick up Joy at the museum. He arrived a few minutes early, parked in the garage, and walked to the agreed upon meeting place. Joy was nowhere in sight. Finally, at 4:45 she came waltzing up, vibrant as always, greeting him as though he were a long-lost friend. Irritated, he scolded her for being late. Offering no apology, she rambled on about the sculpture garden but made no mention of job hunting.

That evening, Roger and Meg were ready for bed, but Joy's loud music made any attempt to sleep futile. Rather than fume, as they did the previous night, Meg went to the guest room to ask Joy to turn down the sound. After a bit, Roger followed, intending to support Meg by adding his own displeasure.

As he approached Joy's room, he heard Meg gasp and saw that Joy was asleep on the bed, completely nude. He stepped behind the bathroom door, wondering what to do. Curiosity got the better of him and he peered around the door as Meg called Joy's name. She didn't answer. Meg walked in and turned off the radio, awakening her.

Joy sat on the edge of the bed and asked Meg to give her a backrub. Meg hesitated, but then began to rub her back. Roger, mesmerized, crept back to his bedroom. After Meg returned, both tossed and turned for a long time before yielding to sleep's caress.

Saturday morning began as had Friday, with the sound of rock music flooding the house before the Smiths' usual time to arise. After dressing, they changed the towels and bedding before going downstairs. The delicious aroma of fresh cinnamon rolls permeated the air, indicating Joy had once again helped herself to their kitchen.

Joy greeted them in her usual jovial fashion and directed them to be seated. The breakfast consisted of coffee, rolls and cheese. Although different from their usual fare of Cheerios and juice, Roger found the food enjoyable and Meg even asked for seconds.

On Saturday, they worked in the yard—he mowing the grass and she tending her flowers. At 12:15 p.m., they went back into the house for lunch. Seeing that Joy had completely rearranged the living room furniture, Roger waved his arms in rage.

"Who in hell do you think you are? You had no right to move our furniture."

Joy merely smiled and pointed out that the new arrangement allowed for a better traffic flow, easier viewing of the TV, and a more intimate feel. Roger was not to be mollified.

"Get your things and get out of our house! You are done upsetting our lives," Roger screamed.

Both of the Smiths shook with rage, but Joy didn't seem particularly upset by his outburst and proceeded to put her new clothes into bags and, smiling at them, departed.

"At last," Meg said, "we can have some peace and quiet around here."

They sat down in their newly rearranged living room. Too upset to eat right away, Roger reached for the TV remote, noticing his magazines were easier to reach, and he didn't have to turn to view the TV from his recliner. Even Meg seemed more comfortable.

They went to the kitchen to prepare a late lunch, deciding to have the remaining cinnamon rolls and a can of soup—quicker and easier than preparing their usual fare. Once finished, they cleared the table and went to the living room, intending to move their furniture back to the way it was. Instead, pausing for a moment, they simply sat down to watch their favorite soap operas.

Over the next two weeks, Roger struggled to regain the level of comfort he had enjoyed before the arrival of their visitor. Meg also voiced her discomfort. They went to bed and arose at their usual times, ate their usual foods, and watched their favorite television shows. They shopped for groceries on Thursday, worked in the yard on Saturday, and went to church on Sunday. As before, Meg worked on her quilting, and Roger in his shop. By all outward appearances, things were back to normal. However, Roger felt a dissatisfaction he couldn't verbalize and noticed Meg also seemed uneasy.

Two weeks later, the doorbell rang as Roger and Meg watched Wheel of Fortune,

"I'll get it," Roger grumbled, ambling to the door. Opening it, he saw Joy, smiling, standing beside several bags. He frowned, sputtering something unintelligible. Then, with a faint smile crossing his lips, he stepped aside to let her in.

Driving through housing developments, I've been amazed at the huge size and similarity of the houses. Many are occupied by couples whose children have left the nest, resulting in much more room than they need. Knowing that, and that older people tend to be set in their ways, I thought it would be interesting to write about a couple who found a way to expand their horizons. The result is this story.

Never is a Long Time

Leon dragged himself out of bed at 11:30 a.m., still wearing his clothes from the previous day. Putting his hands on his head in a futile attempt to quell a hangover, he staggered to the bathroom and threw his clothes on the floor. Leaning against the shower wall, he groaned as water cascaded over his head. As the thirty-year-old son of a wealthy owner of a large construction company, he enjoyed an unemployed-playboy lifestyle.

That evening, Leon was sipping champagne at a party, whose, he had no idea, when he encountered Noel. He tried to ignore him, but Noel was persistent—a huge irritant always critical of whatever he did.

"Well Leon, I didn't expect to see you here. Getting soused again, I see."

"Give me a break! This is only my second drink," Leon groused.

"Yeah, right—you always did have trouble counting." Noel shook his head. "Say, did you ever check into that marketing job?"

"They hired someone else," Leon mumbled. "Besides, I didn't have the required background."

"You didn't even apply, did you?"

Leon's silence was deafening. He had no desire for a mundane job, or any job for that matter. A job would require him to go to work in the morning, a time devoted to sleeping off the previous night's hangover. He escaped Noel's stinging comments by heading to the Outpost Bar where he downed a couple drinks in solitary silence. Only then did he head back to his posh flat.

The following day, Leon got up just after noon and headed for the aspirin bottle. After showering and downing some hair-of-the-dog to quell his hangover, he tried getting a date. Since his egocentric personality turned women off despite his good looks, he sought a fresh start with someone who didn't know him. Accordingly, he checked some online dating apps.

Responding to three prospects, he disingenuously described himself in flattering terms. After exchanging emails with the three women, he called one, Nancy, and arranged to meet her for lunch at the Hungry Crow. Nervous, he thought about not showing up. Pulling himself together, he arrived at the restaurant twenty minutes late. He recognized his date immediately from the description she had given him—a tall brunette wearing a red blouse with a string of pearls around her neck.

"Hi, I'm Leon Eberline. I'm a little late because a business engagement ran over," he lied.

"I'm Nancy—I thought maybe you weren't coming," she said, tapping her fingers and frowning.

The maître d' showed them to a table and handed them menus.

"We'll have a bottle of your best champagne," Leon said.

"Why did you assume I'd want champagne?" Nancy asked after the maître d' left.

If embarrassed by his faux pas, he didn't show it.

"Would you prefer a cocktail?"

"No, I don't drink alcoholic beverages," she replied.

"I recommend the duck a l'orange. It's the specialty of the house," Leon offered.

"I'm sure it's good, but I'm a vegetarian," Nancy replied.

Eventually, they placed their orders.

"Do you work?" Leon asked, in an attempt to break the awkward silence that had settled onto their table.

"Yes, I'm an attorney," she answered. "I work at a law firm specializing in Social Security disability and worker compensation claims."

"You mean, you try to get people who think they're disabled onto Social Security?" Leon interrupted. "Personally, I'm against welfare. The way I look at it, no one is so disabled they can't work at some job," he asserted, oblivious to the irony of his own lack of employment. He continued expounding his world view until Nancy excused herself to go to the restroom. She never returned.

Realizing she had left, he went ahead with his meal and downed the bottle of champagne. Once again, he had bombed with the opposite sex.

On his way to his car, he encountered Noel.

"You are really a crass act," he admonished. "You meet a wonderful woman and treat her like the dirt under your designer shoes."

Offering no defense, Leon returned to his flat and turned on the television. Staring blankly at the screen, he tried to avoid thinking about his disastrous date. Try as he might, he couldn't help feeling distraught over his inability to relate to women. Outwardly, he put on a blustery facade, but he knew he was a charlatan—lacking self-confidence, much less happiness.

A few days later, Leon was walking along Spring Street on his way to The Lion's Head, an upscale watering hole, when he happened upon Father O'Brian.

"Hello, Leon. I haven't seen you in quite a while."

"Hello Father."

"How have you been, Leon?"

"Fine." After a short pause it dawned on him Father O'Brian probably wondered why he hadn't been in church, so he added, "but I've been really busy."

"Oh, what have you been doing?"

Leon racked his brain to come up with something other than partying. Unable to think of anything, he simply said he had been helping his dad.

Father O'Brian set the stage to coax Leon back into church.

"We've missed having your beautiful tenor voice in the choir. We're having a benefit concert for local flood victims—you know, organ, choir, and a few instrumentalists. Our lead tenor has a bad cold and another is out of town. We sure could use your help. Our practice is next Wednesday evening and the concert is the following Saturday night."

Leon's worst fears were realized. He had no interest in going to church or singing in the choir.

"I'm afraid I have prior commitments on those days," he lied.

"Well, you know how to reach me if your commitments change. Take care, now."

Relieved, Leon continued on his way to the Lion's Head. However, his relief was short-lived because he soon ran into Noel.

"Leon—how are things going? You look unhappy."

"You would too if Father O'Brian had just asked you to sing in a concert to benefit flood victims."

"Great! When will it be?"

"It won't be, because I'm not doing it."

"Why not? Lord knows you don't have anything else of importance in your life."

"For one thing, I think churches are filled with weak individuals who grasp at any straw to save their miserable lives. For another, I don't like contributing to a cause rewarding people who don't have enough sense to live somewhere other than in a flood plain."

"You are so cynical, it's pathetic," Noel countered. "Look at it this way. Father O'Brian has steered a lot of business your dad's way and your unwillingness to help him could jeopardize that relationship."

"Yeah, I suppose you have a point. I guess I could sing in this one concert."

"Now you're talking," Noel replied. "See you around."

After a couple of days, Leon called Father O'Brian to inform him he would sing in the concert after all. After the performance, many people congratulated him on his solo parts and thanked him for participating. Nevertheless, Leon wore his usual scowl and did his best to avoid people by slipping out a side door and making his way to the Lion's Head.

Leon had just ordered his fourth Jim Beam when Noel appeared.

"You look miserable," Noel offered.

"Do me a favor and dispense with your insights, okay?"

"Look, I'm just concerned about you. Your drinking is out of hand."

"I'm doing just fine," Leon snapped.

"Then why are you so unhappy?" Noel asked, his voice filled with genuine compassion.

Noel's question took Leon by surprise. His head sank to his hands and he stifled a sob.

"Rich people can never live a normal life," he said, his voice faltering.

"Never is a long time, my friend. Keep working at it, and you will succeed." With that, Noel departed.

"Would you like a refill, Sir?" the waiter asked.

"Yeah" Leon replied.

Nothing changed for Leon over the next several days except that he felt more alone than ever. Even Noel seemed to have disappeared from his life. He went for a jog but soon gasped for air. Alcohol and fast living had taken its toll. Walking back to his flat, he rounded a corner in the hall and collided with an old woman, nearly knocking her over.

"Why don't you watch where you're going, sonny?" she scolded with a clenched jaw and red face.

"If you had stayed on the right side of the hall, I wouldn't have hit you," Leon sputtered.

"Listen, sonny, I walk where I damn please." Then, she wrinkled her nose, her brow furrowed. "You're so damned drunk, you couldn't stay on one side of the hall if you tried, anyway."

"Get lost, grandma."

"I'm not your grandma, thank goodness. If I were, I'd disown you."

Leon took the elevator to his flat and crashed. The next day, he called the concierge to ask why the old woman lived there. He learned she was a widow by the name of May Sanders, who had just moved into one of the apartments designated for low-income renters.

Leon thought about his run in with May. She looked for all the world like a bag lady. He guessed she couldn't be more than 5'2" if standing erect. Bent over with age, she was less than that. A mass of weathered wrinkles crowded onto her tiny face. Her unkempt gray hair hung in strings. On her slight body, she wore long-forgotten treasures from someone's attic. Despite her appearance, he had to admit she exuded an air of confidence. Still, he didn't appreciate having a welfare recipient living in the same building, even if fourteen floors removed from him.

A few days later, Leon encountered May in the elevator. She stepped in, seemingly ignoring Leon at the back, but as she turned around to face the doors, she brought her cane down smartly on Leon's foot.

"Ow! Damn! Watch what you're doing!"

"Eh? You say something, Sonny?" A grin of satisfaction crept across her face, which Leon caught when she looked sideways.

The next weekend, May, juggling two bags of groceries and her cane, struggled to open the door to the apartment complex when Leon approached from behind. He offered no help at first, but eventually became exasperated waiting for her to get out of the way, so he opened the door himself.

"Don't strain yourself there, Sonny. You look rather frail," May chided.

"God, I hate her," Leon muttered under his breath.

Over the weeks, Leon and May had similar acerbic encounters. Although their exchanges had the same sharp edge, Leon came to admire her spunk and even halfway enjoyed their cantankerous exchanges.

On a cold day in January, Leon was in the elevator when it stopped at the third floor—May's floor. The doors opened, but no one entered. As the doors started to close, Leon stopped them with his hand and poked his head into the hallway. May was lying on the floor, unmoving. He rushed to her side and felt for a pulse. She had none. She wasn't breathing either.

Grabbing his cell phone, Leon called 911 for help. He regretted not knowing CPR, but he was accustomed to being helped, not to helping others. Vacillating with indecision, he dropped to his knees. He had seen CPR performed in movies and decided he should at least try something. After a brief pause at the repulsion of putting his mouth over hers, he forced his breath into her. The air exited her nostrils. Pinching her nostrils, he again blew into her mouth. Her chest rose. Then, he pushed on her rib cage enough to stimulate her heart but not so hard he'd break her ribs. He pumped ten times and then blew into her mouth again. He kept yelling for help, but no one came.

After what seemed an eternity, May coughed and regained consciousness, much to Leon's relief.

"Isn't it enough that you run me down? Now you pummel my chest too?"

Leon smiled and bent over to give her a hug.

"Don't squeeze the life out of me, you lug!"

Leon's only answer? The tear trickling down his face. He looked up to see the paramedics spilling from the elevator and explained what had happened. They checked May over and determined her condition to be stable.

"You her son?" they asked.

"Hell no, he ain't my son," May snorted.

"We both live in this building," Leon explained. "I run into her from time to time."

"He not only runs into me, he damned near knocks me down," May barked. She had returned to her feisty self.

"What is your name, Ma'am?" a paramedic asked.

"May Sanders."

"May, it appears this man just saved your life, but we still need to take you to the hospital to have you checked over."

"I don't need no damned hospital. I need for you to leave me alone!" May retorted.

At this point, Leon chimed in.

"You old coot—you damned near died on me. I think you're just afraid of going to the hospital."

"I'm not afraid of anything," May replied defensively.

"Please, May. I think you should get checked over," Leon pleaded, completely out of character for him. "Besides, I'd be rid of you for a while if you went."

Eventually, May relented and was taken to the hospital where she stayed overnight for observation.

Leon started for the Lion's Head, but changed his mind and went home instead. As he walked to the door, Noel appeared. For once, Leon seemed happy to see him.

"Hi, Noel. How's it going?"

"I heard you saved a woman's life, Leon. "That must have been quite an experience,".

"It certainly was. I never thought I'd feel like this. Why don't you come on in and we'll talk about it over a beer?"

When released from the hospital the next morning, Leon arrived just as May asked where she could catch a bus.

"Not you again," she huffed. "At least you had the decency not to run into me this time."

"I phoned the hospital and discovered you were being released, so I came to give you a ride home."

"If you drive the way you walk, we'd both be in the hospital. I'll take a bus."

"There aren't any bus connections from here to your home," Leon replied. "I'm driving you—like it or not."

"Huh," she grunted. "Don't expect me to be friendly with the likes of you."

"Wouldn't think of it," he replied as he escorted her to his waiting car.

After parking his car at the apartment building, he went around to open the door for her, but she beat him to it. He reached down to help her up.

"Get your hands off me! I'm no invalid," she snorted.

"I certainly agree with you," Leon answered.

Against May's protests, Leon escorted her to the door of her apartment.

"Well, I guess you can come in for a cup of tea," she said.

"I'd like that. Promise not to poison it?" Leon said, smiling. They entered her apartment arm in arm, smile matched by smile.

Often, people are repelled by someone less fortunate than they are, perhaps someone on welfare or dressed in shabby clothes. However, if we take the time to get to know them, our opinions might change. Such is the message of this story.

Confession

"Lily, would you please go to the Andersons and borrow three eggs? I'm in the middle of making this recipe and can't leave now."

The twelve-year-old daughter of the Carter's was tall for her age, with dark hair, brown eyes, and a fetching smile.

"Sure, Mom," she said, grabbing a bag for the eggs.

As she crossed the street, a black Mercedes barreled toward her, weaving from one side of the street to the other. Lily tried to jump out of the way, but the car slammed into her, knocking her twenty feet. A jogger saw the accident and ran to her.

"Oh my god, are you okay?"

As Lily opened her mouth, a trickle of blood spilled. Cursing because he didn't have his cell, he put his sweatshirt under her head and ran to the nearest house, frantically knocking on the door until a woman answered.

"A car just struck a little girl. She's bleeding—badly. I don't have my phone. Please call an ambulance—and the police."

After making the call, the woman ran out to the scene of the accident. Recognizing Lily, she dashed to the Carter's house and banged on the door.

"Your daughter has been in a terrible accident; she's over there," she said, pointing.

Mrs. Carter yelled for her husband, and both raced to Lily's side. As they turned her head, their daughter's eyes opened wide, frightened. Her lips quivered; then, her eyes lost focus and she was gone.

Sirens screamed as the ambulance and police arrived.

The EMTs tended to Lily and tried to console the Carter's.

"Did anyone see what happened?" a policeman asked.

"I did," the jogger said. "A black Mercedes, weaving all over, hit her with the left front side of his car and drove away."

"Did you get a look at the driver?"

"No."

"What about the license plate, make of car, year?" the policeman asked, furiously taking notes.

"It all happened so fast. I think it was a newer Mercedes."

"Color?"

"Dark, probably black."

The officer dashed to his cruiser to call in.

"I have a 10-57 at 127 Millrose Avenue. Put an APB within a 20-mile radius for a black Mercedes, probably recent, possible damage to the left front."

"Oh my god, I killed her for three eggs." Mrs. Carter's hysterical cries added to the mournful scene.

"Honey, please. You aren't the guilty one. It was that maniac driver," Mr. Carter answered, embracing his wife.

The APB didn't turn up the Mercedes or the driver. Weeks went by. Fed up with the police's lack of progress, Mr. Carter hired a private investigator.

With his various sources, the PI soon learned there were only three black Mercedes in town. Two belonged to stalwarts in the community, but the third was owned by Mack, a member of a local gang. Concentrating on Mack first, the PI found no evidence of damage to his car, but that didn't rule him out since the damage could have been repaired. No one had seen his car during the three days after the accident, suggesting it may have been in a garage.

It cost the PI a C note to learn a black Mercedes had been in a chop shop the three days in question. A petty thief offered the final link for another C note; he had seen a black Mercedes with dents on the left front entering the shop at 4:10, just two hours after the accident.

Convinced he'd identified the culprit, the PI relayed the info to Mr. Carter, warning him the evidence was circumstantial and would not hold up in court.

Mr. Carter told the police what he had learned. Although they brought Mack in for questioning, it went nowhere. Since no one saw Mack driving the Mercedes at the time of the accident, they released him.

Upon hearing charges wouldn't be filed, Mr. Carter vowed to seek out Mack and wring a confession from him. He went to his bureau to get his gun for protection, knowing Mack was a gang member and could turn violent during a confrontation. Seeing the gun, Mrs. Carter pleaded with him not to challenge the man.

"What are you thinking of? Gang members are dangerous."

Despite her pleadings, Mr. Carter refused to back down. He went to Mack's apartment, intending to do what the police could not—get a confession. Mack answered the door.

"Yeah? Who are you?"

"I'm the father of the girl you ran down and killed."

Mack tried to slam the door, but Mr. Carter lodged his foot between the door and the jam and pushed Mack back into the entry.

"Look mister. I didn't mean to hit her, and I didn't know she died. What do you expect from me now?"

"I want you to go to the police and confess, Mr. Carter snapped. You gang members are all alike. Life means nothing to you,"

"Please, sir. I'm really sorry about your daughter. I should never have joined the gang, but I had no parents. My dad's in prison for life and my mom died when I was eleven. She was no angel, making a living as a prostitute. I never saw much of her. The gang took me in and was the only family I had."

"Why did you drive when you were so drunk you couldn't stay on one side of the street?"

"I wasn't drunk. The gang just got some smack, and everyone got bombed. I didn't want none, but they made me. After they got loaded, I snuck out and got into my car. You know the rest." Sobbing and shaking, he added, "Believe me, I'm sorry for what I did. I ain't no angel, but I ain't no devil neither."

Mack sat with his head in his hands, weeping. Mr. Carter continued to quiz him until absolutely convinced Mack had told the truth. Finally, he realized what he needed to do.

"Mack, I'm an attorney in a law firm. I can arrange for one of my associates to represent you if you'll agree to confess. You might not have intended to hurt anyone, but you'll have to stand trial and will likely be convicted of involuntary manslaughter. However, given what you've told me, and if you testify against the gang, I believe you could make a plea bargain for a lighter sentence, possibly no jail at all, though leaving the scene of an accident may require some time."

Nodding thoughtfully, Mack asked Mr. Carter to tell him about his daughter. Mack, with tears flowing and head hanging, listened for twelve minutes. At that point, Mr. Carter choked up and embraced Mack. A few minutes later, he drove Mack to the police station.

People tend to jump to conclusions in the event of a tragedy. However, often our judgements change upon closer examination of the facts.

Threats

"I know where ya live and I'm coming after ya."

Jack Taylor stared at the message, reading it over and over. Rather effeminate, the skinny fifteen-year-old was prone to ridicule by others his age, particularly Bugsy Cipriano, a known bully and leader of a small group of troublemakers called The Stallions. Bugsy, an imposing figure at six feet two, black hair draping over muscular shoulders, made life miserable for Jack, but he had never before sent threatening messages.

"Where'd you get this?" his mother asked when shown the message.

"In my locker at school."

"Who on earth would make such a threat?"

"I'm not sure, but I suspect Bugsy Cipriano. He has been after me."

"Well, I'm reporting this to the superintendent," she said, reaching for the phone.

Listening sympathetically, the superintendent informed her anyone could have written the note. It might have just been an ill-advised prank. She suggested waiting to see if more threats were made.

Just three days later, another note appeared.

"So, reporting me didn't get ya very far, did it? I'm goin ta make ya pay big time, you wimp."

Jack tried to avoid Bugsy as much as possible, but that afternoon Bugsy intentionally bumped into him in the hall.

"Watch where yer going, punk."

Jack apologized and quickly left the scene.

Alarmed by the second threat, his mother again contacted the superintendent who called Bugsy into her office to question him about the incident.

"I didn't put no message in his locker," Bugsy said, indignantly.

The superintendent turned the message over to the police who checked it for fingerprints, but the only prints were Jack's. Informed of the situation, the school's Security Officer kept an eye on Jack's locker, but saw no suspicious activity.

Two days later, another message appeared.

"Sic'ing the police on me won't help ya. Ya's dead meat."

As before, the note had no fingerprints, except for Jack's, of course, and no one saw the warning being put in his locker.

Since the messages continued, the police installed a security camera focused on the locker, but it revealed nothing. Alarmed and perplexed, the police assigned a daytime guard to Jack, but to no avail. The messages continued.

Worried sick, Jack's mother kept him home from school, but messages then showed up on their porch, and they were getting increasingly alarming, saying he would be tortured and then beheaded.

Desperate, the police arrested Bugsy and took him to the department for questioning.

"Why do you keep writing these notes? You could end up in jail for threatening to kill Jack."

"I never threatened nobody."

The detective tossed the collection of messages on the table.

"You mean to tell me you didn't write these? Come on!"

"Those are printed."

"So?"

"So, I don't have no printer."

"You could have used someone else's printer, or one in the library."

"I ain't never been in no library and I can't type!"

The questioning continued for over an hour before the detective, realizing he had nothing on him, had to let him go.

The Taylors hired a private detective who shadowed Bugsy for two weeks, noting his crass behavior but not tying him to the messages or to harming Jack.

In desperation, the Taylors engaged a realtor to look for housing in Stubinville, a nearby town, even though it would result in a longer commute. They toured a few houses but found nothing they could afford. Houses there were much more expensive.

Then another note arrived on their porch.

"Ya think ya can escape by movin' to Stubinville? I'll get ya wherever ya go."

Once again, the police were called and once again, they were stumped.

"I'm sorry, Mrs. Taylor, but there's not much we can do unless we can prove who sent the messages."

"You damned well better protect my son! I'm sick and tired of hearing you say you can't do anything! You do something or I will," Mr. Taylor exploded.

"Mr. Taylor, I understand your frustration, but we are doing all we legally can. Fortunately, your son hasn't been harmed yet. We'll assign an officer to follow him in the hopes we can catch this Cipriano fellow doing something illegal. Believe me, we are as anxious as you to put an end to this affair."

The following day, another message arrived.

"Yur time's up, punk. Tomorrow's the day. Say yur prayers. Bugsy"

Mrs. Taylor phoned the police immediately.

"Finally, since the note was signed, we have something we can act on," the detective said. "We'll arrest him right away."

When Bugsy's father answered the door, he saw two policemen.

"We have a warrant for the arrest of your son for sending threatening messages to Jack Taylor."

"What? Bugsy, come here," his father bellowed.

"Did you send threatenin' messages to Jack Taylor?"

"I ain't never sent no messages to no one."

"I'm sorry, but you'll have to come with us, son," one of the policemen said.

"He said he didn't send no messages!" Bugsy's father roared.

"I'm sorry, he still has to come with us."

They handcuffed Bugsy and put him in the back seat of the cruiser.

At the station, a detective asked him to sign his name. He looked first at the signature and then at Bugsy.

"Wait here," he said as he left the room to show the message to his chief.

"The Cipriano boy had nothing to do with this message. Compare his signature with the one on the note—totally different."

"Well, I'll be damned," the chief said. "Now we have to figure out who is trying to frame Cipriano."

Two days later, Mrs. Taylor noticed Jack left his computer on. Seeing a file named, "Bugsy," she opened it and saw the most recent note presumably sent by Bugsy. She called Jack into the room to ask him about it, but he claimed he had no idea how it got there. Confused, she called the police to report the incident.

The police confiscated Jack's computer and printer, enabling them to conclude the messages were made by his printer. When questioned, Jack became hysterical, not making sense. The police suggested the Taylors have their son examined by someone familiar with mental issues.

Reluctantly, the Taylors took Jack to a psychologist who gave him a battery of tests. After two sessions, the therapist asked to meet with Jack's parents.

"I'm afraid your son suffers from schizophrenia."

"How can that be? He has always seemed perfectly normal...at least until these messages started," Mr. Taylor protested.

"Well, unless you're trained in detecting mental health issues, you could easily miss the signs. Jack likely had undetected symptoms that were brought to light by the recent bullying he experienced. Logic and reasoning tend to be absent in people with schizophrenia, which accounts for him not realizing the absurdity of his actions and the fact his scheme would eventually unravel."

"I don't understand why he blamed the Cipriano boy."

"Are you aware that he has bullied your son recently?"

"Jack has never said a word about it."

"Your son is not the only one. I had my office assistant call his school, and apparently, Bugsy thrives on bullying. So, Jack felt aggressive toward Cipriano but couldn't express that anger directly.

Instead, he wrote threatening messages, claiming they came from his oppressor.

"What can we do to help him?"

"With therapy, most schizophrenics learn to function quite well, and I expect Jack will also."

About one percent of the population suffers from schizophrenia. Although debilitating, it can usually be managed so that a person can live a relatively normal life. The events described herein are based on recognized psychological principles.

Death's Legacy

As arguments go, it was not the worst, but Rebecca hated to start any day with even a minor disagreement.

"Rebecca, you know I have to go. My job depends on it."

"But you'll miss our anniversary. Isn't that important to you? We have reservations for the Cliff House. Can't you arrange to go another time?"

"I'm sorry, Rebecca. It pains me to skip it, but this trip can't wait. If Smith and Sons don't get the contract, the company may go under and I'd be out of work."

Hurt, Rebecca went to the kitchen after her husband walked out the door. She hadn't even given him a good-bye kiss.

Two hours later, a policewoman rang her doorbell.

"Are you Rebecca Jackson?"

"Yes."

"May I come in?"

"Of course." She directed her to the living room.

"I'm afraid I have some bad news. Your husband was in an automobile accident on the road to the airport."

"Oh no! Is he okay?"

"I'm terribly sorry. He died instantly."

Ashen, Rebecca collapsed. The policewoman caught her and helped her to a chair. Sobbing hysterically, she struggled to speak.

"I…I didn't even…give him…a good-bye kiss." Then her wails grew in intensity.

The funeral came a week later. Teary eyed, Rebecca leaned over the casket to give her husband one final kiss. Her best friend, Susie, slipped an arm around her waist and gently helped her to a seat.

Rebecca had only been married six years. Distraught, she felt empty, as though her very reason for existing had been taken away. Guilt consumed her for arguing with her husband and not kissing him before he left.

Concerned, Susie tried to get her to eat or go to her book club but with little success. Two weeks passed with little change.

Six weeks later, Susie opened her door, mouth agape in wonder, to see a smiling Rebecca.

"It's so good to see you happy again, Rebecca. Why the sudden change?"

"You won't believe it, but I'm pregnant," Rebecca replied, laughing.

"What? Really?"

"Yup, just found out. My husband's baby is growing in my belly."

"Congratulations, Rebecca. What a surprise! I'm so relieved to see you happy again."

Members of her book club welcomed her back, pleased that she seemed like her old self.

As the months passed, the pregnancy became more and more obvious. Around the seventh month, Susie wondered at the corner of a pillowcase protruding below her friend's blouse, but said nothing.

"When are you due?" Susie asked.

"June 21," she replied, smiling broadly.

As the delivery date approached, she called Susie.

"I won't be seeing you for a while. I'm going to my sister's house to have the baby. She offered to help me for a few weeks. I'm so excited!"

"That's great, Rebecca, although I'll miss you."

"I'll miss you too, Susie." In truth, Rebecca had no sister. She preferred to be alone for the delivery.

On June 19, Rebecca rejoiced in her new baby boy.

"Let's see, I believe I'll call you Kasper. That's a nice name. Do you like it, Kasper? What a darling you are." Cradling him in her arms, she sang lullabies to him before putting him down.

After an appropriate time for recovery from birthing, Rebecca took him for a walk in the stroller she had recently purchased. She covered him carefully to protect him from the sun. Heading for Lincoln Park two blocks away, she passed several pedestrians who glanced at the stroller and smiled at her. She was extremely happy to join the ranks of mothers, especially since she viewed Kasper as a gift from her late husband. They had tried unsuccessfully to have a child for three years. It finally had happened.

In the park, she encountered another woman with a baby in a stroller. They visited for thirty minutes before departing.

Back in her rental, Rebecca cuddled Kasper until eventually putting him down to sleep. Then she paced the floor, sat down, and then paced some more.

What's wrong? Why do I feel this way? Should I go home?

Two days later, she loaded the stroller and all of Kasper's things into her car for the trip home. She sat in her car, biting her nails and fidgeting. Then she got out, paced back and forth, re-entered and drove off.

Back home, she did not leave the house for three days, spending all of her time with Kasper—cuddling, singing, changing diapers. Susie had seen Rebecca's car and knew she was in town, but she had not responded to text messages.

Eager to see her friend and her baby, Susie went to her house and rang the bell.

"H...hi, Susie."

"It's so good to see you, Rebecca." She eagerly hugged her. Rebecca hesitated a bit before returning the embrace. They stood looking at each other until Susie broke the silence.

"May I come in?"'

"Oh...yeah...sorry, come on in, Susie."

"How have you been, Rebecca?"

"I've been fine."

"How's the little one? You never told me the baby's name."

"Kasper. His name is Kasper."

"Well, where are you hiding him? Can I see him?"

"I'm sorry, Susie, but this isn't a good time. He's asleep, a light sleeper, and I'm afraid just opening the door would wake him. Another time, perhaps?"

"Darn—let's make it soon."

They visited for an hour before Susie left, wondering why her friend seemed so distant.

Three days later, Rebecca put Kasper in a stroller and headed to the park. She had just gone one block when Susie happened to drive by and stopped.

"Hi, Rebecca. I see you and Kasper are enjoying the sunshine."

"Oh…uh…hi…Susie."

"Let me see that baby of yours."

"I have a cover over him for protection from the sun."

"I'll just take a quick peek."

Before Rebecca could respond, Susie pulled the cover back revealing….

"Oh my god, a doll? Where's Kasper?"

"This is my darling Kasper," Rebecca objected, re-covering him. "There, there, all covered up."

"Rebecca, what is going on? I don't understand…."

"Isn't he beautiful, Susie? I'm so lucky. My husband made sure I'd be happy."

Shocked but recognizing the situation, Susie bade good-bye and drove to the local psychiatric hospital. She was directed to the admissions office where a doctor greeted her.

"May I help you?"

Susie shared her observations of Rebecca with the doctor.

"What do you suggest?"

"Before making any diagnosis, I'd have to see her, of course. People have different ways of coping with the grief of losing someone. Her way may be to imagine she gave birth to her husband's son. I like to refer to such situations as death's legacy, although that's not a formal term. If she's happy thinking she has a baby, there are worse things in life."

"Do you feel she'd benefit from psychiatric care?" Susie asked.

"It's impossible to say, but people often cope better with therapy. You could suggest that she seek help, but if she refuses, she couldn't be committed so long as she's not a danger to herself or others. She might even get better on her own, especially since it hasn't been long since her husband died."

Susie tried unsuccessfully to convince Rebecca to get help, but she was happy with Kasper and saw no need for assistance.

A year later, Susie's husband noticed Rebecca through their living room window.

"Susie, come here. This is the first time since her husband died that I've seen Rebecca without the stroller. She has a tennis racket. It looks like she's headed to the park."

"Well, I'll be. Maybe I finally have my old friend back," Susie replied with a smile.

People have different ways of coping with the loss of a spouse. Sometimes, an individual's defense mechanisms are not up to the task, and they invent elaborate schemes to deal with their pain.

Obsession

After tossing and turning all night, Joe crawled out of bed and sauntered to his window to gaze at the forest. Something about it captivated him—something he had not experienced before. He dressed, ate breakfast, and headed for the woods. There were no trails, but walking was easy due to the lack of undergrowth. The trees, old and gnarled, had crooked branches and numerous burls, adding to their mystique.

Stepping over roots and ducking under limbs, he continued on, drawn by an unseen force. He dared not go too far for fear he wouldn't be able to find his way back. Yet something pulled at him. Incessantly fighting the competing urges to continue and return, he sat down on a log to think. Baffled by his compulsion, he returned home, wind-whipped branches swiping at him as he walked.

That evening, he struggled to comprehend his obsession. He went to bed, his mind working overtime.

The following day, Joe tried to ignore his unsettling experience but met with little success. He stared at the TV for a while, then paced the floor. He lay down on the couch but was unable to sleep. At 3:00, he poured a drink, then another, and another. Nothing dulled his urge until his sixth drink, when he passed out. Waking four hours later, he downed a bottle of wine and slipped into restless slumber.

Over the next few days, Joe tried various things to avoid his strange fixation with the woods. He got into his car. Seeing a theater, he decided to watch a movie but couldn't sit still, so he left. He didn't need groceries, but he stopped by a store to purchase items anyway. Exasperated, he phoned his mother but hung up without saying anything. Once again, he resorted to alcohol to doze fitfully.

Crawling out of bed with a nauseating hangover, he dressed. No longer able to resist the lure of his obsession, he entered the woods. The branches seemed lower and more tangled than previously, as though deliberately attacking him. Nevertheless, compulsion drove him on. Out of breath, he stopped to rest. Realizing he had gone farther than before, fear settled in—he didn't know which way to go. The sun had disappeared behind clouds, making it impossible to tell direction. Growing more anxious with each passing moment, he went in circles, sobbing, wondering what to do. Then, he saw a footprint, and another. At last. Drawing on all his reserves of willpower, he escaped the forest, bedraggled and emotionally drained.

His relief at finding his way out was short lived and soon gave way to the impetus to return. Only with monumental effort did he return home, shaken and exhausted. As before, he took to the bottle to numb his senses and find sleep.

The following day, he awoke, trembling. He knew what he had to do. Not bothering with breakfast, he headed straight for the woods. The limbs waved as he passed, driven by heavy winds. On and on he forged, far beyond the distance he had gone before. He knew there was no turning back this time. Finding his way out would be impossible. He had to go deeper.

Ten hours later, exhausted and unable to continue, he lay down and curled up in a ball, oblivious to the wind and cold.

* * *

Concerned about her friend, Jane wondered why Joe seemed obsessed about finding his way in a forest, especially since there wasn't one within a hundred miles. Also, she'd seen liquor bottles strewn about his apartment during her recent visits. He just didn't seem to be himself.

Determined to understand his behavior, she went to his flat and knocked. No answer. She knocked louder. Still no answer. Turning the knob, she found the door unlocked and entered. She called his name. No reply. She searched several rooms until she found him balled in a fetal position in his bedroom, catatonic. She dialed 911.

The character in this story suffers from schizophrenia, which sometimes is accompanied by catatonia. Those with catatonia may display erratic movement or parroting of what they hear. In the case of this story, it refers to rigidity or inability to respond, where the individual often maintains unusual and seemingly uncomfortable positions for long periods of time.

A Fortunate Accident

The accomplished classical pianist cringed at the hard rock music emanating from her son's room. Mary paced the hallway night after night knowing he was a loner and lacked the discipline to do well in school, especially in mathematics.

As she drove to pick him up from a concert by his favorite group, The Aliens, she couldn't rid her brain of the nagging jitters.

"How was the concert?" her voice quavered as Joel got in the car.

"Fantastic! I picked up a CD of their songs."

"I'm glad you had a good time. Don't forget to fasten your strap."

As they drove down 15th avenue, the CD fell out of Joel's lap onto the floor. He unbuckled his safety belt and leaned down to pick up his new treasure. Mary glanced over to see what he was doing and inadvertently crossed the centerline. She hit a truck. Protected by her safety belt, Mary suffered only minor injuries. Joel was not so lucky.

"Joel," she whimpered. No answer. "Joel? Oh God no! Joel, say something."

Uninjured, the truck driver immediately called 911. The ambulance arrived fifteen minutes later and rushed Joel and Mary to the hospital. After receiving treatment for her superficial wounds, Mary returned to the waiting room, wringing her hands. Hours passed before a neurosurgeon came to tell her about her son's injuries.

"Joel has contusions in the frontal-temporal region of his brain. We took steps to relieve the pressure. Additionally, it appears his corpus callosum is partially severed."

"What is the corpus callosum?" Mary asked.

"It's a bundle of nerve fibers connecting the two sides of the brain."

"What is his prognosis?" Mary asked, through a stream of tears.

"Assuming we can reduce the edema, he should recover considerably. How much we really can't say at this point. We're keeping him in a medically induced coma until he's out of danger. Despite his severe injuries, I feel his chances of a full recovery are better than 50-50."

"May I see him?"

"Of course."

After entering intensive care, Mary kissed him on the forehead and held his hand. Through tears, she told him how sorry she was. She sat with him for hours until a nurse finally suggested she go home to get some rest.

Mary visited her unconscious son every day, holding his hand and talking to him. On the eighth day, the edema largely gone, the doctors ended the coma. It appeared Joel recognized her, but he couldn't talk. Mary asked a nurse to speak with the neurologist in charge. He soon arrived at Joel's room.

Before she could say anything, the neurologist opened the conversation.

"Mary, good to see you. We have encouraging news. The swelling is down and he is progressing nicely."

"But he can't speak," Mary stammered.

"That's to be expected, given his injuries. I anticipate he'll ask you all sorts of questions before long. Give him a couple of more days."

Sure enough, when his mother arrived two days later, he rasped, "What happened. Where am I?" Overjoyed to hear him talk, Mary recounted the accident and what the neurologist had said about his prognosis. Joel continued to improve and went home a few days later. Almost back to normal, he even joked about the accident, which helped assuage Mary's guilt.

Puzzled by the beautiful classical music coming from the living room the following day, Mary went to investigate.

"Oh my god! Joel, where did you learn to play like that?" He had never taken a single lesson.

"I don't know. I heard Debussy's Claire de Lune on the radio and liked it. I thought I'd try playing it."

"But you never...how...."

"It just came to me. Here's another piece I heard." He proceeded to play Chopin's Waltz No.10 in B minor.

Shaking her head in wonder, Mary sat down, staring at Joel and the piano.

Other surprises awaited her. Hearing VE day was May 8, 1945, Joel commented that it fell on a Tuesday, the same day of the week as the 75th anniversary.

"Did you read that somewhere?" Mary asked.

"No, for some reason, it's obvious, just as I know It's been 2,343 days or 56,232 hours since I was born."

Taken aback at his new abilities, Mary needed to understand what the changes meant. Although seemingly positive, she had a nagging feeling they could be harbingers of something bad. Accordingly, she took Joel to the doctor, who suggested seeing Dr. Livingston, a neuropsychologist.

Intrigued by Joel, Dr. Livingston administered a battery of tests, and conversed at length with him, after which he finally called Mary into his office.

"Your son has acquired savant syndrome."

"Oh my, what is that? Is it dangerous?" she asked.

"Savants are people with amazing abilities. One man I worked with could read two pages in eight seconds, one page with his left eye and the other with his right, and remembered them verbatim. He memorized over 22,000 books. Like Joel, some savants can play difficult music without any training after hearing it just once. Others have very specific abilities, such as reciting Pi to thousands of decimal places or extracting square roots instantly. Some suddenly become artistic."

"Does this condition always show up suddenly?"

"In Joel's case, yes—his accident was the trigger. This condition can occur after a brain injury, particularly to the frontal-temporal region or the corpus callosum. However, in most cases, savants are born with their talent. For example, approximately ten percent of autistic individuals are savants. Also, those with frontal-temporal dementia sometimes exhibit savantism. It's common for savants to have a fantastic memory."

"Will his abilities diminish over time?"

"No, he'll be a savant for the rest of his life."

"I don't understand how a person can go from having ordinary abilities to such extreme talents. What accounts for this?"

"We don't know why these skills develop, or why only a few people have them. Some experts think parts of the brain inhibit other parts, and when damage to the inhibitory areas occurs, new abilities are released. However, we really don't know."

As weeks grew into months, Mary rejoiced as she watched Joel prosper in his newfound talent and in all the new musical friends he gained through it. She chuckled to herself as she watched them try, unsuccessfully, to find something he couldn't play. She attended all his music contests, reveling in his superior ratings. She even let him host parties because of his growing popularity. His guests enjoyed asking him mathematical questions such as the number of days or hours since they were born. The sense of guilt Mary had initially gradually faded into full-blown wonder as her son continued to prosper.

> *Consisting of 86 billion neurons, the human brain is an amazingly complex organ. It regulates all of our bodily functions, provides us with information about the outside world via our senses, enables us to think and solve problems, and serves as the seat of our emotions. A few people have brains capable of even more astonishing feats, such as the man who memorized 22,000 books—a real person named Kim Peek. Though most savants are born with their abilities, in a few instances the gifts are acquired though accidents. Lest you think you'd like to have such talents, savantism is generally associated with mental problems, such as autism. Nevertheless, one has to wonder if we might ultimately be able to unleash these remarkable skills.*

Ryan' Secret

"Ryan, you'll roast in a long-sleeved shirt. It's 97 degrees!" his mother admonished.

"I'll be fine, Mom. I don't want to get sunburned either," he replied.

A sophomore at Edgemont High, Ryan Woodson excelled in school. Good looking, some might say handsome, quiet at times, conscientious, and affectionate, at least with family members—a model teenager in many ways.

However, Ryan began to change in a way his mother couldn't quite verbalize. He still exhibited his usual easy interaction with family members but seemed elusive...even secretive. His most obvious new habits: wearing long-sleeved shirts in hot weather and disappearing frequently after dinner.

One morning, his mom went to his room to ask if he needed a ride to school. Because his door was partially open, she walked in without knocking. He had just started to put on his shirt.

"Ryan, what on earth happened to your arm?" she said, alarmed.

Ryan instinctively turned away, quickly slipping his arms in his in his shirt sleeves, but not before his mother saw several ugly scars, one scabbed.

"That's nothing, I cut myself on some broken glass at Joe's house." Joe, his closest friend, was a junior.

That evening, his mother told his father about the scars, who demanded to see them. They didn't believe his explanation of an accident with sharp glass because one cut still had a scab, indicating it was more recent than the others.

"I'm afraid Ryan is cutting himself," his mother said, shaken to the core.

Ryan refused to talk about it the next morning, other than insisting he was okay and had just accidentally cut himself.

A week later, his arms had two more scars, one obviously recent. After discussing the situation, his parents contacted a psychologist.

Despite strenuous objections, Ryan eventually agreed to see her. After three weeks of therapy, she asked for a meeting with the parents.

"I don't know what is going on with Ryan, but I don't believe he's mutilating himself. He doesn't exhibit the symptoms. Generally, self-mutilators have a difficult time expressing emotions. They may feel worthless, angry, lonely, guilty, or hate themselves. Physical pain is a way to deal with psychological pain. Ryan doesn't display those characteristics. I think something else is going on…what I don't know."

The psychologist explained she was bound by law to report the scars to Child Protective Services since abuse might be involved. CPS requested a meeting with Ryan's parents the next night.

"As you may know, we are required to investigate potential abuse of a child," the investigator stated after introductions.

"Wait a minute, this is ridiculous. You think we abused our son?" Ryan's father interrupted.

"Your son reportedly has scars…that's sometimes indicative of abuse. I'm not accusing anyone at this point, just investigating. Can we proceed?"

"Go ahead," he answered defensively.

"Would you say Ryan is a difficult child?"

"Heavens no! He is very caring and cooperative. I can't imagine a better teenager."

"Do you punish him for bad behavior?"

"The extent of our punishment is grounding him when he stays out too late. We've never spanked him or used physical punishment of any kind."

The investigation continued along these lines for an hour, at which point the CPS representative requested a meeting alone with Ryan. His father went to Ryan's room to tell him of the request.

"Why?" Ryan asked.

"It's part of their investigation into the scars on your arms."

Head hanging down, Ryan went to the living room while his parents retired to the kitchen.

"Hi Ryan, is it okay if I ask you a few questions?"

"Sure."

"Do your parents ever get mad at you?"

"I wouldn't use the word, 'mad.' They disapprove of some things, like staying out past my curfew."

"Have they ever physically punished you?"

"Never."

"I hear you have scars on your arms. I need to see them and ask how you got them."

Thirty minutes later, the investigator felt she had enough information and called Ryan's parents into the room where she apologized for the visit. She agreed they were innocent. However, she informed them she'd keep the case open in the event new evidence arose.

"Since the scars might be self-mutilation, I suggest you contact a psychologist."

When informed they had already done that, she persisted, recommending they get a second opinion.

Another meeting was scheduled with a professional specializing in self-mutilation. She came to the same conclusion—that Ryan simply didn't fit the description of a self-mutilator.

At a loss of what to do, Ryan's parents decided to ask his friend, Joe, if he knew anything about the scars. Joe's father answered the door.

"Ryan, has several scars on his arms and refuses to talk about them," they explained. "We're hoping Joe might know what's going on. Two psychologists have concluded he doesn't fit the profile of a self-mutilator. Since Joe is his best friend, would it be okay if we talked with him?"

"We're sorry. Of course, come on in. He's upstairs." His father went to call him.

"Do you know how Ryan got several scars on his arms?" Ryan's mother asked after explaining the purpose of their visit,

Squirming, Joe said he had no idea.

Joe's father intervened.

"Joe, if you know anything, you need to speak up."

"But I swore to keep it a secret. Ryan will never forgive me if I tell."

"Joe, this is one case where you shouldn't keep a promise. This is serious. Ryan may be in trouble and you have to help him if you can."

Reluctantly, Joe admitted they had gone to a meeting, thinking it was just a group of friends getting together. However, it turned out to be a crazy group of people that mixed the blood of members to signify their unity and loyalty to one another.

"After I saw what they did to Ryan, I ran away. Threatened by the other cult members, Ryan didn't know how to get out. They control him. He's afraid to tell you, so he kept going to meetings to avoid further trouble."

Ryan's parents thanked Joe. When they arrived home, Mr. Woodson called the police. A detective came out to interview all of them. He assured Ryan there would be no retribution from the members of the group.

Police arrived at the cult's meeting site in a local wooded area and arrested everyone. After meeting with the parents of all the members, the cult was shut down. Finally, Ryan was free from its domination.

There are thousands of cults in America, the most famous being the Ku Klux Klan and Scientology. However, there are many smaller ones as well. They can exert tremendous sway over people, as in the Jonestown Massacre where 909 individuals died, most by suicide. But there are many small cults that can still exert considerable control over their members.

Missing

One year following the death of his wife, Amos looked at the pile of boxes and furniture, distraught by where to put everything. Independent living facilities didn't have much room. Since the small closet couldn't accommodate all his clothes, he pondered which ones to part with. His couch, favorite recliner, and dining table? Too large for the space. Books? Most would have to go. Opening one of the boxes, he pored over photographs. What could he do with them? Looking at a framed photo of him with his wife on their 50th wedding anniversary, he broke down. Overwhelmed with the move and the realization he would never again hold her in his arms, he sat on a box, crying inconsolably. Making matters worse, he was in quarantine, forced to stay alone in his apartment for two weeks because of Covid-19.

During those interminable days, Amos coped as best he could, discarding belongings and saving those he couldn't bear to part with. In the end, he piled nine boxes in a corner, puzzling over what to do with them. This was it—the place he'd live and die, thousands of miles from his children and anyone who cared for him.

After the end of his quarantine, he tried engaging in the facility's activities. To him, they felt like empty charades—futile attempts to divert attention from the things that count—fulfilling things, things with life.

Attempts to make meaningful contact with others at mealtimes didn't work. Hearing loss prevented him from participating in conversation, especially with all the background noise. To others, he appeared aloof and disinterested.

After a few months, he saw a woman, Maude, sitting in the lounge awaiting the start of a recital. Striking up a conversation, he learned they shared a love of classical music. The visit was cut short by the onset of the program.

Weeks later, he saw Maude sitting alone on a bench in the courtyard. Noticing she seemed unhappy, he stopped to visit.

"Ah, we meet again," he said, pleased to see her.

His greeting was apparently a trigger, for Maude began crying.

"Two years ago today, my husband died. I miss him so!"

"I'm sorry! How long were you married?" he asked.

"Fifty-two years."

"Where did you live?"

"Portland, Oregon," Maude replied.

"That's a nice city. I went there once on vacation."

"Yes. We lived on the edge of a park with a view of downtown."

"Sounds lovely," Amos said.

"It was. My husband and I had short commutes to our jobs. I managed a real estate office; he had a law practice."

"How did you end up here?"

"Our house was too much for me to keep up, especially after I broke my hip. My daughter, who lives nearby, recommended this place."

"How do you like it?" Amos asked.

"Okay, I guess, but I miss the freedom of living in my own house."

"I hear you. There's always someone looking over your shoulder. You have to remember to do this or not to do that. I once accidently tripped the emergency alarm. A woman came barging in, and with no explanation, entered the bathroom to reset the alarm while I was standing in the nude. I didn't find out until later why she was there. An explanation would have been nice."

"Oh, my goodness, how embarrassing! I find it annoying I have to sign out whenever I leave and sign in when I return. I can see the need for people who live in assisted-living facilities, but we're supposed to be independent. Often, I'm gone for just a few minutes."

"Have you noticed how people talk down to us, Maude? I've been called names like dear, honey, darling. And waiters often ask, 'How are *we* doing today?' It is condescending."

"I agree."

"Also, I wish people would quit asking how I am today. Often, I feel lousy. Why not just say good morning or afternoon? They're trying to be polite, but why do we have to be the ones lying by saying we're fine when we aren't? It's as though we're forced to humor our caretakers."

"If I get a large package, I'm warned not to lift it. The assumption is I'm incapable of deciding if something is too heavy," she commented.

"We just want to be treated as adults who haven't lost the ability to think and make decisions. Whatever happened to the 'independent' in independent living?"

They continued talking until mealtime. Since Maude still had problems with her hip, Amos helped her up. Gripping her hand, he realized for the first time the thing he missed the most and for which he desperately longed—touching another individual, holding onto someone's hand while walking in a park, feeling the warmth of another during a hug or a kiss, bodies touching in bed. His thoughts ran on. He held onto her hand longer than necessary to help her up.

A week later, he saw Maude awaiting the start of a movie and sat beside her despite his disinterest in the film. Afterward, she grabbed his hand for help in getting up and continued to hold it after rising.

Maybe she also enjoys touching.

They began eating meals together, conversing in a quiet corner of the dining room. When menu choices were unappealing, Amos asked if she'd like to eat at a restaurant. At one of these outings, he finally brought up the topic of touching.

"Have you thought about the ways our lives have changed since our spouses died? In the womb, we experience touching over our entire bodies. After birth, we're held, fed, hugged, and kissed. As children, we touch others in games, dancing, and more. When dating, we can't get enough touching. After marriage, we touch and kiss one another daily, intimately. But when our spouses die, all of that ends. Now we have to live our last years without it. How cruel! Don't you agree, Maude...Maude?"

As he stared at the empty chair across the table, despair overtook him. There was no Maude, no one to hug, no one to hold hands with, no one at all.

"Do you care for any dessert, sir?" a waiter asked.

"What?" Amos replied, awakening from his reverie. "Oh, no, thank you."

Moving is an emotional experience, especially when one is a senior who has recently lost a spouse. Doing so in the middle of a pandemic is even more upsetting. This story is a highly fictionalized account based on my experience transitioning to an independent living facility. Some of the events actually happened. Considerable research has shown the importance of touch in the physical and emotional development and well-being of both children and adults. Unfortunately, seniors often have very little physical contact with others. Some people find that pets help in this regard.

Nothing Left

Pacing the floor, a man awaited news of his wife's cancer operation. The heavy lines on the surgeon's face as he approached underlined Mark's fears.

"I'm sorry, Mr. Kellogg, we did all we could, but we were unable to save her."

Mark broke into unrestrained sobs and collapsed in a chair, on the verge of hyperventilating. Nothing the surgeon said could console him.

After 55 years, Mark and Nancy were not only husband and wife, they were and always had been best friends since their days as high-school sweethearts. They had done everything together—camping, theater, art collecting, shopping, housework, gardening, and more, much more. In fact, Mark had never done anything without his wife, never giving a thought to making close friends outside of the home. Nancy had fulfilled all his needs. Her death left him numb.

"Can I see her?"

"Of course, follow me."

He tenderly kissed her cheek, tears streaming down his face. Thirty minutes later, he collected himself enough to leave for home. But what was home? Only an empty shell without her. He couldn't bring himself to eat, so he went to bed and cried, unable to sleep. The thought of never again seeing her or holding her in his arms was painful, surreal, beyond comprehension.

The next morning, he lumbered out of bed to fix breakfast but couldn't eat. Her chair, empty as his heart, stared at him. Plodding into the living room, he saw her picture on the mantle and again broke down. Everyplace he looked at reminded him of her. He had to get out of the house.

With morbid thoughts rummaging in his head, he grabbed a few clothes, crammed them into a rucksack, and drove, not thinking of where to go, just going somewhere, anywhere. Hours later and nearly out of gas, he stopped at a decrepit station with only two pumps. The owner greeted him with a friendly "howdy" and filled the tank.

"Where ya headed?"

"Nowhere in particular. Is there a place close by to see the ocean?"

"Sure. Turn right off the highway at the dirt road twelve miles from here. It will take you to some cliffs with great views of the ocean."

"Thanks."

Mark drove to the spot and sat in his car for several minutes, steeling himself. Slowly, he left his car, took off his coat, and walked to the edge of the cliff. The minutes grew long as he stared at the waves crashing against the rocks below. Unable to bring himself to jump, he returned to his car.

After driving five more hours, he encountered a ramshackle motel with only three units. Exhausted, he took two Ambien and got four hours of fitful sleep.

Skipping breakfast, he hopped in his car and started driving again, visions of his wife rummaging in his mind and tears blurring his vision. At 1:30, he stopped at a small diner. The waitress, a woman in her fifties took his order—a hamburger, coffee, and fries. Her heavily-lined face suggested wisdom born of a hard life. With little appetite, he ate half of his burger before putting his head in his hands, overcome by crippling despair.

The waitress sat down across from him, asking if he would like to talk about his troubles. No one else was in the diner.

"Thank you, but it's a private matter," he answered, lifting his head.

"Look, honey," she said, "I've been around the block a few times and heard it all. One thing I've learned is that it helps to talk about your problems. Seeing as how I'm the only one here, how about talking with me?"

Glancing at her, he explained the death of his wife and his difficulty coping after being together so long. He mentioned nothing about his morbid thoughts.

"My son died from pneumonia when he was only seven," she said softly, putting her hand on his. "Always thought I should have taken him to the hospital sooner. I don't think I would have survived without the support of my husband and friends. Do you have anyone close?"

"Not really. I have a brother on the east coast, but we haven't kept in touch. My mother is in a nursing home and very fragile. My wife and I didn't have close friends; we had each other and that's all we needed or wanted."

After talking for 45 minutes and getting a warm hug from the waitress, Mark left, a little lighter of heart, but soon, the numbing despair returned, a relentless companion.

Not knowing or caring where he went, he drove on backroads until he eventually came upon an abandoned cabin in the foothills. He stepped inside. Its emptiness mirrored the emptiness in his heart, but he decided to spend the night there anyway. An old mattress with stuffing coming out served as his bed. As before, he got little sleep, even after taking another dose of Ambien.

His eyes burning from sobbing and lack of sleep, he motored on, high into the mountains, not knowing or caring why. Ten miles after the last occupied house, the road ended. He parked and put his head on the steering wheel, trying to process the pain from the events of the last few days.

With resolve, he got out of the car, put on his jacket, and started up a snow-covered trail. Worn out and lacking food and water, the going was tough, especially since about an inch of the white powder covered the ground, the temperature below freezing. After four hours, the trail ended but he kept going until reaching an alpine lake. He sat thinking, then took off his jacket and shoes and lay on the ground. After shivering for an hour, he no longer felt the cold. As more snow fell, he became sleepy and was finally free from his pain.

> *As anyone who has lost a loved one knows, depression and emotional distress can be intense. That is especially true with the loss of a spouse. If the survivor doesn't have a good support network, the heartache may result in extreme*

measures. However, family and friends can help one cope with the initial despair and ease the transition to a new life.

The Magic Box

There once was a little girl named Kylie who lived in Ashville. The village sat in a valley surrounded by majestic snow-capped peaks. As a typical nine-year-old, Kylie loved to play games with her friends and explore on her bike. However, all kids avoided one place, a house on top of a hill on the edge of town. An old woman, some said a witch, lived there. No one had really seen the house since it was surrounded by many trees and shrubs. There wasn't even a driveway. A winding path led to the house, but no child dared go up it to see.

One day, Kylie and her friend, Ann, rode their bikes near the house on the hill. Stopping by the path, they whispered all the rumors they had heard about the old woman.

"They say she never leaves home," offered Ann.

"Then, how would she get food?" Kylie asked.

"I heard she raises dogs and eats them," Ann replied. "Do you think she really is a witch?"

"She must be. Who else would live in such a place?" Kylie affirmed.

"People say her house has no windows, a moat, and a dungeon in the basement," Ann stated.

They continued to share what they knew, until Ann folded her arms in a huff,

"Let's go up the path just far enough to see the house. Since it's afternoon, she's probably sleeping. Witches sleep during the day."

"No way! I'm not going up there," Kylie protested.

Then Ann came up with an idea,

"Let's draw straws, the short straw goes up the path far enough to see the house. If you meet the witch, just run back as fast as you can. It's not far."

Since they both wanted to know what the house looked like, they finally agreed. Kylie drew the short straw. Although she protested, she had agreed to the plan, and Ann double dared her.

Kylie went up the path a short way but then ran back out. Ann insisted she do what she promised, so she reluctantly did. After she got about fifty feet, she could no longer see her friend because of the curves in the path. Shaking, she continued on but still could not see the house.

"Hello there, little girl."

Startled, Kylie spun to face an old woman on the path with her dog. She didn't look like a witch. Rather, she had a pretty blue dress, neat hair, and a big smile. In fact, Kylie had seen the woman visiting with her mother in Martin's Market.

"My name is Amelia, but you can call me Abbie. What's your name?"

"K-K-Kylie Nelson," she stammered, still a bit shaken despite recognizing the woman.

"You must be Hazel's daughter."

Hesitant, Kylie nodded.

"Your mother and I have visited several times. I was picking up branches when I saw you on the path. I don't get much company. Would you like to have lemonade with me?"

Many questions entered Kylie's mind. Could Abbie be a witch even though she seemed nice? Did she really have a dungeon? Why was the house hidden by trees? Although it seemed unlikely that Amelia was a witch, Kylie couldn't forget the terrible rumors she had just heard from her friend. Nevertheless, she felt drawn to the woman and wanted to find answers to her questions.

Abbie offered a friendly hand to Kylie and led her to a magnificent Victorian house with lots of windows. It had no moat, although it needed paint.

"Come on in, honey. You can keep me company in the kitchen while I make lemonade."

Kylie passed through a lovely living room on the way to the kitchen.

Abbie pointed to a chair and asked her to have a seat.

Although she now realized Abbie wasn't a witch, Kylie couldn't help but ask.

"Do you have a dungeon?"

"Oh honey, that's just a silly rumor. Of course, I don't have a dungeon." Abbie laughed heartily.

After she finished making the lemonade, she handed Kylie a glass along with a plate of cookies.

Thanking her, Kylie started nibbling on the treats.

This woman seems nice.

Kylie couldn't wait to tell Ann she had been wrong about Abbie and her house.

She then told Abbie about her math difficulties and her favorite books. She described her friends and said they enjoyed soccer much more than she did. They talked for more than an hour.

"Abbie, do you mind if I ask you a question?" Kylie asked, now feeling more comfortable.

"Of course not, ask away."

"Why do you have so many trees hiding your house?"

"Well, originally you could see the house from the street. When my husband died, I didn't have enough money to hire people to keep the property up and the trees just kept growing until they hid the house."

"Now, why don't you come into the living room. I have something I'd like to give you to help you with your math and soccer."

There, she handed her guest a tiny box, totally engraved with mysterious symbols,

"I want you to have this. It's a magic box. Carry it with you all the time and it will bring you good fortune."

"Thank you, Abbie. It's beautiful! But it's almost time for dinner, so I'd better go now. Would it be okay if I visited you once in a while?"

"Of course, Kylie, anytime! You are such a sweet girl!"

Kylie thanked her for everything and departed down the path, eager to tell her parents about her adventure.

Her mother laughed when Kylie told her what she and her friend had believed about Abbie.

"She's a wonderful person. Never went out much after her husband died. I see her from time to time in the Market."

Since Ann probably thought she was overcome by the "witch," Kylie phoned her to describe her experience. Ann was amazed and glad she was okay.

For the weeks and months following, Kylie kept the box with her at all times, even at school. Although she had not done well in math, her grades improved to an A-. Rather than holding back at soccer, she became one of the best players. She became more popular with her peers and felt more comfortable asserting herself. In general, she grew in self-confidence and happiness.

It had been some time since Kylie visited Abbie, so one Saturday she picked some flowers and went to her house. When Abbie answered, Kylie gave them to her and asked if she had time for a visit.

"I'll always have time for you, Kylie. Come on in. I just took some brownies out of the oven. Would you like some?"

"You bet!" Kylie replied with an eager smile.

"Have a seat and I'll get them." Returning with a plate of brownies and a glass of milk, she asked, "Well now, how have you been?"

"Abbie, thank you for the magic box. It has changed my life. I'm doing better at school and I'm having more fun with my friends. I even scored the winning goal at our last soccer game. I wonder, though, would the magic disappear if I opened the box?"

"Oh sweetheart, the magic was never in the box—it was always in you! Your belief in it gave you the confidence to believe in yourself."

The idea for this story came from my childhood. A woman in my hometown lived on a hill with trees completely hiding the house. I often wondered what the house looked like. Children frequently attribute mystery to situations they later find are ordinary. I sent this story and a hand-painted trinket box to my granddaughter for Christmas.

The Riddle Murder

Cato saw the headlines in the Milford Times.

Riddle murder investigation halted. Police conclude it's a hoax.

Intrigued, he read the article about police receiving an anonymous note in the form of a riddle.

What once was is no more, find me murdered behind a door.
The place is dark and damp, don't forget to take a lamp.
If you stand by the brew, you will have the best view.

Reading further, he learned that a two-week investigation had turned up nothing. Since there were no reports of anyone missing, the police concluded it must have been someone's idea of a joke.

Cato and his two closest friends, Ray and Shanna were bright juniors who loved intellectual challenges. Considered nerds by most, they excelled at debate and school.

After clipping the article, Cato phoned his pals to propose trying to solve what the police could not. Confident of their abilities, they agreed to work on the puzzle. What if someone really had committed a murder? Perhaps the villain enjoyed playing games with the police and had brought the body to Milford from afar. The trio all agreed that solving a mystery the police couldn't would be immensely satisfying.

That evening, they got together to discuss strategy.

Cato began the discussion.

"It seems to me the last line of the riddle would be the place to start."

"I agree," Shanna replied, "I'll bet standing by the brew refers to the old brewery on the edge of town."

After mulling over the possibilities, they met at Cato's house after school and went to the brewery in his car.

"I wonder if the door mentioned in the riddle could be in the brewery?" Ray asked.

"Perhaps, but why would the riddle mention standing *'by'* provides the best view. If it were inside, wouldn't it be phrased differently?" Cato replied.

"Well, if you stand by the brewery, you would have a good view of the entry door," Shanna said.

"Yes, but it seems unlikely a body would be behind the entry door, especially since it wouldn't be dark because of the windows," Cato interjected.

"Or damp," Ray added.

They discussed more possibilities, eventually deciding the door referenced in the riddle had to be in some structure other than the brewery. Looking around, the only other possibility was an abandoned warehouse across the street.

Since its main door was locked, they walked to the loading docks. Those doors were locked too. As they went around the building, they saw a broken window covered by loose boards which they easily removed. Standing on a nearby crate, they crawled through.

Once inside, the beam of Cato's flashlight was too narrow to see much, so they waited until their eyes adjusted to the dim illumination. The floor creaked, dust flew, and wind whistled through cracks in the structure as they explored the bare space.

"What was that?" Shanna asked, ducking when she heard a loud flapping sound just above her head.

"An owl, I think," Cato replied. "I didn't get a good look at it."

They searched all the rooms, but found no body.

"The riddle mentioned dark and damp. It's certainly dark, but not damp. We must be on the wrong track," Cato said.

"That makes sense, but this is the only building that one can see standing by the brewery," Shanna offered.

They exited the warehouse and stood by the brewery again, not seeing anything different.

"Let's meet at the Blue Heron Café tomorrow after school. How about 4:00?" Cato asked.

All agreed.

Sitting in the café the following day, they sipped drinks, pondering their next move.

"It seems obvious that 'brew' refers to the brewery," said Ray. "What are we missing?"

"I agree," Shanna added. "However, nothing we've seen so far has been damp. I don't think the word damp would have been in the riddle unless ..."

Cato slapped the table, his eyebrows raised.

"Looking at the steam rising from Ray's coffee gave me an idea! What if brew doesn't refer to the brewery?"

"Okay, what else could it be?" Shanna asked,

"The *Coffee Me* stand on the way into town. Coffee is referred to as brew," Cato pointed out, beaming.

"Hey, good thinking!" Shanna said, a big grin on her face.

"Right on," Ray exclaimed. "How about going there tomorrow afternoon? Tonight, is debate practice, so that's out."

Reenergized by the new possibility, they departed for home, each musing over the riddle.

The next morning, rain came in sheets, turning gutters into streams. Yards were cluttered with small branches felled by heavy winds.

After school, Cato asked his friends if they wanted to put off going to *Coffee Me* because of the weather, but they were too excited to wait. Hopping into Cato's car, they headed for the coffee stand.

After parking, they donned their rain gear and walked into the wet weather.

"There aren't many buildings around," Ray commented, zipping his rain jacker, "just the house way back from the street. Think that could be it?"

Shivering, Shanna put her hands in her pockets.

"Maybe, I don't see any other possibilities."

Cato, already crossing the street, motioned for his friends to follow.

The house, an old Victorian, had broken windows, debris lying about, and boards covering doors and windows. Cato stepped back and looked up at the third-story turret, the rain spattering his glasses.

"How can we get in?" Ray asked.

Cato pulled on the boards covering the front door, but they didn't budge.

"Will we get in trouble if we enter?" Shanna asked.

"Not if no one sees us," replied Cato. "Besides, we can't solve the riddle standing outside."

They walked around the house, their shoes squishing in mud and water.

The back door had no boards. Although locked, it opened when Cato put a shoulder to it.

"Voilà, ladies and gentleman, an entrance," Cato said, pleased with himself.

They entered a kitchen with cabinet doors askew and chunks of plaster lying about. The floors creaked and shutters banged as they moved from one dark room to another.

"What was that?" Cato ducked at the flapping sound. Then, he rose, cursing. "Nothing worse than a bat."

"This place is creepy," Shanna whispered.

They searched behind doors on all floors, including the turret, but no body.

"Hey guys, we're forgetting something important," Cato said. "The riddle mentions dark and damp. It has been dark, but dry. We need to find someplace damp."

"I completely forgot about that," Ray said.

"What about a basement?" Shanna offered.

"Great idea, but we haven't seen one," replied Cato.

They combed the house again, finally finding a door they had missed in the dark. Cato tried the handle with no luck. A kick, this time by Ray, solved the problem.

Cato shined the flashlight in the opening, seeing a staircase descending into darkness.

"Look at that!" he said, shining his light. "Those footsteps in the dust suggest someone has been here recently. I'll bet the murderer carried the body into the cellar."

"Do you guys notice the musty smell?" Shanna asked. "I think we've finally found dampness."

They milled around, coughing as their steps stirred up the thick dust. The dirt floor led to shelving on the walls, storage for canned food at some forgotten time. The cellar appeared to meet all the criteria in the riddle except for a door. Cato continued to scan with the light until eventually his beam stopped on a small door.

"I'm not sure I want to know what's behind there," Shanna rasped. "What if there really is a dead body?"

"That's the whole point—to find the body!" Cato said, exasperated.

"I hope we don't become suspects because of being here," said Ray.

"I smell decaying flesh!" Shanna put a handkerchief over her nose.

Cato approached the door and opened it, shining his light in an empty room lined with wine racks.

"But the riddle says to look *behind* the door," Ray pointed out.

Cato swung the door to shine the light behind it. Shanna shrieked. Ray's brow furled and his jaw clenched. Cato bent over in laughter. There it was, the body and the murder weapon. A large rat in a trap.

"What's so funny?" Shanna spouted, her voice raised and fists clenched.

"We've been duped," Cato replied, still laughing.

"Well, I'm not amused," Ray objected. "Spending all this time to find a dead rat?"

The following day, Cato learned a student had found the note and sent it to the police thinking it was real rather than a riddle for a Halloween party. Not surprisingly, it became a top story in the *Milford Times*.

> *I thought it would be fun for someone to investigate a murder by solving a riddle. Then the idea of a dead rat as the murder victim came to me. Since it was light-hearted, it made sense for the "detectives" to be children.*

The Contribution Machine

Melanie Raven loved antiques, so she frequently browsed in stores for unusual items to add to her vast collection. As she searched along Blackstone Street, the home of her town's antique shops, she noticed a small pawnshop with old articles in the window, so she entered.

"Good afternoon," the keeper said. "Is there something I can help you find?"

"No," she replied, "I'm just browsing."

"What's that?" she asked, pointing to a strange looking device.

"Just a curio." he replied. It's not for sale.

"May I see it?" she persisted.

"We don't show not-for-sale items," he explained.

"But you have it on the shelf," she continued. "I'd just like to see it up close."

"Well, if you insist," he said grudgingly, getting the item from the shelf and placing it on the counter in front of her.

It seemed to be a machine of some sort. A small cleaver, about three inches long, could be raised up and down by means of a five-inch handle.

Bas relief of various human and animal faces, adorned its metal framework. The wooden base, about eight by ten inches and 1.5 inches thick, had small holes and grooves in it, as if some wood-eating beetles had used it for a playground. An ornate dish rested on the wood base under the blade.

"What is it?" Melanie asked.

"I don't know," he said, picking it up to replace it on the shelf. "I shouldn't have shown it to you."

Melanie did not know why, but she was drawn to the device.

"I'll give you $20 for it."

"Sorry—not for sale," he said.

"40?"

"Nope."

"$60?"

"Lady, believe me, you don't want this," he countered.

"Not high enough? Okay, I'll give you $200 for it."

The shopkeeper paused upon hearing her last offer, his resistance weakening. Sales had been slow for months.

Before he could reply, she blurted out, "Three hundred dollars."

"Okay, lady, it's yours," he said reluctantly. "But I warn you, objects like this require strong willpower."

He placed it in a cardboard box, wrapped the dish carefully to prevent breakage, and taped it shut.

"I urge you to put this in a drawer and forget about it," he cautioned. "It's not something to fool with."

Melanie took her purchase home, removed it from the box, and placed it on her coffee table. She examined the dish, thinking something on its bottom might indicate its origin, but found nothing. She moved the handle up and down and ran her fingers across the blade, finding it surprisingly sharp. Examining the base and metal frame with its bas-relief, she found the human faces vacant and nondescript. Lining its rim were strange symbols unlike any she had seen before. Turning the base over, she noted indentations in the wood. She placed a piece of paper over it and rubbed with a pencil to reveal writing. "La Machine de Contribution, 1337."

"Contribution machine?" she thought. "What on earth is a contribution machine?" She left it on the coffee table and went to the kitchen to prepare dinner. After the meal, she again examined it but saw nothing she had not seen before. Placing it on the mantel, she turned on the television.

As days passed, Melanie found herself thinking about the machine more and more. After a couple of weeks, she took it from the mantel to examine it by the window. In the bright sunlight, she discerned a fine line outlining a rectangle on the base, possibly a door. She tried pushing on it in various ways, but nothing moved. Then she forced a knife blade in the crack and tried prying. To her surprise, it moved about 1/16 of an inch revealing a hollow cavity in the base, but she could not open it farther.

She got a wood chisel from the basement, inserted the blade in the crack, and twisted it with a pair of pliers. The door opened another quarter of an inch.

The wood appeared to have swelled, making the door extremely tight. With repeated attempts, she finally opened it halfway. On the inside was a piece of paper, brown and brittle with age. She carefully removed it. Although written in French, she understood most words. As nearly as she could tell, it read, "To make a contribution, remove the blade from the machine by removing the pivot pin. Heat the blade until it is red hot. Replace blade by reinserting the pivot pin. Raise blade. Insert finger in trough with knuckle immediately below the blade. Lower blade. Hold finger end against the blade briefly."

A chill ran down Melanie's spine. The contribution machine seemed to be some sort of device to cut off fingers. She guessed the dish caught the lopped off finger part, and the hot blade cauterized the wound.

"Who would use such a grisly device," she shivered, "some medieval doctor?" Medicine had been very crude at one time. After all, doctors used to drill holes in people's skulls to let out evil spirits, so this was really no more bizarre. Still, she found it disturbing, and calling it a contribution machine baffled her further.

Melanie placed the gruesome item in a bureau drawer. But even though it was out of sight, she could not get it out of her mind. She thought about it more and more as days passed. It intruded on her sleep and affected her work. She considered throwing it away, but something compelled her to keep it. She examined it again to look for anything she had not previously noticed, but saw nothing. She puzzled over the bas-relief faces and symbols, but again came up blank. Her hands trembling, she replaced the machine in the drawer.

A few days later, Melanie was a wreck. The machine pervaded her every thought and virtually forced her to retrieve it from the drawer and set it on the kitchen counter. Slowly, hypnotically, she removed the pin holding the blade in place and heated it in the gas flames of her cooktop until it glowed red. She replaced the blade by inserting the pivot pin, raised the blade, placed her left index finger in the trough with the distal joint immediately below the blade, and jammed the blade down emphatically.

Howling in pain and shaking, she pushed the stub of her finger against the blade to stop the bleeding. After bandaging her finger stub, she cleaned the apparatus and put it back in the bureau.

Melanie felt serenity for the first time in weeks. She could sleep again, concentrate on work, and felt wonderful. When her friends asked about her finger, she replied she had crushed it badly in her car door, requiring amputation.

Over the next few months, Melanie's obsession with the machine gradually increased until again reaching a fever pitch. Realizing what she had to do, she removed the machine from the drawer and prepared to make another contribution, regretting she hadn't heeded the shopkeeper's advice.

As a youth, I was enamored with the stories of Edgar Allen Poe. This tale combines the gruesomeness of Poe with a psychological theme.

The Hand

My ears rang from the deafening noise of artillery. The ground shook as a shell landed nearby, scattering body parts and more. Landing at my feet was a left hand, still clutching a photo. Tendons and bone protruded from the wrist, blood oozing from its veins. Retching, I looked away, but I couldn't erase the grisly scene from my mind.

The photo, of a man and woman on their wedding day, made me choke up. Not wanting the photo to be destroyed in the chaos, I removed it from the hand and put it in my pocket, freaked out at how tightly the fingers still gripped it. Then I noticed the ring. Suppressing the urge to vomit, I removed it with difficulty from the warm, flexible fingers. A man's wedding band, studded with five small diamonds, bore the inscription, "My beloved Dav. Kat-1968."

"Move out," a sergeant's voice boomed as more artillery rained from above. I pocketed the ring and crawled from my foxhole, shivering at the thought of the gruesome hand. The rest of that day remains a blank in my memory.

I thought about reporting it to my superiors, but I felt the items would probably get lost in army bureaucracy. If they were to be returned to Kat, I would have to do it.

A few days later, shrapnel pelleted my right leg, providing me with a purple heart and a medical discharge. Images of the dismembered hand clutching the photo continued to haunt me, especially at night.

I often removed the photo and ring from their resting place in my bureau drawer, wondering about the man to whom they belonged and how to return them to Kat. It seemed doubtful she received any information about him other than that he was lost in battle and presumed dead. I had to find her. She would want to know the last thing her husband saw was their wedding picture.

To start, I searched records of soldiers who had died in the battle. I discovered 297 men had perished that day but found nothing of use.

Unfortunately, there were no photographs of the men and no names beginning with Dav. The authorities might not even have known on what day he had died, considering all the chaos and the obliteration of his body by the shells.

Sending a copy of the photo to the Secretary of the Army proved unfruitful. Months later, I was informed that they had no way of identifying photos. They didn't even bother to answer a follow-up letter asking whom I should contact.

How could I find the name of a soldier named Dav? Was his name David, Davis, Davon, or something else? Kat could have been a nickname for Kate, Katie, Katrina, Katelin, or dozens of other possibilities. It could also have been a pet name.

Hours of online searches produced nothing of use, either. Nevertheless, the more roadblocks I encountered, the more determined I became. Following the suggestion of a friend, I posted the photo on Facebook, together with the date, the names Kat and Dav, and a request to forward the info to anyone who might be able to help identify them.

Several months passed before I received a call from someone in The Dalles, Oregon, a town of 15,000. The caller mentioned she knew of a Katrina Moore, a widow who might be the person for whom I looked. I called the number she gave me but immediately got transferred to a message box. Reluctant to leave a message with sensitive information, I hung up. After several more tries, I decided I'd have to leave a message, hoping she'd call me back.

The following day, the phone rang. A trembling voice asked if I had left a message about a photo. Assuring her I did, I explained that I had served in the same battalion as her husband and had a wedding band with an inscription. Since she knew the exact wording on it, I realized I'd at long last found Kat and asked if she'd like to get together so I could return the objects to her. She was more than eager. Since I lived in Cheyenne, I booked a flight to Portland where Katrina agreed to meet me.

Recognizing her from the description she gave, I shook her hand and asked if she'd like to go somewhere quiet. Seeing the mementos was bound to be an emotional experience. She suggested we go to her home, about one hour and twenty minutes from the airport.

Along the way, we refrained from any mention of her husband, instead making small talk about the weather, scenery, and our trips. Kat showed me to her living room, offering refreshments.

We sipped coffee for a few uneasy moments until I brought up the purpose of my visit. Showing her the photo, I told her he was holding it when he died, avoiding any mention of the severed hand. She held the photo, her hand shaking, her eyes wet. After regaining her composure, she showed me an eight by ten-inch framed version of the same picture prominently displayed on her grand piano.

She told me about her husband, his work with disadvantaged children, his little-league coaching, many things. Then, reaching in my pocket, I pulled out the ring and handed it to her. She held it next to her heart while her weeping began anew. I offered a consoling hand.

Reading the inscription, she struggled to talk.

"You don't know how much this means to me. I can't thank you enough. Did you get any other items? His billfold? Dog tags?"

Refusing to upset her more by telling her all I saw was Dav's hand, I responded with my well-rehearsed lie.

"After grabbing his tags, I was about to check for his billfold when we got the order to move out. With artillery landing all around, I dropped the tags."

After dinner, we spent the evening talking. She told me how they met in college, sitting beside each other in a philosophy class. From that point on, they were inseparable. They were married the following summer. Not having much money, they honeymooned in the Wallowa mountains in eastern Oregon, after which they returned to Oregon State University for their senior year.

After staying in Kat's guest room for the night, she drove me to the airport. As we parted, she cried again, thanking me for taking the time to contact her. I had a few tears of my own.

Horrible things happen during wars, but what could be more gruesome than a severed hand still holding a wedding picture? Starting with that, I wrote this story.

The Mysterious Trunks

Heavy rain pelted the ground as Nick Macario and Claire Padilla approached Leo Gadzinski's, mansion. The edifice, situated in a remote cove on Catalina Island, enjoyed an expansive view of the Pacific. They admired the eloquent mansion, Greco Roman in style with a large portico and a courtyard sporting a fountain. It had obviously cost a fortune to build, a fortune gained from illegal trade in Egyptian artifacts and paintings of the masters.

The IRS had long suspected Leo of tax evasion but had no proof until a purchaser of an Egyptian artifact ratted on him in a plea bargain. Claire and Nick had been assigned the task of inventorying the contents of the manor prior to an auction. Opening the eight-foot-high bas-relief doors, they entered a huge hall with marble statues in alcoves and a grand staircase. The second floor had six bedrooms, each with a private balcony.

They started on the upper floor and worked their way down. It was slow going because of all the belongings. On the third day, they entered a large basement with several rooms, mostly filled with furniture except for an expansive wine cellar. Nick, working in the last room, tripped on small box and fell. Bothered by his own clumsiness, he shoved a chair against the wall. He stopped. The hollow sound of the chair hitting the wall caught his attention. Nick tapped on the wall in several places, all of which produced sounds suggestive of a void.

"Claire, come here."

"What?" she asked.

"Listen." He tapped on the wall.

"Are you practicing your drumming skills?"

"This sounds like there's an empty space beyond," he replied.

After talking it over, they retrieved an axe from a nearby room and, after many blows, succeeded in making an opening about three feet in diameter. Darkness made it impossible to see inside.

"I'll get a flashlight from the car," Claire offered.

Returning, she shined the light around the hidden space, empty except for two large trunks, each with three huge padlocks. They used the axe to enlarge the hole enough for them to enter.

They tried moving the trunks, but they were too heavy.

"What could be in there, gold bricks?" Nick pondered.

"Perhaps," Claire answered, "Leo was worth billions."

They reported the trunks to their supervisor, IRS Special Agent Michael Smith, who told them he would check into it and get back to them. Because the authorities knew Leo dealt in Egyptian artifacts, Smith also contacted the Cairo Ministry of Antiquities. They informed the IRS that the trunks should not be opened until a representative of the Ministry could be present. If the trunks did indeed contain Egyptian artifacts, they insisted on repatriating them to Egypt. Additionally, special care had to be taken because some items might be fragile or might deteriorate in light.

Arrangements were made for Agent Smith and a representative from the Ministry of Antiquities, Dr. Baahir Abadi, to go to Catalina Island. Because Dr. Abadi was the world's leading authority on Egyptian antiquities, had numerous teaching obligations, and ongoing artifact-repatriation negotiations, it took three months before he could travel to California.

Both arrived at the mansion, finding Nick and Claire waiting to let them in. After introductions, the foursome went to the basement to examine the trunks. The huge padlocks resisted the bolt cutters they had brought. They talked it over and decided to try an acetylene torch, if one existed on the small island. They inquired at The Chamber of Commerce in Avalon, the only village on the island, and were told that Sonlight Auto Repair, a short distance southeast of town, was their best bet.

The shop had a torch, but the owner worked by himself and said he only had time to come on the weekend. Dr. Abadi and Michael checked into Hotel Metropole to await the following Saturday morning.

Arriving about 10:00 a.m., the auto shop owner was escorted to the basement by Nick and Claire, who watched as he worked on the six locks.

It was tricky business since care had to be taken not to set the wood trunks on fire. Eventually they succeeded; the auto shop owner, paid $425, left around 2:00 p.m.

Dr, Abadi and Agent Smith looked at each other nervously. Claire and Nick held their breaths as Dr. Abadi reached down to lift the lid of the first trunk. It was filled with bricks. Immediately, he opened the second trunk. More bricks. Speechless, they emptied the trunks to see if anything was underneath the bricks. Nothing. They examined the trunks carefully but saw nothing noteworthy. Why anyone would hide two heavily padlocked trunks full of bricks behind a fake wall? Disgusted, Dr. Abadi, stormed out, leaving the other three in stunned silence.

* * *

At Pebbly Beach Landfill, a bailer operator noticed two trunks. The lid of one had been crushed, revealing the edge of something colorful. Checking further, he saw that the lid consisted of two pieces of wood that looked for all the world like one piece. He grabbed a prybar from his toolbox and separated them, revealing a painting. Checking the other trunk, which looked identical, he found that it also had a hidden compartment containing another painting. The paintings ripped at the edges as he yanked them free. Noticing "Van Gogh," he struggled to pronounce the name.

"Van Gogg? Must be some kid who can't even draw," he muttered aloud as he tossed the pieces into the pit with the rest of the rotting trash.

Intrigued by criminals imprisoned for nonpayment of taxes on their ill-gotten gains, I wanted to write a story about a thief of priceless items. I cast the story on Catalina Island off the coast of California. All place names were real at the time of writing.

The Pinochle Game

To arrange the card game, Gladys called Irene, Miles, and Ed, reminding them that they would gather at 6:00 p.m. in the lounge. At the designated time, only Gladys and Miles had shown up.

"Did you remember to indicate the time?" Miles asked.

"I did. After all, you came at the right time."

At 6:50, Irene entered.

"I see I'm not the only one that's early," she said.

"Early? We were supposed to meet at 6:00," Gladys piped.

"What? I thought it was 7:00, sorry."

At 7:10, Ed appeared, huffing and puffing.

"I've wondered where you all were. I was waiting in the rec room by myself. No one told me about the change in location."

"The room wasn't changed. I told you we were meeting in the lounge," Gladys sighed. "Well, now that we're finally all here, let's play. Miles, you and Irene can be partners."

"Wait a minute, we were partners last time. I think it is my turn to be paired with Ed," Miles protested.

"No, it's my turn to be partners with Ed. We haven't been partners for a long time," Irene argued.

Gladys looked at the ceiling and rolled her eyes.

"Okay, here's what we'll do. I'll write each of your names on a piece of paper. Ed, can I borrow your hat? Now I'll draw a name out to be my partner. Are all of you okay with that?"

Once they agreed, she drew Miles' name, and all took their places. Gladys shuffled and dealt the cards.

"I have five nines and no meld," Irene proclaimed, throwing her cards on the table. "By rule, you have to deal again." Gladys shuffled the cards, grumbling under her breath.

"Wait a minute, I was supposed to cut the deck," Ed interjected.

"That's right," Irene stated. "I saw the bottom card. You'll have to deal over."

"Oh, for Pete's sake," Gladys moaned, throwing down her cards. She shuffled and dealt them for the third time.

"I bid 150," Irene announced.

"You are under, which means you automatically bid, but not 150, 250," Gladys admonished.

The bidding continued, with Ed winning at 310. He named hearts trump.

After passing cards, play commenced.

"You don't have trump?" Gladys asked Miles, a little later.

"What's trump, clubs?" he asked.

"No, it's hearts," Ed said.

"Oh dear, I thought it was diamonds," Miles exclaimed. "I've made several wrong plays. We'd better start over."

Since everyone else had decided to replay the hand, Gladys shuffled and dealt—for the fourth time.

Everyone sat looking at their cards; no one started bidding.

"Are you going to bid or pass, Miles?" Gladys asked.

"Me? I thought Irene was first."

"Irene is under, Miles. It's up to you to bid or pass." Gladys took a deep breath.

"My apologies."

At long last, they finished bidding and actually played a hand. Then, they counted the pointers they had taken.

"We have six," Gladys said.

"Give us eighteen," Ed piped.

"You couldn't have eighteen since there are 25 total and that only comes to 24." Gladys threw up her arms, exasperated.

"There's one point for the last trick. Who took it?" Irene asked.

"I think I did," replied Miles.

"No," Ed corrected. "It was me. I played the king of clubs and no one had clubs or trump. That makes nineteen for us." At last, they were ready to play the next hand.

"Who dealt last?" Ed asked, looking around.

"I did—four times," Gladys answered, her voice edgy.

Despite several more interruptions, they managed to play another hand.

"That's all for me—its past my bedtime." Irene yawned and got up.

"Me too," piped Miles.

"This has been really fun. When can we play again?" Ed asked.

"Not in my lifetime," Gladys muttered under her breath.

Have you ever had trouble remembering who did what in a game? Well, I have. I thought it would be fun to write a story about people who kept forgetting what they were doing.

ACKNOWLEDGEMENTS

I wish to offer heartfelt appreciation to Gerrit Hansen, without whose help and encouragement this book would not have been possible. Serving as my mentor and friend, he patiently guided me along the path to better writing skills. I also want to express my appreciation to my son Craig Wollen for designing the cover art.

Made in United States
Troutdale, OR
08/19/2024

22086059R00136